ADDLED

Adventures of a Reluctant Mystic

Jessica Davidson

JesDharma Books

Photo by Robert Aichinger

Published by JesDharma Books
Printed by CreateSpace
www.jessicadavidson.co.uk

To my mother and father
~ without you there would be no me.

The birds have vanished down the sky.
Now the last cloud drains away.
We sit together, the mountain and me,
Until only the mountain remains.

- Li Po

Jonah and the Whale

This story isn't easy to tell. It's a bit like one of those obscure films where nothing happens for hours but then you realise that, somehow, everything has changed.

It started the day I met Jonah. He was coming out of the tunnel by the bridge and heading for the quay. I'd been cleaning in Gateshead and was walking down to the bars to hand out business cards before I went home. He was beautiful and almost invisible in the darkness. The streetlamps made his face glow like living mahogany. He scowled at his phone and shoved it back in a pocket, hunkering down into his black duffel coat. A sharp cloud of breath rose over his head and hung there like a half-hearted halo. His coat didn't seem to be giving him much protection from the December chill because he shivered violently as he stepped into the road.

I wanted to catch up, say something, break the ice, but he was moving too fast. Plus, I'm only small and my little legs were no match. Rush hour had morphed into a multi-headed metal monster, sucking the oxygen out of the air. I watched him slide between cars and buses with the grace of a bad-tempered panther.

At the top of the bank leading down to the quayside, he stopped, eyes on the bridge. I had been so intent on watching him, like a crazed stalker, I hadn't noticed what was happening. The green steel of the Tyne Bridge rose ahead of us into the starless sky. A helicopter was buzzing overhead, the searchlight bouncing off the stone structure. Police swarmed the bridge, the traffic snaking into Gateshead.

A man was threatening to jump. He was on one of the ledges, clinging to the side, his back to the road below. Terrified.

I caught up with my quarry and stood beside him.

'He'll not jump,' I said.

The beautiful dark face turned and I risked a look into his eyes. He was surprised by something.

'It's just attention-seeking,' I continued.

The scowl returned and he looked like he was about to have a massive go at me, so I bolted and left him standing there with his mouth open. So much for breaking the ice. I marched down Bottle Bank towards the river, my backpack rebounding against the base of my spine, like I was flagellating myself for being such an idiot. It always went like this. I tried to fit in, be a good little cog, but I was incapable of being normal.

I crossed the Millennium Bridge, rainbow lights dancing over the arch high above my head, and made for the nearest bar. Normally I wouldn't be seen dead in the Pitcher and Piano. It's not for the likes of me: self-employed cleaner and professional freak, second-hand clothes and messed up hair. Bars like this are for people with aspirations, people with futures, people clambering over each other on every available ladder, people with money, people who would rather die than clean their own toilet.

Normal people.

I pulled off my purple beanie and slunk through the glass doors, scanning the patrons for potentials. Flames flickered in the artificial fire, the mantelpiece arrayed with candles destined never to burn. The swanky bar was filling with Friday-nighters determined to wipe every trace of the week out of their heads. In an hour it would be too busy to conduct business, so I got to work.

I made my way around the tables and was so intent on hustling I didn't see Jonah come in. There was a group of rowdy execs in cheap suits hogging the sagging brown leather sofas. They were already drunk so I should've known better than to speak to them, but what the hell. They surrounded me in seconds and I had to do my best impression of my mother to get them to back down. The one with a pink face to match his tie took a card and squinted at it. He leered up at me. I knew what was coming.

'You can clean me up, pet. S'long as you do it naked.'

His mates jeered and clapped. I had no intention of mopping up after this oaf. I could imagine the mess, and the smell. Out of the corner of my eye I noticed his hand reaching for my bum. I waited until he was precariously balanced on the edge of his seat, then stepped aside. For a fraction he appeared suspended, then gravity did its work and he hit the floor in a bewildered heap. I fixed him with my best withering look and plucked the business card from his sweaty fingers.

'For that, you can clean up your own bloody mess.' I turned away as the men hooted and pelted their hapless friend with nuts and pretzels.

That was when I saw him. Duffel coat slung over a stool, suit unbuttoned and tie crooked, he was sitting at one of the high tables, picking at the label on his Stella and watching me, a faint smile frozen on his lips. I started towards him and he looked away, swigging from his bottle.

'Did he jump?' I said, trying to look like I cared.

He looked surprised again. 'I don't know. You seemed pretty sure he wouldn't.'

'You don't kill yourself in rush hour.' I handed over my card. 'I'm Zoe. I clean stuff.'

My business cards are pretty basic. They read 'Get your house Green Clean. Zoe Popper' and have my phone number along with a picture of the mops and buckets from Disney's Sorcerer's Apprentice. You know, the one where Mickey Mouse gets in trouble for messing up his magic. All he wants is to clean up without having to do any work, but the spells go wrong and he ends up with hundreds of mops and hundreds of buckets all marching about the place causing mayhem.

'So d'you use magic to clean stuff then?' he said.

'If only.' I plonked myself on the stool opposite and gave him a long searching look. My blood was buzzing around my body and I wanted to work out whether it was the start of something special or just my ovaries acting up. This seemed to unnerve him and he took another long slug of beer.

'What's a guy like you doing in a bar full of wankers?' I said.

He gagged but managed to swallow, then looked a bit lost, which made me smile. I should explain something about my smile, and I'm only going on what I've been told; never been on the receiving end. It's a smile that can stop a man at twenty paces, make him forget his own name and give away all his worldly possessions.

Apparently.

It seemed to do the trick anyway, because he relaxed and smiled back.

'Can I get you a drink?' he said.

'I thought you'd never ask,' I beamed back.

He returned from the bar with another beer and a glass of red wine for me. I don't normally drink, but this was a special occasion and it gave me the opportunity to watch him twinkle-toe to the bar and back. He moved as if his body were made of music and my heart sung at the sight of his neatly tied brogues dancing across the floor.

'I'm Jonah.' He set my glass down.

'Like the whale. No, the whale wasn't Jonah. No-one knows what the whale was called. No-one thought to ask, I expect.' *Stop rambling, Zoe.*

I put my bag on the floor, then picked it up, put it down again. I couldn't settle. Jonah went off into his own little world while I was trying to make myself comfortable, so I sipped my wine and watched him. He pulled out his phone and checked something, sighed then slammed it shut with more force than it merited. I guessed women trouble.

'Was she mean?'

Jonah looked up sharply, surprise all over his face. I had to stop doing that to the poor guy.

'You some kind of psychic?'

I scoffed into my wine. 'Hardly.'

'She dumped me by text. Can you believe that?'

'Coward. Passive-aggressive.'

'There were three kisses.' He held up the phone. The text read: 'Snot wrkin ur doin head in. Sorry xxx'

I duly grimaced. 'She thinks you're too good for her. Hates herself, probably, but then a lot of women do. A lot of people. You're better off without her.'

Jonah nodded. I think he'd already figured that one out for himself.

'So Zoe, what do you do when you're not cleaning?'

'I clean a lot,' I shrugged. 'What do you do when you're not hanging around bars moping about being egregiously dumped by a bitch?'

Jonah laughed. It was a beautiful laugh, deep and resonant, with the tiniest hint of a little boy delighted and excited just to be alive.

'I'm a paper pusher in the barren corridors of toothless bureaucracy. Riding a desk until overtaken by pension or senility,' he said.

'You're a poet.'

'Singer-songwriter. My band's called Dionysus Wept.'

'Did he? Weep, I mean. I didn't know that.'

'Yeah, it's all about divine craziness,' he said, dark eyes flashing. 'He's a power of nature, a mad, furious inspirer, descended from fire. He was born with horns and a crown of serpents, torn to pieces and boiled.'

'Ouch.' My wine was finished. I clutched the glass in my hand and leaned forward, all mock concern. 'What happened?'

'Don't worry,' he continued with a smirk. 'He was reborn and raised as a girl, but his stepparents were driven mad. Someone or other turned him into a ram and he was looked after by nymphs, which can't be a bad thing, and then he invented wine.'

He tapped a fingernail against my empty glass, letting it ring out. As if set free by the sound, my mind relaxed and opened out, and I felt myself retreating down a long corridor, the bar becoming an echo chamber. I tried to hang on to something solid, something real: the sound of his voice, the glass stem in my fingers, but it was too late. I was going.

I can't do this, not here, not with him watching. What will he think? What will he do?

My eyes left Jonah's face and drifted up. His voice came to me as if underwater, each word sending out ripples into the space around us and tremors through my body.

'Got a bad rep for driving people nuts if they didn't honour him. A bunch of pirates jumped ship and became dolphins, which sounds more like fun to me. But to get to the point, when his friend and lover Ampelos died, Dionysus wept. Either his tears were wine, or they turned into wine, or a vine grew where they fell, depending on which story...'

He stopped talking. My mind unravelled into tendrils of vines wrapping themselves around the furniture and up the walls. Plump golden grapes hung, glistening from the vine. I wanted to reach out and pluck them, devour them, but I knew that was taboo. They must be offered, freely given to those who pass through the narrow gate.

I felt Jonah shake me. I couldn't respond. It was the beginning of the end.

When I came to my mind was fuzzy with warmth, like I was wrapped in slowly baking pastry. It wasn't unpleasant so I lay there until the flames reached my face. Someone was shining a light in my eyes. I squeezed them open. Above my head was a square patch of sky, the sun blasting me awake. Clouds ambled past, hiding the sun long enough for panic to hit me in the chest. *Where the hell am I?*

I jerked my head around. I was on a futon in the middle of a room directly beneath a large roof window, the eaves stretching away over my feet. The walls were soft violet, there were a couple of dark purple lamps and a generous wooden wardrobe. A gentle ticking came from a small clock perched on a chest of drawers, above which hung a mirror framed with photographs. No clutter. No mess.

I lifted the covers and peered down, relieved to find I was still fully dressed. Someone had removed my battered trainers. I went back to watching the clouds change shape and tried to remember what had happened. The usual sickening blankness rose up and my mind reeled away.

Focus Zoe. Think.

A guitar was being played somewhere, possibly downstairs, and it all came back: the bar, the wine, the sadness in his eyes. Jonah had taken care of me.

I smiled and threw back the covers. It was good to meet a man who knew how to tie his own shoelaces, and the trance hadn't freaked him out. At least he hadn't abandoned me to the bar, or worse, called the police, or worse still, the hospital. How long had I been gone? Had I made a fool of myself? Most people kept away from me once they knew what I was like. Jonah had brought me home.

The guitar stopped and footsteps approached, coming up the stairs. My heart started pounding so I took a couple of deep breaths, tucked my hands behind my head and tried to act normal, whatever that meant under these circumstances. There was a soft knock at the door, then it opened a crack.

'Hey,' I said, trying to sound casual.

Jonah came in carrying a steaming mug of something. In place of the natty suit he was wearing jeans and a black vest. He perched on the edge of the futon, looking nervous.

'Hey.' He put the mug on the floor behind my head. 'Coffee.'

'Thanks. Not for the coffee, for the... well, yes, thanks for the coffee too, but... y'know, for last night, for looking after me.'

He smiled and a warmth spread through my chest and down to my fingers. Heat flared in my cheeks so I sat up to distract myself. Jonah glanced away and scratched at his head like a confused puppy.

'Does that happen a lot?' he said.

I was startled for a second, then realised he meant the trances.

'On and off since I was a kid. Doesn't usually happen in public like that. It's, um... well, I'm just bonkers.' I laughed, hysteria bubbling too close to the surface for comfort.

I took another deep breath and willed myself to be calm. It was always like this on Re-entry, like coming down off a drug high. The trance itself felt great, like nothing could ever be wrong, like coming home. Then on Re-entry you crash, hurtling back to earth, your body weighs a ton and the world is too loud and in your face.

I never told anyone about my little trips away. Even when I was a kid I knew that was risky, I mean, look at what happened to Dad. And here I was going the same way. I tried to keep busy, keep thinking, but it wasn't working. My mind was determined to betray me. I would be found, like my dad, standing in a field wearing nothing but boots and a poncho reading poetry to cows, and when they tried to take me away I would clobber the poor doctor over the head with Leaves of Grass.

Walt Whitman had a lot to answer for.

Jonah cleared his throat and shifted anxiously, bringing me back to the present. He probably wanted this crazy woman out of his flat so he could get on with his life. I opened my mouth to apologise and secure a hasty exit, but Jonah cut across me and we spluttered into confusion.

'Sorry about...'

'I'll leave you to...'

I wanted to dive under the duvet and hide. When the silence had become unbearable, I tried again.

'Um... can I ask? You've been so kind, and I was just wondering, I don't know, maybe you're as crazy as me underneath, or something, but, why did you bring me home?'

He gave a tiny shrug, like it was nothing, 'I didn't know where you lived and I didn't want to call the police.' A shadow fell across his face, then was gone. 'And besides, I couldn't leave you there. Not in a bar full of wankers.'

We laughed and the tension between us evaporated. He was about to stand when I noticed the tattoo on his arm. A vine, like the one in my trance, wound around his left biceps opening in a flower on his shoulder. Peeping from under his vest I could see a hummingbird in flight, its long beak poised to drink nectar from the flower. Without thinking, I reached out to touch.

'This is beautiful. Can I?'

He smiled assent and I ran my fingers up the vine, following the contour of his arm. I slowed as I reached the flower and the edge of his vest, and wanted to sink my teeth into the smooth dark chocolate of his neck. I snapped my hand back and felt my face glow.

'Grab a shower if you want.' Jonah stood, flashed another brilliant white smile and left the room.

I clasped the coffee mug in my hands and inhaled. Steam curled across the opaque surface and I felt my mind loosen, as if I were the one twisting and folding over and around myself, turning to vapour, edges blurred, spreading out, fading...

Shit. Focus. This couldn't keep happening. I didn't even understand what was happening.

I glanced at the clock. I was going to be late.

Popper Originals

Jonah's red and rusting transit van was a treasury of sweet wrappers, empty crisp packets and assorted fluff and sticky stuff. I was surprised. His flat was an oasis of order and cleanliness. I shot him a questioning glance as we drove into town.

'Not me,' he said.

'The text writing bitch?'

He chuckled and shook his head, and pulled into the kerb outside Popper Originals. The shop window contained a display of vaguely phallic sculptures, a couple of Northumbrian landscape paintings, and the knotted face of Rebecca Popper – my mother. She was waiting for me. My agitated state cranked up a gear. I grabbed my backpack, shot Jonah a grateful smile and jumped out the van.

'Must be the band then,' I said.

'The same.'

We grinned awkwardly at each other for a bit and I twirled my bag in my hands, desperate for something to say.

'Thanks again,' I said, feeling idiotic.

'You busy tomorrow?' he shouted over the engine.

'Yeah. I'm seeing you.'

Jonah laughed and pulled my card out of his back pocket. 'I'll call you.'

I slammed the van door and rushed into the shop. Popper Originals sold arts and crafts made by local artists, and occupied two adjoined buildings on Osborne Road in Jesmond. Mum bought the shop not long after we arrived in Newcastle from Brighton, and with the persistence of water torture had made it work. She had the gift of being gentle with the artistic egos but mercenary with the galleries and customers. The latter she classified as Bored Wealth, convincing the likes of Crispin and Zenobia that what they really needed, what would make their life and converted barn complete, was a few aspirational art objects.

'You're late,' said Mum.

'I know.'

I opened my backpack, dumping cloths, dusters and home-made eco-sprays on the counter. Mum still had her face pressed to the window.

'Was that Danny? When did he get a van?'

'It wasn't Dan, Mum.'

I cleaned in a blur around the shop, leaving a trail of white wine vinegar and lemon juice in my wake. Mum followed, like she always does, checking every object and surface. She doesn't believe something is clean unless it's been sluiced down with a chemical cosh. I had to train her to stop using those artificial air fresheners that leave my eyes stinging and make everything smell like a toilet, teaching her about essential oils and how to, you know, open a window.

This hyper-vigilance was accompanied by the usual stream of criticism aimed at Danny – my brother and twin. Two sperm, apparently. We even look a little alike now I've chopped my hair short. Anyway, a year ago Danny walked out of a job on a building site: said the gaffer was a bully, there was a conflict of personalities, he always got the shitty jobs and why should he have to put up with that kind of crap. Turned out, Danny had been caught smoking the wrong kind of cigarettes. He quit before they could fire him. Mum hadn't spoken to him since.

'He's been stealing again. He comes into the house when I'm busy here. He obviously thinks I'm stupid. Does he think I don't notice? Zoe?'

'No. I doubt he thinks that.'

'Well, then what does he think he's doing? When is he going to get a job like a proper person?'

My fist tightened around the cloth. Always the same argument. It was pointless to get involved, neither of them listened. I tried to stay out of it, but they kept dragging me back, like a couple of kids in the playground squabbling over whose turn it was to play with the marbles.

'You can't wash your hands of him then start making demands,' I said with a sigh, knowing Mum would take this as a cue to turn her attention on me.

'When are you going to come home? You can't stay with your brother, he's a bad influence. I hate not knowing where you are. At least give me the address.'

'I promised Danny I wouldn't.'

'He wouldn't have to know.'

'And how would that work, Mum. Think it through.'

After the Big Fight, Danny left home. His name had reached the top of the housing list so he moved into a squalid flat in Elswick and 'forgot' to tell Mum where he was going.

I finished packing my cleaning things away while Mum continued the offensive. Why had I cut off my beautiful hair, I should have paid someone to do a decent job of it, I looked like a boy, when was I going to start doing something useful with my life, what was I doing cleaning when I'm so much smarter than any of my customers. I smiled inwardly at that one. *Smarter than you, Mum?*

'You can always pay someone else to clean for you.' I held out my hand.

She looked affronted. 'Can I give you the lot next time you do the house?'

'It isn't pocket money. This is my business.'

She sighed and opened the till. Credit where it's due, without Mum I couldn't have got the business started. A lot of my customers are her customers, some are her friends. She was the first to take me on and then talked me up so aggressively to everyone she met it wasn't long before I was having to turn people away. I think she was just happy I was doing something after the Big Disappointment of me dropping out of university. She probably thought I was going to end up like Dan.

The bell above the door jangled and in walked Popper Original's only shop assistant. Kayleigh had violent blue hair and vivid green six inch heels, her ears were plugged with headphones and she was chewing gum. She always chewed gum. In fact, I'd never seen her eat. She seemed to gain all her sustenance from aspartame.

'Hiya Becks,' said Kayleigh as she breezed through to the back room.

'I've told you a thousand times not to call me that,' shouted Mum.

Kayleigh reappeared without coat and headphones and winked at me. She'd worked here for a couple of years after leaving school with only two GCSEs, Art and English, having failed everything else. With bleak prospects, she bulldozed Mum into giving her a job. For her part, Mum had recognised a fellow hustler and wanted to neutralise the competition.

'Alreet Zo,' said Kayleigh between chomps on her gum. 'Did I miss the big birth rant yet?'

'No. You're in luck. Today we're trying to get away without paying the staff.'

'There,' said Mum, thrusting the cash into my hands. 'You girls enjoy picking on a poor defenceless old woman?'

This was so far from the truth on every level that I felt a surge of affection for my mother and almost hugged her. Almost. Instead, I retreated to the door.

'I don't always talk about your birth, do I?' she said. 'I mean, it was pretty unforgettable. It went on and on. I thought it would never end.'

I slipped out the door. 'Bye, Mum.'

My birth. Our birth. We will forever be one, even now. No matter what life throws between us.

The story was a classic of maternal exaggeration. Mum told it so often I'd started to believe I could actually remember it: the muffled sounds, the whooshing heartbeat and endless darkness.

The prenatal world was crowded. We were locked in a nine month long embrace. The space shrunk daily and I was desperate to get out, to breathe the air and feel something other than his slippery limbs wrapped around mine. Convulsions, unbearable pressure, and still Danny wouldn't budge. I tried to shove him out of the way, the embrace transformed into a wrestling match.

In the end, the doctors dragged him out. Mum said he was born with two black eyes. Is that possible? Did I do that to my fractionally bigger brother? Anyway, once they had him, he was making such a fuss no-one noticed when I flopped out fifteen minutes later, exhausted and thinking there had to be an easier way. Probably.

Things hadn't changed much since then. Thirty-three years later I was trapped between my mother, who wanted to turn me into herself, and my brother, who also wanted to turn me into his mother. All I wanted to do was be Zoe, but I didn't know who that was.

I walked into town from the shop. I walk a lot. I have no idea how much ground I cover day to day, but can wear through a pair of trainers in six months. I reckon if I knew how far I walked between customers, I would convince myself it couldn't be done and get the bus. I'd get lazy, get fat, and die. So I walk and think about something else.

I hiked up Westgate Road thinking about this and that and barely noticing where I was, and fell into step behind a pair of lads shambling along, jeans around the tops of their legs. They could hardly walk. I had to stop myself running forward to yank up their trousers and deliver a stern lecture about the virtues of a belt, or at the very least braces, as I did so. They were embroiled in a heated discussion about something or other, which required the use of more profanity than I cared to know. I tried to extract the gist of the argument from between the cascade of fucks and bastards, but didn't know where to start.

They shuffled forward as if wearing leg manacles, shoulders hunched, stabbing at the air with the exaggerated gestures of the chronically insecure or the drunk. Condemned men firing out tiny globules of spit left and right.

I wanted to overtake, but was worried I'd be hit in the back by a mucus pellet, so slowed down and hoped they weren't going all the way to Elswick. Their movements were curiously synchronised, like they were engaged in a strange aggressive ballet. Something was tugging at my awareness, something I'd noticed but hadn't really seen, so I glanced down.

A jolt of electricity hit my heart. The one on the left hadn't tied his laces. They were flapping around his ankles. How was he not standing on them, falling over, breaking his neck?

Pain seared across my chest. My heart was trying to smash through my ribs. I yanked at my jacket to pull it away from my throat. I couldn't breathe. I was going to pass out. I couldn't pass out, not in the street. I wanted to run. I wanted to jump into the road, screaming.

Keep it together. One foot in front of the other.

I forced myself to look away, look at the houses, the cars, the yellow line in the road, anything but those stupid laces. They're just bloody laces, for goodness sake.

I dropped my backpack in the hall and pressed my forehead against the wall. It was safe now. I stood with my eyes closed for a moment, the resistance in the wall making me feel more solid. The flat was silent, perhaps Danny was still in bed.

It wasn't a bad place to live, but it was small and felt all the more so with both of us there. Since I'd moved in, I'd done my best to liven it up with curtains and cushions, but Danny had a way of messing everything up without even trying. He spent the little he got from the dole on skunk and booze, so I hadn't been surprised to find he'd been stealing from Mum. He drifted day to week to month, waiting for something, who knew what.

I glanced at the clock in the kitchen down the hall. *Three twenty?* I shook my head and checked my mobile. Every clock in the flat told a different time. I'd synchronised them once, but somehow over the months they had drifted, with Danny, into timelessness.

I went through to the living room and squeezed between the TV and the coffee table heaped with empty Carling cans, congealed takeaway cartons and stuffed ashtrays. Blankets of sweet smelling smoke hung in the air, lasers of sunlight piercing the nimbus through a chink in the closed curtains. I flapped my arms pointlessly and flopped into a chair.

Danny was asleep on the sofa looking pale and ruffled, like an unkempt vampire. One of his laces was undone. In a rush, I lunged forward and tied it. He stirred and peered up at me, rubbing his eyes.

'Can I borrow some money?' he said.

'What did you take from Mum?'

He groaned. 'Just some food from the fridge.'

'Dan, you have to stop this. You're 33 years old, you can't keep rebelling like a fourteen-'

'Don't start with your psycho-bollocks,' he said, cutting across me. 'Lend us some cash, Zo.'

'No. I need it. I've got a date.'

Danny sat up and leaned over the end of the sofa in my direction. 'May I remind you, you live here rent free.'

'You get benefit.'

'So?'

I sighed. I knew how this was going to go. It always ended the same way. I was a mug. Danny slid off the sofa and plonked himself in front of me, his head in my lap. He gazed into my eyes, a lost dog, and I did what I always do. I gave him half what I had.

'Don't you want to hear about my date?'

Danny leapt to his feet and grabbed his coat from the floor.

'Later. Gotta go. See ya, sis.'

He kissed the top of my head and was gone.

Three Scary Monsters

The tide was coming in at Tynemouth and the water-logged sand reflected the cold blue sun, dazzling the handful of hardy dog walkers trudging up the beach, wrapped tightly against the wind. Their dogs ran and leapt and barked at the sea, which crashed and rolled as it advanced.

Jonah and I ran down the steps to Long Sands clutching 99 cones and giggling at the absurdity of eating ice cream in winter. Turns out he's a southerner too. I've lived here most of my life but still can't get my head around wearing nothing in sub-zero temperatures, like the locals. Eating ice cream in all weathers, however, is fine by me, even if today it proved impossible. The wind was whipping the sand up and throwing it in our faces, so we walked backwards into the wind and ignored the crunches in our teeth.

Jonah was intent on finding out more about me, so I bombarded him with questions and kept him talking. He came to Newcastle to study music at college, then stayed for his band. His aunt Sofia had given him his first guitar after he'd run off one day and scared his mother silly. He was seven. They'd been shopping at the market on Electric Avenue and he was getting bored watching his mum stock up on okra, sweet potatoes and ackee, enough for a feast – her sisters were coming round. His mum gave him a bag of plantain and spices to carry, then got talking to a man with a shiny mouth. That's how he said it – he had the sun in his mouth. I guessed gold teeth.

Anyway, little Jonah wandered off through the crowds and stalls and around the curve in the street, watching the people and listening to the different voices. It was like a conversation between the whole world. He didn't sound like his mum; sometimes he would try to mimic her Caribbean cadences but it never felt right. He was a London boy. The sound of guitar music drifted through the bodies and legs, so he followed his ears and found a half-starved old man sitting on the pavement playing blues guitar and singing with his eyes closed, like he was about to be executed.

The hubbub of caterwauling stallholders, people haggling, laughing and arguing, faded into nothing. Jonah was encased in a bubble. All he could hear was blissful music. He sank to the kerb and sat there amongst the discarded chip wrappers and fag ends, the plastic bag stuffed with plantain between his knees, and wept with joy. Half an hour later, although it seemed a lifetime, he thought an avalanche had landed on him when his mum found him, swept him up and dragged him home.

That evening they had their feast and his favourite aunt gave him a replica Gibson hummingbird acoustic made from rosewood. A week later, Sofia took him back to the market in search of the old blues master, and found him the worse for rum in a pub. After some nifty wrangling and more rum, Steve, for that was his name, agreed to teach Jonah to play guitar.

'Turned out Steve wasn't that old,' said Jonah, shoving the last of his ice cream cone into his mouth. 'He was only about 45, but to a seven year old, that's ancient.'

Just then, a spaniel came running up to us, dripping sea water and trying to bark with a stick in its mouth. Jonah grabbed the stick and hurled it back towards the water, sending the dog gambolling away, barking with happiness, tail threatening to come loose from wagging. All of which distracted me so well I didn't see Jonah's question coming and was completely unprepared for it.

'What are you hiding?'

My mouth dropped open – not a good idea in a high wind on a north east beach.

'I'm not having a go,' he continued. 'It's just – I like you, but I have no idea why. And I'd like some clues.'

'Will you write me a song?'

'Come on, Zoe. I'm going to smoke you out. Why d'you end up cleaning people's houses? Why d'you live with your brother? What's it like being a twin? What do your trances feel like? What do you see?'

I folded my arms in protest and stopped walking. 'Which question would you like me to answer first?'

I couldn't understand why I was being so perverse. Surely this was what I wanted. Here was someone genuinely interested in me and I was pushing him away. I didn't have anything to lose, so why was I building a wall around myself? Did I want to end up like Danny, whose only friends were his dealer and Big Davinder, the Sikh who ran the chippy. I took a deep breath and prepared to kick out a couple of bricks.

'I clean people's homes because I'm not qualified to do anything else. Did psychology at uni but I dropped out. I live with my brother because I can't afford my own place. Being a twin means you're never really alone, even if you want to be, so – a pain in the arse. The trances...'

I looked at my feet. Two tiny heaps of sand had piled themselves onto the tips of my trainers, like mini sandcastles. I stared at them feeling disoriented. Warm fingers touched my cheek and I looked up. Jonah was smiling at me with such kindness I almost told him everything.

'It's not easy to talk about, you know,' I said.

He shoved his hand back into his coat and we continued along the beach.

'Why d'you drop out of uni?'

He was obviously as stubborn as me and I couldn't hold out forever. I took a deep breath and tried to decide what not to tell him.

'I left early in the third year. Couldn't concentrate. There was too much going on in my head.'

'The trances?'

I nodded. 'And some other stuff. There are some things you can't tell someone you've known less than 48 hours.'

'Now I'm even more curious.'

'Look, I'm just a nobody, probably insane, who knows how to get a wicked shine on a mahogany table,' I said, wishing the sand would quicken and swallow me whole.

'I don't think you're crazy.'

'Based on what evidence? You saw me the other night. I'm useless. No good for anything in the normal world, full of normal people and their normal lives. I can't live like that. I'm broken. I'm caught in the grip of one of the biggest, scariest monsters and I'm not strong enough to fight my way free.'

'Scary monsters?'

'There are three.'

He grinned.

'I'm serious.' I counted them off on my fingers, 'Love, Death and Madness.'

'Love's not a monster,' he said, frowning and looking ready for a fight.

'It is scary though.' I wasn't about to be argued out of my best psychological theory. 'It's about control. All the things that matter the most are the things we have the least control over. Love – everyone wants it, nobody understands it, and once it's got you, you're buggered.'

'Buggered?' The grin was back.

'Well, y'know. You can't control who you fall in love with or whether they'll return the favour or how it'll change your life.'

Jonah shrugged, 'Granted.'

I stuck up two fingers. 'Death – there's no escaping that one. Although, it's not death itself that's the problem. Once you're dead, you're dead, so fuck it, right? No, it's the actual dying that scares people, the loss of control. And then there's madness.'

'I'm not scared of madness.'

'Never thought your mind would unravel at the slightest touch? Never thought you could end up being one of those crazy fruit loops wandering the streets shouting at your imaginary enemies and smelling of wee?'

Jonah laughed. 'No, never.'

'You're lucky.'

'I put all my craziness into my music,' he said. 'Music is big enough to contain anything I need it to. It's my sanctuary.'

I gazed over the fast disappearing sand. 'I need that. I need a sanctuary.'

Jonah watched me thoughtfully. We had been walking in a shambolic way along the beach and had almost reached Cullercoats. He stopped to pick up the stick discarded by the overexcited spaniel we met earlier, and drew a large circle in the sand. He stood in the centre and waved for me to join him. I didn't know what he was up to, but obeyed.

'I think it's only scary if you make it so,' he said.

'Easy for you to say.' The old defences were sliding back into place.

'D'you think you could run your business if you were crazy?'

'It's not that simple, Jonah. Things can seem fine and then, Bang. Most people have no idea how precarious everything is, especially their own sanity.'

'Have you seen a doctor?'

I took a step back. His face was pure innocence; he didn't know, how could he? But it was like he had taken a knife and slashed open my guts. I stood there, blank, staring at him while my intestines piled around my feet.

He moved towards me, concern and confusion in his eyes. 'Zoe, I didn't...'

I spun away and stumbled out of the circle. 'You can't make me see a doctor.'

The sea roared in my ears as I tried to run but the uneven sand kept throwing me off balance. Jonah was shouting apologies and imploring me to come back when I remembered I had no way of getting home. He was driving and I had no money left for the Metro.

I turned around and slowly walked back to the circle in the sand where Jonah waited, shivering, hands in his pockets, wind smacking his dreadlocks into his cheeks.

'You can't make me see a doctor,' I said, unable to meet his eyes. 'You just can't.'

'I won't,' he said. 'I promise.'

He rested his hands on my shoulders, gentle and reassuring, and lifted my face to his. 'Tell me about it.'

I had to look away. The waves tearing up the beach pulled at me. To be churned about and smashed to pieces on the rocks would be a relief.

'My dad was an artist,' I said, eyes fixed on the sea. 'That's how Mum met him, in a gallery shop in Brighton. Daniel Popper. Completely unknown, mad and dead. A true artist. He was a paranoid schizophrenic. Hanged himself. We were nine.'

I told the whole tale and Jonah listened so selflessly I almost forgot I was talking, like he'd climbed inside my head to share the nightmare.

Danny and I were walking home from school with Mum. A day the same as every other. I was carrying my Sleeping Beauty lunch box which I'd covered with drawings from my favourite TV show: *Monkey*. There was Monkey himself, with his magic wishing staff, Pigsy with his silly piggy nose, and Sandy with his skull necklace. I liked the horse too, but it wasn't a real horse. It was a dragon in disguise, obviously.

I'd spent the day pondering what the clever man on the show said: 'Like a mountain, a good man is visible from afar.' Knickers, or rather Mr Nickelson, was as big as a mountain, so you could see him from a distance, but I didn't think that was what it meant.

Danny was kicking a stone along and we were both holding Mum's hands. We arrived home, Danny gave his little stone a final kick and it thwacked against the front door. Mum yanked his arm and tutted. She seemed to communicate mostly in tuts and sighs, a kind of Mummy Morse Code. I had learnt to decipher it early. Mum unlocked the door and we all went in.

The first thing I remember seeing was Dad's feet in mid-air. One of his laces was undone, dangling like the light switch in the bathroom. I couldn't understand what was going on. Why were Dad's feet in the air?

Mum fell down on the floor between me and Danny, like she'd fallen asleep. I looked up and Dad was hanging from the second floor landing, a rope digging into his neck and his purple tongue sticking out, like he was playing a joke, pulling a face to make us laugh.

Jonah's warm fingers touched my hand. I looked at him and finished my story. 'After the funeral we left Brighton and moved north, as far away as we could get. Mum couldn't stand being there, dealing with the nasty looks and people muttering behind her back, as if madness was contagious.'

Jonah's arms were around me before I could stop him. The wind was determined to push us over, like an invisible sumo wrestler, but Jonah dug in his heels and held me tight. I fought the tears gathering in the reservoir in my heart. They're always there, if I let myself feel them, but I never cry and had no intention of starting now. I pushed against Jonah and wriggled free of his embrace.

'He was 33 when he died. I was 33 in September. What if I go the same way? Maybe this is how it starts, with the zoning out and the visions.'

'You're not your dad,' he said softly.

But I wasn't listening. 'I don't know what to do. Danny's doing my head in but I can't go back to Mum's, I'd end up murdering her, or... I need to get myself sorted but it's just fucking chaos, in here.' I whacked my fingers against my stupid forehead. 'I'm terrified that the next trance will be the end of me and I'll float off, like a lost balloon, never to be seen again.'

'You need somewhere to tie your string,' said Jonah. 'Tie it to my finger.' He held out one finger and waggled it.

I stared at him like he was the one losing his mind. Into the awkward silence erupted a shimmering series of pings from Jonah's mobile. He ignored it.

'I have a spare room,' he said. 'I could use some help with the bills. You're welcome to stay. It could be your sanctuary.'

I stood very still and watched the churning sea. The offer sounded casual enough but I could feel something else underneath. Or was that wishful thinking? He pulled his phone out of a pocket and flipped it open. Irritation bubbled in his eyes and he snapped it shut again.

'Problems?' I said.

'Just my ex.'

'Ah, the bitch.'

We grinned at each other and I relaxed; this could work.

'What d'you say?' he said.

'Give me a week to smooth things over with Danny.'

We walked out of the circle in the sand and up the beach to the steps.

'For someone who's just dumped you in one of the shittiest ways possible, she does seem very keen to keep in touch,' I said.

'She wants me to pick up my stuff from her place.' He made it sound like she was asking him to give her slimy uncle a thorough bed bath with his favourite flannel.

'I could come with you. Bit of psychological warfare?'

Jonah chuckled and took my hand, giving it a squeeze.

Behind us, the tide rippled forward dissolving the line in the sand, leaving no trace we were ever there.

We drove back into Newcastle, aiming for the red, white and blue triangle of the Byker Wall, jutting into the sky like a Lego-brick ski jump. Jonah left the van in the Morrisons car park under the watchful eye of the CCTV, and we walked to the estate past endless discount stores and shuttered shops.

From the outside, the Byker Wall looked like a brightly coloured prison, but once inside it opened out, with muddy grass and trees enclosed by ranks of blue or green balconies and walkways. Jonah ducked into a stairwell and I followed, bracing myself for what was coming.

He stopped at a door and took a deep breath, no doubt gathering his thoughts. I hung back, loitering on the walkway overhanging the courtyard. Despite the weakness of the winter sun, it had warmed through the wooden rail running around the terrace. I leaned into it and let the warmth ooze through my old coat and into the small of my back.

Jonah knocked. We waited. No response.

He got on his knees and looked through the letterbox, calling out, 'Nisha, it's me.'

I cupped my hands to the window and peered in, but couldn't see anything through the net curtains. I joined Jonah as he stood up and hammered on the door again.

'Why'd she text and say come round and then not be here?' he said.

'I think she's playing silly buggers,' I said, rather unhelpfully.

Jonah shot me a look so mangled and strange I started to wonder what I was getting into. Admittedly, it was a bit late to begin worrying, considering I'd just agreed to move in with him, even just as friends. He seemed so harmless and sweet, but they were the ones to watch, the ones you never saw coming. I decided to tackle it head on.

'Why did Nisha dump you anyway?' I said, trying to sound casual.

'She was a cow.'

'Yes, but apart from that.'

Jonah pushed past me onto the walkway and leaned on the railing, glowering at the leafless trees below.

'It's just that, despite you being Mr Nice Guy, and I'm very grateful and all that stuff, it's just... well, for all I know, Nisha could be lying in there in bits and this is some ruse you've cooked up to get an alibi to cover your tracks, 'cos really you're this crazed axe murderer and you're planning on turning me into dog food next.'

Jonah was shaking. His hands gripped the wooden rail as he vibrated with laughter. He turned to face me, grinning like an escaped lunatic.

'Dog food?'

I shrugged. 'I had to ask.'

He calmed down. 'Fair enough. For the record, I asked Nisha to move in with me, thought it would be better than living here, but she said no. After that, it kind of fell apart.'

'And now you want your stuff back.'

Jonah sunk onto the wooden bench on the walkway and rested his head against the sill of the window above, rubbing his hand over his face. 'I can't even remember what she's got.'

I went back to the front door and peered through the letterbox. In the hallway, I could see a cardboard box on the floor containing an ornate picture frame, an orange bear wearing a sombrero, and what looked like the sleeve of a shirt. It was hard to tell in the gloom. Someone, presumably Nisha, had written the word 'Oxfam' on the box. Jonah appeared and crouched beside me.

'I think she's offloading your gifts.' I said, and stood up.

Jonah looked through the letterbox and whimpered. 'That's my purple shirt. I wondered where that'd got to.' He stood and gave me puppy dog eyes. 'I love that shirt.'

'It's just a shirt.'

'It's silk.'

'Is that the sum total of your relationship?'

'Doesn't look good, does it?' he said, as we left the estate.

We walked back down Shields Road, dodging pushchairs and drunks. I glanced up at Jonah. He was deep in thought, a frown scrunching his face, his poetic soul brooding on his latest humiliation. I felt duty bound to cheer him up.

'Promise me something?' I said.

'Anything.'

'Promise you'll never give me a sombrero wearing bear.'

He laughed all the way back to the van.

Little Miss Ouseburn

I stood before the open wardrobe and ran my eyes along the desultory collection of clothes huddled inside. Moving out was the perfect opportunity to get rid of my junk. There was stuff in here I hadn't worn in years and couldn't remember buying. I was going to have to be systematic and ruthless. Jonah had found some cardboard boxes and they sat behind me expectantly. I'd already packed my collection of psychology books and there was a small box of mementos, with bits of old jewellery, a couple of seashells and a pebble. I was surprised by how little I had accumulated over the years and even toyed with the idea of chucking the lot, but then found I couldn't let go of the tiny pebble. Literally. I held it over the bin and stared at it.

I found it on the beach in Brighton. Mum told us we were leaving while we were on one of our walks beside the sea. Danny cried and clung to her, pleading and devastated. He didn't want to leave his friends. I was listening to my feet clattering over the shingle and the sea rolling the pebbles, dragging them to their doom in the depths. I felt resigned. We were leaving and there was nothing I could do about it.

Up ahead I spotted a funny looking pebble and ran to pick it up. It was smooth and grey and shaped like a heart. A jagged line of white cut across the stone from top to bottom, like a lightning bolt. I slipped it into my pocket.

The pebble was small in my hand now. Maybe it was time to move on. I plonked it decisively on the window sill and turned to the open boxes. I took a deep breath and started to fill them with clothes, one for me, one for charity, and by lunchtime had everything under control. Everything except Danny.

I had been waiting for the right moment to tell him I was moving out and here I was, ready to go and I hadn't said a word. I knew he'd be difficult, demanding and selfish. I was scared I would relent and stay.

I picked up one of the smaller boxes and carried it through to the front door. Jonah was waiting for me in the living room, sitting beside

Danny on the sofa. Danny was already stoned and I wondered, with a pang of guilt, if I could get away without telling him. He puzzled as I walked past with the box, inhaled deeply from his spliff then offered it to Jonah, who waved it off.

'You need a hand?' said Jonah, as I returned for the next box.

'I'm nearly done, but you could bring some of the heavier ones through.'

'She's doing her bit for charity,' said Danny. 'Buys her clothes, takes 'em back. Like a library, but with clothes.' He erupted into a fit of giggling.

As we carried the last couple of boxes out to the van, I noticed Jonah looking troubled and started to worry he'd changed his mind about me moving in.

'Is there a reason he thinks you're taking this lot to charity?' he said.

'Some of it I am.' I slammed the back door of the van.

Jonah raised an eyebrow. I wasn't fooling anyone.

'D'you think I could move out without him noticing?'

'Zoe, you have to tell him.'

I sloped back into the flat and found Danny almost passed out on the sofa. I took the spliff from his fingers and stubbed it out. He opened his bloodshot eyes and peered at me, with a crooked smile.

'What would I do without you, sis?'

'Danny, pay attention.'

He nodded lazily, eyelids drooping.

'I'm moving out. Okay?'

Danny raised one hand and waved, curling his fingers over like a child.

'Bye, bye,' he said, and closed his eyes.

My insides had turned to sludge. I could feel them lurching and slopping about as Jonah drove us into town. I knew Danny's reaction was temporary. As soon as he came to and realised I was gone, there'd be hell on. I didn't want to think about it but my guts had other ideas.

The Mind shop gratefully took custody of my old clothes, (I'd have to be careful not to accidently buy them back again in a couple of months), then Jonah took me home. I was supposed to be paying attention to the route so I could remember where I lived but was so caught up in a feverish rationalisation of what I was doing to Danny, it passed in a blur of traffic lights, bus lanes and shop signs.

Jonah's flat was bigger than I remembered. The living room seemed enormous, two large windows filling it with sunlight. Last time I'd been too preoccupied to notice; now I could relax and spread out. We carried the boxes upstairs into the spare room. Jonah unlatched the futon sofa and placed it directly beneath the skylight so I could watch the stars. Then he ran back into town and picked up a basic clothes rail, while I stacked my books in piles by the bed. It was spartan, but brightened by my bizarre collection of mismatched rags hanging in the corner.

The flat was in a converted warehouse, an old boot factory in Ouseburn. Next door were the stables. I had already seen a line of ponies walking down the street, children carried aloft, riding helmets perched on their heads (the children's heads, not the horses). And Jonah had warned me about the horseshit. You had to be careful where you put your feet in this neighbourhood.

With the skylight open, if I stood on my tiptoes, I could see across the valley to the scrap metal yard hidden behind the old flour mill, now called The Cluny and home to artists and creative types. To the left was the huge brick chimney of the old forge, and behind that, the farm with its grass roof and solar panels, and beyond to the three bridges: brick, iron and concrete. The whole area was an evolving time capsule, an oasis of animals and art in the centre of town.

I flattened my cardboard boxes and took them down to the recycling bins. Stepney Bank's equestrians were hard at work, but with the shutters down I couldn't see them. The shouts from the instructor mingled with birdsong and the low hiss and hum from the road bridge, and I felt a noisy kind of peace creeping up on me. Jonah had been right: this could be my sanctuary.

'What d'you think?' Jonah shouted.

I turned. He was watching me from the long Velux window.

'I want to explore,' I shouted back.

'I'm coming down.' He disappeared and shut the window.

We sauntered down to the river Ouse, navigating the lumpy cobbled pathways. Shaggy goats munched grass in an enclosure under the Byker

Bridge, the tall brick archways vaulting over us, carrying the traffic away into the city.

'Did you know, all round here used to be fields?' I said.

Jonah grinned and leaned over the edge of the stone footbridge, watching the river bubble and swirl beneath and away to the Tyne.

'I'm serious,' I continued. 'It started out agricultural, outside the walls of the city, then the industrial revolution happened and it was all barges and slums and shitting in a bucket, and now it's gone creative.'

'Listen to you. Little Miss Ouseburn.'

We rounded the corner, following the cobbles, and stopped at the seats beside the river. Four curved concrete slabs were arranged in a circle, etched with one word each: DREAM WITH OPEN EYES. A pair of white willow trees leaned over the seats from the riverbank, their branches stripped clean and nodding in the wind. With the gentle bleating of the goats and the rush of water flowing past, my mind fell into stillness. I wandered into the centre of the circle and stood, turning on the spot. I felt strangely drawn to this place, like I was meant to be here for something important.

I closed my eyes and the stillness rippled. Goose bumps rose on my skin despite my jumper and jacket. A change was coming, a new life, a new way of seeing. But that meant something else too: death. I opened my eyes but found looking at the seats gave me vertigo. I lurched towards Jonah, and pushed against the encroaching darkness in my mind. *I am not going mad.*

'You okay?' said Jonah, as I stumbled past him.

I spun round and gave him the brightest, least mad smile I could muster. 'Fine.'

We walked back along the river past the ramshackle collection of warehouses and pigeon lofts, some dilapidated, some renovated. Everywhere I looked, nature was reclaiming the buildings, growing anywhere it could get its roots down. In the spring and summer it would come alive even as the buildings decayed. A crow cawed and swooped overhead, and I looked up. A flock of pigeons circled round and round, surging at the rooftops and then over, playing in the wind.

'I reckon I belong in a place like this,' I said. 'Shabby and neglected.'

Jonah gave me a sidelong glance and smiled.

'Not so much of the neglected,' he said, and took my hand.

You could almost believe the houses weren't there, such was the darkness spread all about us. It was as if the terraces had turned their faces from us as we passed in our little car. Jonah was driving and I sat beside him, staring into the gloom like I was searching for a lost treasure. All the streetlamps were off; the only light came from the headlights on the car, but these barely illuminated the road before us.

In the murk up ahead I could make out a shape. Our pathetic lights reached out, throwing back wild imaginings. What was out there in the darkness? As we drew closer, I could see the form of a man emerging out of the shadows, as if he were made from the night itself. He was standing with his back to us.

The car sped forwards; the man loomed closer. I shouted at Jonah to stop and he hit the brakes, just in time. The car shuddered and stopped right in front of the man. He didn't seem perturbed and calmly turned to face us. In the headlights, I could see he was in his 60s with greying hair, and was well-dressed. In fact, he was wearing a full pinstripe suit, including a waistcoat with tiny buttons and a lilac cravat. He looked at us curiously, like we were animals in a zoo, but when his eyes fell on me, a smile exploded across his face. A smile unlike any I had ever seen.

I woke with a start and sat up. I was struggling to get comfortable in my new bed and the dreams had been wild and erratic. This latest was the strangest. There was something familiar about the man but I knew I'd never seen him before. I felt sure I'd remember that cravat.

I lay back and gazed up at the stars through the skylight. It was so peaceful here despite being in the middle of the city. My mind turned fuzzy and heavy again, sleep tugging at my consciousness. A star winked, my eyes drooped. I pushed aside a thought about Jonah sleeping in the next room, and allowed the warmth and softness of the bed to pull me under into oblivion.

Maya

I was walking into Heaton, my backpack heavy on my shoulders, when my mobile rang. I knew it was Danny without looking and braced myself for the onslaught. Reality had penetrated the fug in his head and he wasn't happy.

'I'm not abandoning you, Dan. You're not a child.'

I hung up feeling guilty. Then felt bad for feeling guilty. Then felt stupid for feeling bad about feeling guilty.

Things didn't improve through the day. Danny bombarded me with texts, pleading, whining, and angry by turns, until my phone was choking with petulant rage. I stopped reading them after a while. Surely he'd run out of credit by now.

I cleaned in a frenzy, hoovering, polishing and ironing my way through two houses in Heaton and another in Jesmond. Finally, exhausted, I headed home. In fact, I was so tired I almost forgot I'd moved, and was halfway through town when I remembered and had to turn around and drag myself back to Ouseburn.

Later that evening I found myself sitting in the front seat of Jonah's van clutching a huge casserole dish wrapped in a tea towel. We were driving up to The Village in Fenham for his band practice, his guitar and amp strapped down in the back. Jonah had cooked jerk chicken while I hovered in the kitchen and watched his sinuous fingers chopping chillies and onions as he danced between the benches in a cloud of allspice and ginger. Now I could feel the heat from the chicken radiating through my hands and thighs while I listened to him talk. His smooth, deep voice slipped into my ears and around my brain like honey laced with rum.

'Cosmic plays bass like a demon possessed by an angel. He's a total, locked down funky motherfucker. The original Unmoved Mover.'

'I'm guessing he wasn't christened Cosmic,' I said.

'Na-ah. His wife calls him Ray. D'you see what we did there?' He shot me a smirk.

I grinned back. 'I dread to think what you call his wife.'

'Linda. She's looking forward to meeting you.'

'Is that so?' He'd been talking about me behind my back. 'What about the other one, the drummer?'

'Daylight plays drums like an angel possessed by a demon.'

'Daylight?'

'Short for Daylight Robbery,' he said, as if that explained everything. 'He's called Robin.'

'Right. And what do Cosmic and Daylight call you?'

'Never you mind.'

'Not much of an alias.'

Jonah laughed and shifted gears with a crunch. We crept through the traffic in spasms and finally arrived at The Village, which turned out to be a standard terraced house with peeling window frames and a garden left to the whims of nature. Ray and Linda had bought the house with the inheritance Linda received when her parents died. While Ray worked with Jonah in bureaucratic purgatory, Linda ran The Village as a B&B cum commune, with paying guests and friends staying from all over the world. Right now, they had two Norwegian scientists visiting, studying climate change at the university. Meanwhile, Robin ran a recording studio back in Ouseburn.

'It's a bit of a mad house,' said Jonah, as we clambered out the van. 'That's why I moved out. Needed some space to think, for the lyrics, y'know. It's hard to concentrate when you're living in Clapham Junction.'

He led the way to the front door, laden with his guitar and amp; I followed with the chicken. From amongst the winter stripped bushes I heard a plaintive mewling and turned. I searched the ravaged garden for the source of the sound. Golden almond eyes watched me through a thicket of branches and dead leaves.

'You've found the cat,' said Jonah. 'She's feral. Won't let anyone near her, comes in when she wants, eats and buggers off. She loves jerk.'

'What's she called?'

'Erm... That's complicated.'

Jonah pushed his key into the lock just as the door swung open. Two giants emanating the kind of health and vigour rarely seen in the British, burst through the open door. Jonah stepped aside as they slapped him on the back and plunged down the path to the gate, without breaking off their intense, incomprehensible discussion.

'Morgan and Henrik have had a breakthrough. It's very exciting.'

The female voice pulled my attention away from the babbling titans and I turned to the door. A voluptuous woman with a mass of wavy auburn hair was leaning on the door frame smiling vaguely at the retreating scientists.

'I don't understand a word of it,' she said, 'but they insist they're going to save the world.'

'Linda, this is Zoe,' said Jonah.

Linda's face froze in amazed awe for a fraction, then burst into smiles. She flew down the step from the door and engulfed me in an awkward, hairy hug; awkward because of the casserole dish in my hands.

'Oh, this is so exciting. Jonah's told me all about you. Come in, please.'

Linda ushered us both into the house and absently closed the door behind her. Suddenly, she lunged at the door in alarm and pulled it open again. The cat slipped through the gap and slunk between our legs.

'Goodness, Fluffy,' said Linda. 'I nearly chopped you in two.'

Fluffy was black with white paws and white tufts on her ears. Her name didn't seem complicated to me, although I doubted she was very pleased with it. She ignored the humans and ran straight up the stairs, which were, to my surprise, bright purple with red hearts painted at intervals all the way up.

Every wall was painted a different colour, as if the decorator couldn't decide which scheme to go for and had randomly allocated colours to walls, heedless of the result. Spread over the floor and walls were rugs and drapes showing elaborate geometric patterns, mainly from Tibet and the east. I had entered my worst nightmare – a hippy paradise.

Standing at the top of the stairs was a wiry man in jeans and stretched tight T-shirt; a powerhouse of muscle waiting to explode. I felt sure this must be Daylight, the drummer.

'Hey there, Luke,' he said, as the cat slunk by his feet.

'Robin, honestly. She's a girl,' said Linda, as we followed her up the stairs.

'She's a lady,' said another man, emerging from the kitchen down the hall ahead of us. 'And she's called Stella.'

By a process of elimination, I guessed this was Cosmic Ray. He towered over the rest of them, easily as tall as the Norwegians, and was solid, with long fingers, like Jonah's. I could see he would make a good bassist. I could also see the problem with the cat's moniker.

'I'm confused,' I said. 'Has anyone asked the cat what she would like to be called? Jonah, what do you call her?'

Linda beamed at Jonah. Ray and Robin exchanged amused glances.

'Oh, yes Jone, do tell,' said Robin.

Jonah looked like he wanted to disappear. Fluffy/Luke/Stella sat down in the open doorway to the kitchen and watched us. She yawned and licked a paw.

'Zoe,' said Jonah simply. He flashed me an apologetic smile, although I don't know why, and shrugged. 'It means life, and it's, ah... always been my favourite name.'

If I hadn't been holding the casserole dish in my arms I'd have thrown them around his neck and kissed him. I felt my cheeks redden. It had suddenly gone very quiet and everyone seemed to be looking at me.

Ray cleared his throat and took Jonah's amp. 'To work.' He disappeared up the next flight of stairs.

'Yes, the quicker you boys get started, the sooner we can eat,' said Linda, taking me by the arm and leading me to the kitchen. 'We have lots to talk about.'

The kitchen was built from mismatched pre-war units spread around the walls and piled on top of one another. The same anarchic colour scheme applied here, and the effect was galvanising. Everywhere I turned, my senses were assaulted and shaken, and I found myself hoping I didn't have a trance. Who knew what would happen under such stimulation? Perhaps my brain would pop.

The far end of the room opened into a windowed alcove filled with climbing vines and tomato plants. In the centre of the recess was a huge table made from what looked like old railway sleepers, sanded smooth, and surrounded by a higgledy-piggledy collection of chairs and stools.

I put the casserole dish in the oven, as directed, and accepted a bowl of potatoes to peel, sitting on a stool at the great slab of a table. It was like sitting in a greenhouse. Linda stood at the sink washing up plates and cutlery.

'I've always wanted to meet someone like you,' she said.

'Someone like me?' I dropped a peeled and slippery potato back into the bowl.

'Mmmm. I just do the cards, y'know. And crystals, aromatherapy, colour therapy, that kind of thing.'

'So you're responsible for all this incredible colour?'

'Good, isn't it?'

I put on my best fixed smile and nodded, a little too enthusiastically. 'I've never seen anything like it.' Linda seemed incapable of detecting irony.

'I'm training myself to see auras. I expect you see them all the time, it must be normal for you. I wish I could see like that, can you see mine now? What does it look like, have I got any murky bits, are my chakras spinning okay?'

I'm sorry to say my mouth dropped open. I stared at Linda like she was an escaped lunatic, until I realised how rude that must seem. She probably thought I was checking out her chakras.

'What exactly has Jonah told you about me?'

Linda grabbed a tea towel and dried her hands, joining me at the table, her cheeks pink with excitement.

'That you're a visionary.' She rested her hand on my arm. 'They used to hide themselves away in monasteries. Even the other monks would keep away from them, because they saw such awesome and terrifying sights. But these days, they're out in the world. Loose. Like you.'

'Erm... I'm not really religious, Linda. Don't know anything about monks.'

'Yes, yes, but that's the point. Don't you see?'

'Not really.'

'Shall I do you a reading? I'm sure it'll come up.' She reached across the table and picked up a bundle of cards wrapped in a silk scarf. After laying the scarf out between us, she shuffled the deck.

I was starting to squirm, and desperate to escape, took the potatoes to the sink to give them a wash.

'I don't want to disappoint you, Linda, but there's nothing special about my trances. They're more annoying than anything else. They just get in the way.'

'Have you got a teacher?'

I shook my head and turned off the tap, setting the potatoes to drain on the side and drying my hands on my jeans. I leaned against the sink, determined not to get drawn into this ludicrous tarot thing.

'They say when the pupil is ready, the teacher appears,' she said, and stopped shuffling, turning over three cards in quick succession. 'Oh.'

Linda laid the cards out on the scarf and beamed at me. I tried to look enthusiastic and encouraging, but probably just looked constipated.

'Past, present, future,' she said, indicating each card in turn. 'The Fool in the Past means you've recently started a new phase in your life, a leap into the unknown. Next, the Present is the Star, a great card. It shows inspiration and help. You'll meet your guardian angel or develop a hidden talent. Then, the Future is the World, the end of a cycle and reaching your goal.'

It sounded pretty vague to me and I didn't know what to make of it (nothing), so I smiled and nodded. Linda leapt from her chair and wrapped me in a bear hug, her curls finding their way into every orifice in my head.

'Whatever happens, Zoe, it's going to be amazing. You'll see.'

While Linda finished preparing dinner, I sat at the table, idly going through the tarot cards and looking at the pictures. The music of Dionysus Wept throbbed and pulsed through the house. They stopped and started and experimented. I found myself fascinated by the process: how did they know when it worked? What were they listening for? The three of them seemed perfectly locked together: the way the music would suddenly shift, speed up or slow, subtle changes in rhythm – it was almost like they were mind readers.

And when Jonah started to sing I couldn't resist. He was an angel, a banshee, a raging torrent of beauty. Like Odysseus, I had to get closer. I drifted up the stairs and sat outside the door of the rehearsal room, my head resting against the quivering wall. Remembering what Jonah had said about music being his sanctuary, I closed my eyes, for once not frightened of my mind loosening its moorings. I allowed myself to be carried and churned, plunged downwards then lifted, exulted.

A shrill ringing punctured the glorious cacophony pulling me back to my seat on the stairs. My phone was ringing. It was Danny. I sighed and watched the phone go off when he hung up. I closed my eyes again, but again the phone rang, and again, and again. Finally, I snatched it up and switched if off.

I was settling back into my uncomfortable perch when the cat appeared at my feet.

'Hello you.'

The cat purred and rubbed herself around my legs, pushing her bony head into my hand and running her rough little tongue over my fingers.

'Thought you didn't like people,' I said, scratching the cat behind its ears. 'I think it's about time we found out your real name. What d'you reckon?'

I watched the cat thoughtfully as she stretched out a paw to demand more petting. She was the least feral feral cat I had ever met. Perhaps she was faking it, or maybe she just recognised a fellow uncivilised creature in me.

'How about Maya?'

She looked at me and blinked, then up came the paw again. I obliged and rubbed under her chin.

'Maya it is.'

I ran the cloth over Buddha's belly and smiled at him. Buddha smiled his chubby wooden smile back. The figure in question belonged to Ella Richmond and I cleaned him once a week, leaving his belly and pate gleaming. Ella had picked him up in Thailand on holiday, and knew nothing about Buddhism. I knew nothing about it either, only what I could remember from *Monkey* when I was a kid, and that all seemed to be about fighting demons and flying around on magic clouds, and I was pretty sure Buddha had never done that, not literally at least. Ella had proudly placed the foot high statuette on the mantelpiece and declared, 'He looked so cheerful, I simply had to have him.'

Ella was far from cheerful. She was deep into a mid-life crisis, subsisting on anti-depressants and cake, while her husband kept disappearing to what he euphemistically called the office. Ella had the gaunt appearance of a woman trying to look younger and firmer than she was; a failed attempt to defy gravity. Her misery broadcast from her eyes no matter how wide her wretched smile. The thinner she got, the more desperate her eyes, and the longer Martin stayed away. I'd watched this mutual torture unfold over the last two years, gently cajoling Ella to get a life of her own, but she was more interested in buying stuff. She was the perfect customer for Popper Originals.

I transferred my attention to the bookshelves, although they didn't contain many books. Ella was clanging about in the kitchen, baking. In between bouts of starvation, she had baking binges, filling Tupperware boxes with flapjacks and cupcakes and all manner of sponges. She said it calmed her.

The doorbell trilled and the clanging stopped as Ella went to the front door. I could hear muffled voices, then the living room door was flung open. Ella stood in the doorway in a crimson pinny, smoothing back her hair with floury fingers. She looked flushed, even happy.

'Why didn't you tell me you had such a handsome brother?' she said.

Standing behind her was Danny, looking nervous. He shot me a wan smile and squeezed past Ella into the room.

'Hey, sis.'

'Make yourself at home, Daniel,' said Ella. 'I'll put the kettle on. Tea, yes?'

'Tea would be lovely, thank you, Mrs Richmond.'

Ella flushed the same colour as her apron. 'Oh please, call me Ella.' She left the room giggling to herself like a teenager.

I stood transfixed, duster clenched in my fist, and stared at Danny in disbelief.

'What?' he said.

'She actually giggled.'

Danny grinned. 'Long time since I've had that effect on a woman.'

'Oh, for goodness sake.' I wanted to spray him in the face with my polish. It was only olive oil and lemon juice, but still… I squirted a shelf instead.

Ella bustled back into the room carrying a tray laden with teapot, sugar and milk, three cups, cake and biscuits. She had taken off her apron, straightened out her hair and reapplied her lipstick. She poured the tea and handed a plate containing a generous wedge of chocolate cake to Danny.

'It's the last piece. I have another baking now.' She gazed at him expectantly.

Danny seemed to realise what was required of him and took an enormous bite of cake. He closed his eyes and chewed, crumbs and dark icing smeared around his mouth. He made all the right noises and gave Ella a thumbs up.

She giggled.

I rolled my eyes and grabbed a custard cream. A ping sounded from the kitchen. Ella gave Danny a sultry smile and winked.

'Don't go away. Another one coming right up,' she said, and disappeared through the door.

Danny watched her go, his eyes vacant, jaws chomping away on cake. I knew exactly what he was thinking.

'Stop that,' I said.

Danny looked genuinely perplexed. He took a swig of tea to wash down the cake. 'Don't know what you're talking about.'

'Yes you do. You're an opportunistic little fuckhead. Free cake and sex on tap. Husband away all the time, off her tits on Prozac. She's desperate.'

'That makes two of us. When are you coming home?'

'I'm not.' I turned back to my polishing. 'It's time you grew up.'

'Fine. In that case, you can't tell me what to do. Or not.'

I spun back round. Danny was exasperating. I wanted him to be happy, but he always chased after the wrong things: booze, drugs, breasts. He didn't know what he wanted. Well, not in the long term, anyway. He knew very well what he wanted in the short term.

'It'll end in tears,' I said. 'It always does.'

'You don't know everything,' he said, and stuffed a whole chocolate digestive into his mouth.

'Nobody does,' I said, my eyes falling on the beaming Buddha.

False Pretences

The lights had been up since October but it was only with the Big Day looming, that the mania set in. Everybody was getting stressed. I'd already had three desperate calls from panicked clients freaking out over poultry or puddings or oversized trees.

Town was heaving. I dribbled forward like a snail, squeezing between crazed Christmas shoppers, each with their own gravitational orbit caused by the multitude of bags stuffed in hands and under arms. I had a couple of bags myself but had finished shopping.

I was on my way to a last minute bonus clean for one of Mum's friends. Trudy was my first client, after Mum, and if I'd known who she was I wouldn't have taken her on. By the time I realised, it was too late and I was committed. She was the wife of my old psychology tutor at university; the one man I did not want to see. This meant carefully timing my visits to coincide with his lectures to be sure I didn't run into him. However, this being the holidays, I was worried. They had a visitor for Christmas and needed the place sprucing up; I just had to hope the professor was out shopping like everyone else.

I stopped to look at the Fenwick's window display. Carols screamed from the speakers on a loop and the animatronics jerked and whirled. This year it was scenes from the nativity: an angel bobbed on a wire, dangling before a surprised Mary, Joseph looked murderous, and there was a shepherd doing something unspeakable to a sheep.

All around kids giggled and pointed while their parents pretended not to notice. I was laughing along with them when I started to feel odd. Time seemed to slow, like I'd been dropped into a vat of treacle, and I sensed the presence of another mind pressing against mine.

Someone was watching me.

My blood froze, skin prickling in waves of unease. I scanned the faces reflected in the glass, looking for my stalker. Laughing faces, eyes wide and smiling, cheeks rosy with cold and happiness. All were watching the debauched shepherd.

I felt the pressure of the bodies surrounding me and clamped my jaw shut to stop myself crying out.

There's nobody there, you're imagining things.

Deck the Halls blasted from the speaker above my head, piercing the gloop in my brain and making me jump. I spun round to escape from the crush and came within kissing distance of a grinning middle-aged baby-man with two day stubble and a belly bigger than Father Christmas.

'Easy, pet,' he said. 'Where's your mistletoe?'

I laughed mechanically, then with a final desperate push, broke free.

I arrived at my tutor's house and held my breath, sliding the key into the lock as quietly as I could. My ears strained for the slightest noise. There were voices: two men arguing.

He was here.

My heart started fluttering wildly. I fought to get the key out of the lock and retreat before they heard me, but one of my shopping bags crashed into the doorframe. I yanked out the keys and dropped them with a clatter.

The living room door burst open and slippered feet appeared in the hallway.

'Ah, Zoe. Good. Trudy told me you'd be coming in.'

I retrieved my keys and stood up straight, taking a deep breath and trying to stay calm.

'Long time no see, Professor.'

Professor Charles Harrison looked just the same, if slightly podgier round the middle. He must be nearing retirement now but still had dark hair and an unkempt beard. The avuncular look was misleading. Hidden under the hair was a mind capable of laser-like destruction. He smiled and offered his hand. I took it.

'Good to see you again, Zoe.'

The last time I spoke to my tutor I was leaving university and trying to explain myself without letting on what was really happening. It hadn't gone well. And following my miniature paranoid freak out in town, I wasn't overjoyed at being in the company of a psychiatrist.

'Come and meet Felix,' he said. 'I think you'll find him interesting.'

I followed him into the spacious living room, the walls lined with shelves bulging with books. Sitting in an armchair was a man with the most extravagant facial hair I had ever seen. In contrast to Professor Harrison, his hair was pearly white and tied in a long pony tail. His moustache was enormous and lovingly coiffed into glossy arches. I couldn't stop staring at it.

'Dr Felix Baldwin,' said my tutor, 'this is the young lady about whom I was telling you. Zoe Popper.'

Dr Baldwin sprang out of the armchair, skirted the chunky coffee table and enveloped me in a warm embrace before I had a chance to even say hello. What had the professor told him? And what kind of doctor was he? He released me and gave me a long, appraising look.

'Grab yourself a cup and join us Zoe,' he said. 'You can back me up against old Charlie here. He really is quite mad.'

'I'd love to, but I'm here to clean,' I said, desperate to escape.

Dr Baldwin screwed up his face and made a noise like a pregnant buffalo.

'Balls,' he said. 'They want it clean for me. But which of us will care about a little dust when we're drunk as hell on port and stuffed like turkeys with mince pies and novelty chocolates?'

Professor Harrison rolled his eyes then shot me a look I could only describe as guilty. What was going on?

'To tell you the truth,' he said, 'we don't need any cleaning. You do such a good job at keeping the place spotless, Zoe, and I feel bad for bringing you here under false pretences. I'll pay you for cleaning anyway, if that's acceptable?'

False pretences?

'Let me at least do the bathroom.' I wanted to run from the room.

The professor smiled his agreement then put his hand on my shoulder so I couldn't escape. The three of us stood in silence for a moment and the two men smiled down at me in the most disconcerting way; like they were sizing me up for a coffin. Finally, the professor broke the silence.

'Felix is a psychiatrist, Zoe.'

Shit, shit, shit. SHIT.

I had been ambushed. Someone must have told them about me. But who? I kept the serious craziness hidden from Mum, so it couldn't have come via Trudy. Was it Jonah? Maybe he had been checking up on me.

I had to get out of there.

'Professor, I really-'

'Zoe, please. I'm not your tutor any more. We're all friends. Call me Charles.' He removed his hand from my shoulder. 'I'll get you a cup. Tea okay?'

I managed to nod. Panic was making me stiff with fear. I could barely breathe. What were they up to? Dr Baldwin was still smiling benignly at me through his abundant facial furniture. I hovered next to him, mind racing, trying to look relaxed and normal and sane.

'I think we both know you must call me Felix, eh Zoe? None of this doctor bollocks from you.'

He winked, and despite my anxiety, I found I liked him. A warning bell tinkled in the back of my mind. I must be careful not to let my guard down. That's how they get you. They trick you into relaxing then next thing you know you've got a syringe jabbed in your arse. I smiled at Felix and tried to stop thinking.

'Charlie tells me you were one of his best students,' he said.

The professor reappeared with a cup and filled it with tea from the pot. Struggling to see the Prof as a Charles, let alone a Charlie, I inched over to the armchair beyond the table and perched on the edge of the seat. I was now too far from the door to make a run for it. I was going to have to brazen it out.

Charles handed me the cup, 'You did good work, Zoe. You'd make an excellent psychologist. Good instincts.'

'That's rare,' said Felix, slurping his tea. 'He even compared you to Jung. In a complimentary way, I hasten to add. You know how he feels about all that, quote: mystical eyewash.'

'I kept a place open for you,' said Charles. 'I was disappointed when you didn't return. Did you succeed in rearranging your priorities?'

That day in his office had been one of the most humiliating moments of my life. I told him I wanted to leave due to family problems, but then Trudy had talked to Mum and I was called in to explain myself. The official line was that I had been unwell. My priorities were changing and I needed some time to sort myself out.

I wasn't sure he'd bought it at the time, and now, sitting here in this Kafkaesque ordeal, I knew he hadn't. They were both watching me, waiting for me to betray myself.

'Yes. I run my own business now.' *I mop up other people's shit.* Not a million miles from being a psychologist. 'Things are much better.'

'Waste of a good mind, if you ask me,' said Felix.

'You sound like my mother,' I blurted, then wished I hadn't.

Charles leaned back on the sofa and cleared his throat. I remembered this behavioural habit. It meant he was about to say something confrontational just to see your reaction.

'Your father was schizophrenic, was he not?' he said.

'He was dead long before I dropped out of university, professor.' My hands started to shake. I was keeping it together, but it was just a matter of time.

'You misunderstand,' he continued. 'The age your problems started. Might there be a connection?'

My tea cup started to rattle in its saucer. I leaned forward and placed it on the table, spilling half of it in the process. I took a deep breath.

'What are you insinuating?'

'Why do you think I'm insinuating something?'

I clamped my hands to my knees to keep them still and stared at the moat of tea surrounding my cup.

'Why have you brought me here?' My voice was tiny, shrunken by fear.

'You're scaring the poor girl half to death, Charles. For goodness sake, what the devil is wrong with you?'

'This is a delicate area, Felix. I'm not blundering into this the way you would.'

'Looks a lot like blundering to me, my friend.'

'Zoe,' Charles sat forward and smiled at me in a way he obviously believed conveyed empathy and compassion. It didn't. 'I'm sorry, but there's no easy way to say this.'

'You think I dropped out because I'm schizophrenic like my dad?'

Felix was shaking his head, a volcano bursting to erupt.

'This is exactly what I was talking about,' he said, rounding on Charles. 'How are you supposed to understand anything about the individual's lived experience if you expect everything they do to make sense according to your priorities? It's no wonder Zoe, and countless others like her, is unable to be honest. You force her into an Apollonian straightjacket made from monotheism and fallacies about normality and sanity, and watch her try to wriggle free. And then you have the audacity to claim it's her who is insane.'

'I have never claimed any such thing, Felix. You are putting words into my mouth, as usual.'

'You know very well sanity is culturally defined,' continued Felix, 'but you refuse to take the cultural context into account when diagnosing patients, or even to question the validity of our cultural constructions in the first place.'

He lunged forward, nearly flying out of the armchair. I thought he was about to throttle Charles, but he just continued to rant. They appeared to have forgotten I was there. Perhaps I could sneak out while they fought. With my eyes on the door, I rose from my seat in slow motion, their dispute raging in a world parallel to mine.

'You lean too heavily on that damn book,' said Felix, thumping the table with his fist and making the tea things jump like startled bunnies. 'They add the Spiritual Problem category and then fail to adequately train practitioners in recognising the problem. Just because an experience is painful, or difficult, or hard to understand, doesn't mean it should be medicated out of existence.'

'Which was precisely your approach for 25 years,' said Charles. 'The DSM is useful. It works.'

'Balls.'

'Well, we all know you want to tear up the rule book, but give me some credit.'

I was on my feet and about to dive behind the sofa and bolt for the door, when Charles looked up and caught me.

'Zoe, I didn't invite you here today to humiliate you.'

I froze.

'You sure about that, old boy?' said Felix.

Charles glared at his friend then turned back to me. I was ready to throw up all over the coffee table.

'Just answer one question,' he said.

I reluctantly returned to my seat.

'Are dreams real?'

Was this a trick question? I knew Professor Harrison was a hardcore reductionist materialist. As far as he was concerned it's all just a load of chemicals sloshing around in your brain. All your experience comes down to neurons and genes.

This must be what they'd been arguing about when I arrived. I swallowed my nausea and took a deep breath. If this was some kind of test they would need more than my beliefs on the nature of dreams to section me. So far, I hadn't done anything to alarm them. As long as I didn't have a trance, I'd be safe.

'I know you don't think dreams are real,' I said carefully, 'but then why use them in treatment? Why consider them meaningful at all if they're just produced by a bunch of randomly firing neurons. There may be a correlation between brain states and conscious experience, but correlation doesn't equal cause. Dreams are real because we experience them as such, just as we experience our own consciousness – from the inside. Also, dreams have real effects in the real world. How many times have you woken with a racing heart, or sweating, or with a massive boner?'

Felix chuckled and patted Charles on the knee. 'Not so often these days, eh, Charlie boy?'

'How do you know you're not dreaming now?' I continued. 'You only know you've *been* dreaming. Any minute you could wake up and realise: it was all a dream. That's what I'm hoping will happen now, at any rate.'

'Quite so,' said Felix, leaning across to Charles and pinching him.

'Ow!' Charles clutched at his arm.

'Is one of you going to tell me what, in the name of Freud, I'm doing here?' I said, getting some sense of myself back and relaxing a fraction.

'I'd like to offer you a job, Zoe,' said Felix. 'It wouldn't be until next academic year, but I need a research assistant with an open mind. With your background and experience I think we could do good work together.'

'What are you researching?'

'The epistemology and technologies of shamanic states of consciousness and their effects on healing individuals and communities. Been travelling round tribes in America, Africa, Siberia, and I want to compare it to our experience in Western medicine. Shamans were the first psychotherapists, first artists, first doctors, first storytellers, first everything. And yet, their skills are derided by the likes of our friend Charlie, here. Interested?'

'I never qualified. I mean, I don't have a degree.'

'Doesn't matter.' He grinned at me. 'I need your mind, not your subservience to a system of mind control.'

Charles rolled his eyes and coughed. 'Really Felix, you'll be the death of us.'

Felix whipped out a business card and handed it to me. 'Give me a call and we'll get organised.'

I looked at the card in my fingers, an alternative future unspooling itself in my imagination, one that didn't involve hours on my knees with an arm shoved down somebody's U-bend. I could explore, create new ideas. I could be happy.

Would that even be possible? Could I keep it together long enough to convince them I was capable of doing the job?

'Let me think about it,' I said, hoping my voice sounded reasonable and businesslike.

Felix smiled and twitched his whiskers. 'Absolutely. Take your time.'

Thumbprint of God

Fragmented images flashed and swirled about me, none of them lasting long enough to decipher. It was the tail end of a convoluted dream that had confused me even while I was having it, and I wanted to wake up and get back to reliable, linear reality. At last, I struggled into consciousness and lay with my eyes squeezed shut. I wanted to be awake, but didn't want to get up. The weather had been frigid lately, and I knew once I emerged from the duvet, bits of me would start to freeze. The acidic tang of coffee hit my nose and made me think I was lying on the sofa downstairs. Disoriented, I opened my eyes and saw an envelope with my name on it leaning against a steaming mug on the floor beside the futon. I frowned at it, utterly baffled, until I remembered it was Christmas Day.

I propped myself up on the pillows and opened my card. Jonah had sneaked in while I was sleeping. I smiled at the snowman on the card. Last night I left Jonah's card on his computer keyboard because I didn't trust myself to go into his room. His present was hidden in a plastic bag bundled up beside my bed and I was a little anxious over his reaction.

I was on my regular trawl of the charity shops, looking for Christmas presents and bargains, when I found it. I worked my way methodically through Scope, Mind and Shelter, and a bunch of others – the names all blurred into one after a while. Each shop was more depressing than the last. No number of brightly coloured signs or jolly window displays of mannequins in wigs at a jaunty angle, prepared you for the smell. These were shops of death, the clientele shuffling between the fusty racks like vultures picking clean a carcass.

By the time I reached Oxfam I'd found two tops and a skirt for me; a chunky ashtray made from recycled glass in the shape of a four-leaf clover, a perfect present for Danny; and a faux-fur jacket that would look great on Mum, once I'd given it a clean. All I needed was something for Jonah, and I was struggling.

I was zipping through a rack of men's stuff when, out of the corner of my eye, I saw a dark purple sleeve poking out from the shirts. I dove on it and yanked it out, holding it up for inspection. It was silk and looked the right size. Could this be the actual shirt? What would happen if it wasn't? Would it just remind him of his horrible ex? We could always ceremonially burn it if he hated it.

I put my snowman card on top of the pile of books beside the bed and picked up my coffee. There was a soft knock at the door, then Jonah's head appeared, smiling.

'Merry Christmas,' he said. 'Ready for your present?'

I put the coffee back down and nodded eagerly. He came in holding a large box wrapped in gold and silver paper. He was still in his pyjama bottoms, dressing gown hanging open showing off a muscular torso. I took a deep breath and kept my eyes fixed on his face. He perched on the edge of the bed and put the box into my lap.

'If they don't fit we can exchange them,' he said, beaming with anticipation.

I tore at the paper and opened the box to reveal a pair of hiking boots. They were the right size. I was dumbstruck. Jonah must be the first person ever to give me something I really needed. I hadn't even asked for them. I wanted to cry.

'Jonah, they're fantastic. I don't know what to say. I mean, thank you.' Tears started to roll down my cheeks. I felt ridiculous crying over a pair of boots. What was wrong with me? 'Now look. You've made me cry. I never cry.'

I lifted a hand to wipe my cheeks but Jonah beat me to it. He leaned across and gently ran his fingers under my eyes. There was a pause. We both seemed to hold our breath. I became absurdly aware of the mess of box, paper and boots piled between us, and wanted to push it all onto the floor and lunge at him. Instead, I turned and grabbed the plastic bag from the other side of the bed, thrusting it into his hands.

'Sorry I didn't wrap it. I don't know if it's the one, but... well...'

Jonah opened the bag and peered in, his eyes opening wide in astonishment. He pulled out the shirt and held it up, letting the bag fall to the floor. He pressed the silky fabric to his face and inhaled.

'They washed it,' he said in surprise. 'I can't believe you found it.'

He grinned at me then shoved the box of boots and accompanying jumble onto the floor, and dropped the shirt on top.

'Are you sure it's the right one?' I said.

My heart was doing back flips. Jonah shunted up the bed and took my face in his hands, looking deep into my eyes. There was no way he was thinking about the shirt.

'Positive.'

The heat from his fingers on my cheeks tingled and I felt sparks spread through my body and bounce around my belly as I leaned towards him. His breath felt warm and soft on my lips. He tasted of coffee. I could feel his heart pounding through the air between us, the heat from his body rising in waves. I ruthlessly quashed a stray thought about how my coffee was going cold, then all thoughts dissolved into skin and hands, limbs and tongues, and I didn't care about the coffee, or the boots, or the shirt, or anything.

I opened the door to Danny's flat and had to take a step back as a putrid stench engulfed my senses. Since I'd moved out the place had descended into olfactory anarchy.

I found Danny sprawled on the sofa nursing a bottle of Glenfiddich tied with a red bow. He was surrounded by the usual carnage of half-eaten takeouts and crushed cans. On the coffee table was a jumbo pack of condoms. What had he been up to?

'Don't you ever clean anything?' I said.

He belched.

'Where d'you get expensive booze like that?'

'Present.'

I'd guessed that from the bow, but who was responsible? An image of Ella flashed into my mind and I pushed it aside. It seemed unlikely.

'What's with the jollies?' I said.

Danny grimaced and looked like he might be sick. The sooner we got some food into him, the better. I stepped across the mess and stood over him, took hold of his wrist and pulled.

'Come on, time for dinner.'

He yanked his arm back. 'Not going in that bitch's house. She'll poison me.'

'Not at Mum's, you idiot. The Village.'

'The where?'

I dragged Danny to the van parked outside, where Jonah was waiting patiently. I bundled him into the back and got him strapped into a seat. He was still clutching the whiskey bottle. I hadn't been able to liberate it from his sticky fingers, but had managed to replace the cap. He hadn't noticed and tried to drink from the bottle without removing it. There were a few confused moments before he realised what had happened. He looked at me reproachfully.

'Where's this village, then?' he said.

'It's just a house.'

'Stupid,' slurred Danny.

Jonah drove us the short distance into Fenham. I sat beside him in the passenger seat and grinned. I'd been grinning all morning. I hadn't felt this good in a long time. I stole tiny glances at Jonah as we drove. Every time I looked at him, he was looking at me. He was grinning too.

Danny held onto his bottle and watched the grins bounce back and forth: the happiest tennis match ever played.

'What in the name of Glenfiddich has got into you two?' he said.

The Village was swamped with tinsel and streamers, hundreds of cards clustered on every flat surface, and incense thickened the air with frankincense and myrrh. The rum flambéed chicken stuffed with plantain went down without touching the sides and every plate was licked clean. Replete and bloated with food and wine, the party moved to the more comfortable seats in the living room so we could spread out and loosen belts.

I curled up with Jonah on the sofa, Lucy, Ray and Robin stretched out in arm chairs, and Danny sprawled on a beanbag in the middle of the room. Everyone ignored the flickering TV. We were waiting for Doctor Who.

The cat slipped through the door and jumped onto my lap. Maya turned round a couple of times then dropped into a ball on my belly and began purring so loudly everyone turned to see what was making the noise. Eyebrows shot up all round and Jonah smiled.

'Traitor,' said Ray.

'Apparently, she would like to be called Maya,' I said.

'You come round here,' said Robin, 'eat our food, name our cat, shag our guitarist, making him all happy and shit.'

A chuckle purred deep in Jonah's chest.

'Where are the songs going to come from now? We'll have to disband,' said Ray, hamming it up. 'Or find an unhappy replacement.'

'Don't fret,' said Jonah. 'It works just as well with joy. Better, possibly.' He crooked his neck to look down at me, nestled against his chest. 'I've never tried it before.'

I smiled up at him and saw my happiness reflected in his eyes. My toes tingled and a yawning relaxation spread through my body. I recognised the feeling immediately. It was the beginning of a trance. I could feel it creeping up on me but was too comfortable to fight it. The whole room seemed to breathe out. I closed my eyes and sensed the others close by, breathing with me. Danny began to snore, someone chuckled softly, another shifted in their seat.

My body suddenly felt very heavy. I was pulled into the sofa, like I was made of stone. It felt like falling asleep and staying awake at the same time: the body relaxes and the mind sharpens. My mind opened into an endless space, an infinite panorama; and I could see – like my eyes had snapped open, even though I knew they were closed. Shapes and patterns formed and shifted in front of my open/closed eyes.

It started in black and white with basic geometric forms, zigzags and squiggles. As the patterns became more complex, they changed, in a flash, to colour. I slowed my breathing and relaxed further. Intricate and exquisite patterns hung in the air around me, fractals twisting and evolving into new explosive shapes. The whole display was revolving clockwise, like I was inside a vast tube, watching the patterns on a screen, sliding slowly past, a couple of feet from my face. The fractals pulsed and the display moved gently towards me then away again, as if it were breathing.

With a surge of joy, I noticed this movement matched my own breath. All through childhood I had seen these patterns in the air. I had lain in bed, with my eyes open, and enjoyed the show. It was better than television. Later, when I found pictures in books of the same patterns, I was overjoyed. There were many different types, but one had stood out:

the Mandelbrot set, the Thumbprint of God. I was looking at the mathematical foundations of the universe, of life.

I opened my eyes and the fractals continued their dance. It was the coolest thing I'd ever seen and I wanted to cry with joy. I could see the room behind the translucent patterns, and was dimly aware of voices.

'What's she doing?' said Robin.

'Is she epileptic?' said Ray.

'She's fine,' said Jonah. 'It'll pass.'

'I wish I could see what she's seeing,' said Linda. 'Oh, this is so exciting, to be here and see it happen.'

'Shush, now,' said Jonah.

I could feel him stroking my hair. He was watching over me, keeping me safe. The fractals were beginning to fade and I felt a momentary panic; I didn't want them to go. Something else was circling in the darkness. I could feel the presence of someone powerful, someone trying to push into my consciousness. My stalker was back. I concentrated on the softness of the cat's fur against my fingers and tried to resurface, come back to reality, but something stronger gripped my mind.

'Pay attention.'

The shock of the man's voice jolted me upright. Linda was crouched beside the sofa, watching me with rapt eyes. I felt Jonah's hand rub my back, and I sank, gratefully, into his arms.

'Okay?' he said.

I nodded, but it felt like two thousand volts had just detonated through my body. I ran my hands over Maya's quivering form and tried to synchronise my heartbeat with Jonah's. Slowly, calm returned. I didn't want to deal with the avalanche of questions I had no doubt Linda would assail me with, so I pressed my cheek to the warmth of Jonah's skin and pretended to be asleep, one hand buried in the cat's fur.

Maya continued to purr.

The Ultimate Subversion

As soon as I walked through the supermarket doors I wanted to turn around and walk out again. I was still feeling jangled from my latest encounter with weirdness, like my skin had been pulled off. It was early, so Morrisons wasn't too busy, but the light still hurt my eyes and the vacuous music still made me want to shove radishes in my ears. I couldn't filter out the noise like I normally would. I couldn't filter anything out. Walking down the aisles was an assault course, stacks of products all screaming for attention, arranged deliberately to confuse, so you end up buying stuff you don't want, let alone need. Nobody needed this much choice. It was a conspiracy of consumption. It was unhealthy.

I consulted my list. I had carefully prepared it to match the order of the shelves so I could get in and out as quickly as possible. But here I was, basket in one hand, list in the other, lost in soup and canned meat. This should be cereal. They had moved everything. Again.

'I need an au pair,' said a joyful man's voice behind me.

I shivered. The voice sounded familiar but I couldn't place it. As I turned, it hit me: it was the voice from the trance. The powerful, overwhelming voice commanding me to Pay Attention. I almost bolted for the doors, but instead found myself looking into the face of a super-spruce gentleman who was smiling at me with great amusement. His hair was grey and his pinstripe suit expensive, with a waistcoat with tiny buttons and a sleek lilac cravat. He looked like he'd stepped straight out of my dream into the shop.

I fumbled around in a pocket and pulled out one of my business cards, holding it out for him. Maybe he thought au pairs were cleaners and had got confused. Maybe he was just posh. He made no move to take the card – just stood there, smiling.

'Adam Kadmon,' he said, with a nod of his head. 'At your service.'

I felt stupid standing there holding out my card, so put it back in my jacket. My mind had gone into slow motion trying to work out what was going on. Why was this man talking to me? Why had I dreamed about him? Was he following me? Had it really been him speaking to me through my trance the other day? And why did he have such a strange name? Whoever he was, he seemed out of place, like he didn't quite belong here.

He looked about, amused by something. 'You'll not find what you need in here.'

'Oh?' I was intrigued despite myself. 'And what do I need?'

'Don't you know?'

He fixed me with a look so deep, so unfathomable, I had to look away. I fumbled around, looking for a response.

'I've seen you before. In a dream.' I felt foolish telling him this, but his smile grew warm.

'Meet with me on Sunday,' he said.

Part of me wanted to argue, to run. This was too outlandish. My brain wanted to shut down and sleep. But another part of me, a deeper part, understood what was happening. I needed to talk to his man but couldn't do it here surrounded by oxtail, minestrone and spam. His eyes twinkled and yet he was absolutely serious. I knew in my bones I couldn't argue with him, or at least not win an argument with him.

'Where and when?' I said.

'The circle seats by the river at noon.'

I glanced away for a second to work out where he meant. Why was he being so obscure? There was that set of concrete seats arranged in a circle beside the river Ouse just down the street from my flat, the ones with the words about dreaming carved into them. *Did he know where I lived?*

I looked back and the aisle was deserted. I rushed down to the end and searched left and right. There was no sign of him.

He had vanished.

That evening I hung around the kitchen while Jonah cooked rice and beans. I still had the jitters and kept getting in his way. I managed to be standing in the wrong place at the wrong time over and over, and could tell he was getting annoyed but I wanted to tell him about Adam.

'Why would I dream about him and then meet him? What's going on?'

Jonah shrugged and poked at the boiling rice. 'You're the visionary, babe.'

'I know I need to talk to him, but I'm scared of what he'll say.'

'The fear of madness stuff again?'

I nodded and chewed on a fingernail.

'How old was he?' he said.

'Hard to say.' This had been puzzling me all day. 'He could be in his sixties, but then, he seemed younger and kind of older too. It doesn't make sense.'

'So what does an old bloke want with a young woman?' said Jonah, taking the rice off the stove.

'He's harmless.'

'And you know that because?'

'Because... I don't know, Joe. If you saw him, you'd understand.'

'Y'know, you shouldn't trust a man just 'cos he's wearing a natty suit,' he said, with a smirk. He drained the rice, disappearing in a cloud of steam.

I remembered the first time I'd seen Jonah, standing by the Tyne Bridge, shivering in his best suit. I hadn't been remotely interested in his clothes. I smiled to myself and hooked my arms around his waist as he stood at the sink, slipping a hand under his T-shirt and running my fingers across his belly.

'I'm sure it'll be fine,' I said, and almost believed myself.

Sunday arrived and I made my way down the cobbles behind The Ship Inn. The lumpy path was so uneven, one tiny slip and I could be laid up for days with a twisted ankle and unable to work, which would mean no money, so I concentrated hard on where I was putting my feet. It was a welcome distraction from the sickness in my stomach. I hadn't managed breakfast that morning because I was too nervous to eat, and now I was regretting it.

I crossed the footbridge and rounded the corner. Adam Kadmon was sitting on the seat marked DREAM, waiting for me. I had an impulse to turn back, but it was too late, he had seen me. I entered the circle and sat opposite him, on the seat marked OPEN.

'I wasn't sure I should come, I mean, I don't know... you could be... not that I think you're a...' *Stop rambling, Zoe.* 'I don't know you from Adam.' I laughed my best hysterical laugh and stared at the cobbles at my feet like they were the most fascinating thing I'd ever seen.

Adam didn't move. He sat listening and watching in the same suit and cravat as before. *Didn't he have any other clothes?* It was profoundly disquieting. He was doing the therapist thing: sitting in silence and waiting for you to figure it out for yourself. Well, if I was capable of figuring it out for myself, I wouldn't be here, would I?

'Why did you come?' he said.

'I don't know.'

'What do you want, more than anything?'

Peace on earth? Everlasting happiness? To win the lottery? A flat stomach? There were a million answers to that question, but I knew we were talking ultimates. The bottom line. The non-negotiable, deal breakers. I didn't even know how to begin answering. I felt completely lost.

'I just want to understand who I am. Underneath all the madness.'

'You must stop running away.'

I laughed again. 'I'm not running away. I came here, despite myself. I'm sitting here.'

'Are you?'

In a snap, my mind kicked into high alert. I did want to run away. Every nerve, every muscle in my body was straining because I was repressing a violent desire to flee. Adam gave me a look so intense and focused I couldn't hold his gaze. It felt as if the earth was moving beneath my feet. I pushed my hands against the rough, freezing concrete. It felt solid enough, but it didn't help, the ground was still reeling. I jumped up and started to pace.

'Why are you staring at me like that?' I said, panic making my voice thin. 'It makes me feel like, I don't know, like-'

'Like you're standing on the edge of the world,' he said softly, 'and one tiny gust will send you tumbling over into nothing.'

'Who are you?' I spun round to face him, anxiety making me tremble.

'Sit down.' His voice was gentle, like a caress. 'If I'm going to help, we need to establish where you are right now.'

I sat.

'But I understand,' he continued. 'You need some reassurance. I could be a nutcase, right?' He chuckled heartily and light flickered in his eyes.

I nodded and smiled. His laugh was infectious and I felt a bubble of joy burst in my belly and spread. The idea that he could be a lunatic suddenly seemed absurd.

'I ran for a long time too,' he said.

Adam had been a broker, one of those traders surrounded by screens and telephones and blinking numbers. It explained the big ticket suit. He made lots of people lots of money, and stashed a canny sum for himself in the process. On his way to work one morning on the M25, his Ferrari started to splutter, so he pulled over. Smoke was pouring from the engine. He sat at the side of the road and watched the flames lick around his tyres while he waited for rescue. By the time they arrived, the engine had damn near exploded, and so had he.

His blood pressure was off the scale and he hadn't slept properly for years. Being a superstitious sort in those days, he took it as an omen and quit his job. He got out in time to miss the stupendous crash which was just around the corner and would have cost him, and his clients, a fortune.

This made him think. And the more he thought, the more he realised his life was out of balance and he needed to do something about it. He travelled the world but couldn't settle anywhere. He started to ponder the meaning of life and found himself in a woodland monastery in Japan. He was stripped of his belongings and his beloved suits, and threw himself into monastic life with the fervour of a recent convert.

'That's where things got interesting. I struggled and fought and ran. I made life very hard for myself.' He chuckled. 'But you can't outrun the process.'

'What process?'

'Liberation.'

'From what?'

'You.' He smiled, as if to be free from yourself would be the most wonderful, glorious thing in the world.

'But I don't want to be free of myself. I want to know who I am.'

He laughed. 'And who is that?'

'Well, I don't know, that's why I'm here.'

'Precisely. You're already on the path, Zoe. You're a mystic. You just need a little training.'

A what?

Being labelled insane was one thing. Being labelled a religious crackpot was another.

'No. I don't believe in all that God shit.' I spat the words at him and stood. 'You've made a mistake.'

My head was swirling with heat and confusion. I marched away from the seats, vibrating with anger and embarrassment. Why had I come here? It was such a stupid thing to do.

Adam shouted after me, his voice echoing round the valley and implanting itself in my mind, 'Same again next week.'

I didn't look back.

I slammed the front door behind me, swept through to the living room, and flung myself on the sofa. Jonah was composing on his synth at his computer in the corner, headphones clamped to his ears. He slipped them off and spun his chair to face me.

'What happened?' he said, looking worried.

'He's a nut job.'

Jonah leapt to his feet. 'What did he do?'

'Nothing. He didn't do anything.'

I rubbed my hands over my face in frustration. I didn't want to think about what Adam had said, it couldn't be true. I was a rational human being, not some brain dead, wishy-washy hippy mystic imbecile, floating about being all mysterious and talking gibberish.

'He said I was a mystic. A fucking mystic.'

'Didn't you talk to Linda?'

'She just babbled about monks and tarot cards, and you were the one who told her I was a visionary, Joe.'

'What if it's true?' he said. 'He might be able to help. You do keep having those experiences.' He flicked his index fingers up to emphasise the last word. 'Being a mystic could be cool, like being a shaman. That shrink with the tache, maybe that's why he wants to work with you. In the old days, or in a different culture, like the ones he's been studying, you'd be revered.'

'Yes, and sent to live in a hut on the edge of the village away from everyone so I don't upset them with my craziness.'

'You are a bit psychic, you know.' He sat on the sofa and scooched me towards him. I snuggled against his chest and listened to his heart beating.

'I am not,' I said, pretending to sulk.

'You're always saying things I'm thinking. Sometimes I think you're in my head.'

I sat up and looked at him. 'Isn't that a bit weird? Doesn't it freak you out?'

Jonah shook his head and smiled. 'It's cool, babe. You're part of me.'

I cleaned my way through the week trying not to think about Adam and his ridiculous assertion, but in reality, thinking of little else. It felt like an accusation, a slanderous taunt designed to undermine every truth I knew about myself. Thousands of years of evolution, of struggle, of fear and superstition, and only recently had humans succeeded in wrestling rationality from the maw of the dragon of irrational authority: religion. I wasn't going to be another convert to the backward march to insanity and fundamentalism. Just because life was chaotic and confusing, people thought they were justified in switching off their brains.

Well, not me. No matter how confused I got, I refused to stop thinking. Trouble was, it was starting to feel like I was being followed around by a gibbering idiot, running the same arguments back and forth.

It was true, I kept having weird trances I didn't understand, and it wasn't like I could ignore them, people were starting to notice. Sooner or later it would happen in front of the wrong person and they would lock me up in a secure ward doped up on hardcore anti-psychotic pharmaceuticals. All my worst case scenarios involved losing my autonomy, being at the mercy of some other person. Worse still, a psychiatrist. Most of them were not like Felix Baldwin.

I'd read of an experiment where a bunch of people got themselves diagnosed schizophrenic by reporting the usual symptoms to their doctors. Once hospitalised, they started to behave in a totally normal way. But because they'd been diagnosed, everything they did was seen as symptomatic of their illness. You get a new label, a new identity, and you're written off.

Even when things got intensely screwed up at university, I avoided doctors, convinced they would shunt me onto pills. How could I think straight if my mind was warped by chemicals? How would I know I was even me anymore? I'd become a list of characteristics, behavioural quirks and compulsions, my humanity reduced to a diagnosis. I remembered how Dad was when they put him on the serious stuff. He didn't paint, he didn't do anything, just sat and stared out the window. That's why he kept throwing out the pills. That's why he killed himself.

But what if I really was mad? What if my mind was already warped? Calling it mysticism didn't make it any less insane. Then again, what if the culture I'd grown up in had it wrong? What if the secular worldview was incomplete or false? What if, and I could barely bring myself to think it, what if I really was a mystic? My mind baulked at the thought, but it persisted. The rational thing would be to find out more. All I knew about mysticism came from psychiatric books and papers, and I guessed they weren't exactly experts on the subject.

At worst, it was regressive and infantile: the patient escapes reality by sliding back to the oceanic oneness felt in the womb, into a kind of nihilism. Thank you, Freud. At best, it was a search for God. Thank you, Jung.

If I knew one thing, I knew I definitely wasn't looking for God. There was no such thing, so it would be futile, and by definition, mad. It would be the same as going off hunting unicorns or fairies. Besides, I felt close enough to madness as it was; why would I walk straight into it, willingly open myself to disintegration?

I ran my cloth back and forth across the mirror, rubbing viciously at every tiny speck. The mirror was enormous and dominated the hallway of my favourite customer. I thought, vaguely, that I shouldn't have favourites, that everyone's home should be equally cleaned and cared for, but Dorothy was different. Outwardly, she appeared shrunken and shrivelled, but in reality she was formidable. Unlike most older people, she never mentioned her age. I had tried to find out once, but Dot had batted it away as irrelevant. Most people never grew up, some people were never young. And that was that.

'You keep polishing like that there'll be no mirror left.'

Dorothy was watching me from the doorway to the living room, leaning awkwardly on her stick. Her arthritis must be playing up again. I stopped polishing and stood back to admire my work.

'Come and sit,' said Dorothy. 'You have something to get off your chest.'

'I need to get your shopping in. Is the list in the kitchen?' I escaped down the hall then disappeared out the back door to the shop.

Dorothy was waiting for me when I got back. She hobbled about helping to put the shopping away. There was no sense in telling her to go and sit down. The woman was unstoppable, and I knew I wasn't going to get away with not telling her what was on my mind.

'Right then. Make us a cuppa and come and sit down,' she said, as she limped back down the hall.

I obeyed, and joined her in the living room. After practically wrestling the teapot from her hands, I poured the tea and we settled back on the chintzy sofa, dunking our way through a plate of chocolate chip cookies. I tried to describe my experiences to Dot. It was farcical and embarrassing, the limits of my vocabulary and understanding making me sound like I didn't know English. I told of my meeting with Adam, and my doubts over what he had said.

'I don't know which would be worse, finding out I really am crazy, or finding out I'm a religious nut in denial, a God Botherer in disguise,' I said, dunking another cookie.

Dorothy roared with laughter, almost spilling her tea, and had to put her cup back on the coffee table.

'How much thought have you given this, young lady?'

'Loads.'

She shook her head. 'You've studied the Bible, the Koran and the Torah, you've debated with theologians and philosophers, and grappled with the ultimate metaphysical questions of existence?'

'Well... no.'

'So how can you be sure?'

'It's obvious, isn't it? I mean...' I searched in vain for an answer. I had been an atheist all my life, it had never occurred to me to actually think about it or question it. Back in Brighton, I went to church with my maternal grandmother; she liked me to keep her company. I dangled my legs in the uncomfortable pews and gawped at the patterns in the stained glass windows, while the huddled and ageing congregation groaned through hymns and mumbled through prayers. Then they would troop up to the altar to take communion. I never joined them; couldn't think why I would. It was just another bizarre ritual, another thing grown-ups did that made no sense, like putting out a mince pie and a carrot for Father Christmas. Sitting there in church, I felt like an alien from another culture. What did they think they were doing? It baffled me.

I had never doubted my lack of faith. Religion didn't seem necessary. As far I as was concerned, God was as real as Santa. I couldn't believe I was even having this conversation.

'It's just not rational,' I spluttered.

Dorothy exploded in laughter again, then grew serious and gripped my hand. The strength in those gnarled fingers surprised me, and I turned to face the old woman.

'It's not rational to exclude the irrational,' she said. 'Who are you to decide the truth of something without investigating first? Is that rational?'

'No. No it isn't.'

'That said, most of us don't have the wherewithal to answer these questions. We're not inclined or we don't have the time, so we rely on folks who can. Folks like you, Zoe.' She released her grip and took the last cookie.

'You have a gift,' she said. 'Use it.'

Dorothy almost had me convinced, but I wanted more information, so when Jonah's band practice came around again, I tagged along. I was determined to pin Linda down and get some sense out of her. While the maestros rehearsed, I told her about Adam.

'See,' she said, her smile so wide it threatened to tear her head in two. 'What did I tell you? This is brilliant.'

Linda threw her arms around me and hung on like a drowning woman. I twitched free and sat down at the kitchen table, while she opened a bottle of wine.

'He said I was a mystic.'

'I knew it,' she said, and poured two generous glasses of red, then slid one under my nose.

'Can you tell me what a mystic actually is?'

Linda sat down with a bump and stared into space for a moment, twirling her glass in her hand.

'A mystic is someone who wants to discover the truth about reality. The same as scientists, really, but working with the inner world instead of the outer.'

'Is that all?'

She nodded and took a sip of wine. 'It's probably not at all straightforward.'

'No,' I said. 'If it were obvious, everybody would be at it.'

Linda jumped up and opened a lurid pink cupboard. It was stuffed with a jumble of recipe books, assorted odd ends and a battered Scrabble box. She pulled out an equally battered dictionary and searched the pages, scanning down the words with an index finger.

'Here we are.' She sat down. 'Mystic: a person who seeks by contemplation and self-surrender to obtain unity with or absorption into the Deity or the absolute, or who believes in the spiritual apprehension of truths that are beyond the intellect.'

She snapped the book shut and bounced to the cupboard to put it back. 'Of course, mystics say it is obvious. I don't really get it, but they say the truth is hidden in plain sight, an open secret. I thought you might know, Zoe.'

'Sorry.' I shrugged.

'But you've got a teacher now,' she said, joining me back at the table. 'All will be revealed.'

I sipped my wine. So far, this conversation hadn't been very reassuring. All this talk of deities and self-surrender was making my head spin. Or perhaps that was the wine.

'If all they're doing is looking for the truth,' I said, 'why are they so vilified? You'd think we'd be queuing up to find out what's really going on in the world.'

'That's just it,' she said. 'Zen is the ultimate subversion. Mystics are ignored because most of us don't have the guts to follow through on what they show us. Which is the death of our ego. People don't like that. Not one little bit. It undermines all our assumptions, everything we've built society on. Because once you know the truth, there's no going back. Everything has to change.'

That was exactly what I feared.

A Grand Prix of Cogitation

Adam wasn't there when I arrived at the concrete seats. I leaned over the fence and watched the river tumble by, my breath condensing in the frigid air. A polite cough sounded behind me and I turned. Adam was sitting on one of the seats dressed in his usual exquisite tailored suit, having made no concession to the weather. I blew into my gloved hands and sat opposite him.

'Aren't you cold?'

'You came back.'

I started to unwind my fluffy purple scarf. 'D'you want this?'

Adam smiled. 'I'm just fine. But thank you.'

'Seriously, you must be freezing.'

'Still running, I see.'

I threw my scarf back around my throat and sat very still. Maybe he was one of those yogis who can control their body temperature. They sit outside in the middle of winter, completely naked, while other monks wrap wet blankets around them. They generate so much heat within their bodies, the blankets dry out in minutes. Adam didn't look cold at all, but I couldn't ask him about it now, he'd think I was still dodging something. There was no getting away from it.

'Jonah said you might be able to help me control my trances.'

Adam watched me closely, and I shifted in my seat. It felt like he was looking straight through me. I wasn't sure he was even blinking.

'Erm... Jonah's my boyfriend. He, well... I, um...' This wasn't going well.

'Start at the beginning.' Adam's voice was gentle and soothing, like he understood how hard this was for me. I took a deep breath and began.

'When I was about 7, or maybe 8, not sure, probably doesn't matter, I used to see fractals in the air, still do sometimes, when I trance. You know fractals?'

Adam nodded.

'So, anyway, that stopped for a bit, when I was a teenager. And then everything was normal, well, y'know, normal for a teenager. Mood swings, hormonal apocalypse. Lots of crying, mainly. Never cried since, well, once over some boots, but that's not... relevant. Anyway, I went to university and that's when it all went wrong.'

I looked down at my shaking hands. I had never told anyone what happened that summer, just before my 21st birthday. I knew how it sounded. I knew they'd think I was insane. I didn't want people to look at me the way they looked at Dad, with that stupid fixed smile and the fear in their eyes that said: please don't do anything crazy, please don't make me uncomfortable.

'It's okay,' said Adam. 'Take your time.'

He spoke so softly I almost didn't hear him. I took another deep breath. I knew I had to tell it all, but it was hard to keep it straight in my head. In a sense, I had made myself forget. It was the only way to keep moving forward.

It was the end of the second year, summer break, and Mum was away on an art buying trip. She left me in charge of the house. I don't know how it started, it came out of nowhere. One minute, I'm studying the development of syntaxical-membership cognition and the next, I'm hearing voices and having massive panic attacks. A room full of people had invaded my head and were all talking at once; a tape playing backwards at speed, gibberish ripping my mind to shreds. I had amnesia and lost pockets of time. There was just a kind of blankness; my brain sucked into a black hole. I'd sort of wake up walking down the street with no idea where I was going or why. I would turn around and go home, only to discover we'd run out of milk and have to go back out again.

Then there were the days everything glowed. It was as if the world had become more real, more alive, like it was shouting at me, pulsing with an inner light, buzzing with an energy I could sense rather than see. Even inanimate objects seemed alive, and it was all connected up, somehow. But then, the next day the light would be gone and everything was back to being dead and empty; a hollowed out travesty of the world.

My mind swung back and forth. I fell into a void: I was nothing, an absence of anything meaningful. I didn't even recognise myself; the face in the mirror was a stranger. I would stand there, staring into frightened eyes, and in the back of my mind there's a voice, a reasonable, rational voice, saying don't be ridiculous, that's you, that's how mirrors work, but it looked like a crazy person, and I wasn't a crazy person, so how could that be me?

I'd read all the books so knew what was happening. I was dissociated, ontologically insecure, it was a psychotic break, a regression in service of the ego. But I didn't want to service my ego, I wanted to kill it. I had no control, no understanding, and I wanted it to end. I planned my death with fanatical precision, careful not to draw attention or alarm anyone. I stockpiled painkillers, squirreling them away in my knickers drawer where Danny wouldn't find them. I had so many I could've killed myself several times over. But when it came to it, I was stopped.

'Someone found you in time?' said Adam.

'No. I'd been extra careful about that. I was determined to die and didn't want some well-meaning person spoiling it.'

'So what stopped you?'

'I don't know. One minute, I'm sat feeling numb, pills crushed up and ready to go, and the next... I was calm and peaceful, like something had lifted me up. I felt light and kind of protected. And it was as if there were two of me. One was screwed up beyond belief and the other was cool and serene. And I knew, without a doubt, that the cool, serene me was the real me, and that no matter what happened, no matter what I did to myself, or what others did, I would be all right. Because the real me was untouchable. It had always been and always would be. It's haunted me ever since. I don't know what it was and I want to know.'

'Good,' said Adam, like he was congratulating me for a job well done.

'Good?'

'First, you're not insane. Second, you need grounding. Third, you lack discipline.'

'How do you know I'm not crazy?'

'I've been through something similar. Your perception is transforming. At a certain point in the development of our consciousness it becomes possible for us to evolve to the next level, to wake up. Without training this can be, shall we say, messy.'

'This doesn't happen to everyone, though.'

'It can,' he said. 'There's a taboo against transcendence. We grow up and develop an ego, a centre from which to observe the world. There's nothing wrong with this. But consciousness doesn't stop evolving just because we think it does. Transcendence cannot be repressed. It finds another route, often destructive – alcohol, drugs, and so on. Mostly evolution doesn't happen beyond ego because people aren't aware it's possible. You, on the other hand, have an abnormally endowed mind.'

'Great,' I said, a bit heavy on the sarcasm.

'Your only choice is to work with it, or not. But be aware,' Adam grew severe, 'if you choose not to follow the path, this process, the one you're already undergoing, will continue. It will continue whether you cooperate or not.'

'And if I don't cooperate?'

'I think you've already had a taste.'

It didn't sound like much of a choice to me. I could ignore what was happening, repress it, rationalise it, run the hell away from it with everything I had, and it would pursue me and rip me to pieces, like a pack of rabid wolves. Or I could embrace it and learn to master it, even if that meant entering scary territory and slaughtering a few sacred cows. I still didn't feel comfortable calling myself a mystic, so I put that aside for the time being. This was an experiment. I would enter into it in the spirit of a scientist. I would lay out my evidence, then seek to falsify it. I would discover the truth. What other choice did I have?

'What do I need to do?'

'I'm going to teach you a basic mindfulness meditation. I want you to watch your breath. The breath will always bring you back to your body, stop you getting lost in that big head of yours.' Adam smiled at last, his eyes twinkling with mischief.

I relaxed. He said he had been through the same thing; he understood. Relief flooded my body and I wanted to jump up and hug this inscrutable man sitting so still in front of me. Instead, I stayed in my seat and listened as Adam gave strict instructions on how to meditate.

'You must practise,' he said. 'It is most important.'

I stood and whipped off one of my gloves. I wanted to shake his hand, but he wouldn't play along.

I stood there feeling foolish, then put my glove back on. 'Thanks, Adam.'

He smiled up at me. 'See you next week.'

I sat in a pool of sunlight pouring through the long Velux, amplified and focused by the glass. Propped up on a cushion, struggling to keep my back straight, I fidgeted and rubbed my knees. I was supposed to be watching my breath. Adam said I could count them if it helped, but I kept getting lost. How could I lose count when I'm only counting to ten? I looked at the dust encrusted smudges on the window vaulting over my head and fought the urge to jump up and get out my cleaning kit.

The idea behind meditation was to simply be aware of whatever was present, in your mind, body and surroundings, sounds and smells and so on. My mind was crammed with shit. It was worse than the window. As soon as I sat down my mind had gone into hyperdrive, spinning and churning, throwing up images and thoughts ranging from spectacular mundanity to outrageous fantasy and everything in between. Closing my eyes made it worse. I had no control. My mind surged, giddy with its own stupidity.

I opened my eyes and glowered at the dirty window. Strange swooping and popping noises were coming from downstairs. It sounded like aliens were landing in the living room. I stretched out my legs in relief, and giving up on the meditation, went to investigate.

At the far end of the room stood a line of shelves stuffed to overflowing with books and DVDs, a high-tech stereo having pride of place in the centre. A generous sofa curved across the olive green carpet, dividing the room in two. Nearest the door was Jonah's workstation, a jumble of computer and synths with flashing lights and wires tangled like spaghetti.

Here Jonah sat, hunched over a synthesizer, his fingers fluttering over banks of knobs and faders, unabashed glee playing over his face. There were no aliens.

'What you doing?' I said.

'Noodling.'

'I thought the aliens had come for me.'

Jonah chuckled and turned a knob causing the sound pulsing from the speakers to plunge down, dragging my insides with it. I wandered over to the sofa from where I watched him tweak and twiddle until the air was filled with static, the noise of an untamed radio. He continued fiddling, making tiny adjustments and I listened, entranced, as new sounds sprung from the speakers. Another couple of tweaks and the air was filled with the warble of a demented blackbird.

Something was trying to worm its way into my consciousness; the way he was filtering the frequencies of sounds reminded me of...

'It's the brain,' I said, with a surge of clarity.

Jonah looked up, surprised and not a little confused. 'What is, babe?'

'This is how it works, only without all the knobs and stuff, obviously.'

He grinned and I thought I'd better explain myself.

'Scientists used to think the brain just converted all your sensory inputs into what you think of as reality,' I said, 'but then they found it changes it. As well as adding stuff and filling in the gaps, your brain filters what you hear and see and sense, and gives you an approximate version of reality. What you think is reality is just what your brain tells you is there. We have no way of knowing what reality is *really* like. What we see is just enough for us to get around, not bump into the furniture or get eaten by a tiger. The brain has to filter reality or you'd be overwhelmed – there's so much of it. Reality, that is. Not brain.'

Jonah continued to experiment, making bleeps and squelches, while I went over my conversation with Adam. Meditation changes the way you think, so what effect would it have on my brain? Jonah's assault on noise whimpered and fell silent, and he turned to face me, stretching his arms over his head and arching his back like a big sexy cat.

'What's up?'

'Just thinking about my filter.' I tapped my fingers against my head. 'Adam said my perception is shifting. Maybe the idea behind meditation is to open your filter so you can see more reality.'

Jonah nodded. 'Sounds reasonable.' He finished stretching and joined me on the sofa.

'But... do I *want* to see more reality?'

'You already do, babe.' He took my hand. 'You're filtering it different to other people, that's all. No need to worry about it. After all, there's no tigers gonna eat you. Not in Newcastle.'

Jonah kissed my hand softly, then rained down a flurry of smackers up my arm to my neck, where he started growling and nuzzling, until I collapsed in a fit of giggles. This drove him wild, and he took to licking my neck, yanking at my jumper and trying to climb into my jeans, so the only sensible thing to do was stop laughing, join in and pull him to the floor.

The smell of hot cotton rose from the pile of ironing as I carried it upstairs. I took each step carefully and deliberately, feeling my way. I had never felt so present or so alive. Every contraction and release of muscle, the tightening of tendons, the movement of air through my lungs, even the beat of my heart, all working together, propelling me forward.

I practised meditating whenever I could and discovered it was much easier if I was up and moving about, rather than sitting with aching back and knees. I was too restless to sit still and it seemed to make my mind worse. When I had managed to sit, I either dozed off or started seeing lights. There was a translucent lilac pulse of liquid light which would gyrate before my eyes. Like the aurora borealis encircling my head in a chrysalis of electromagnetic luminosity. Once, I was dazzled by a crescendo of colours, a rainbow rising over my head, one tone following the next, a scintillating ladder lifting me out of this world.

I opened Ella's wardrobe, sweeping back the doors, a blast of air wafting the hair from my face. Despite being mindful of every little detail, I still found my mind raced, thoughts piled upon thoughts, racing to get to the point, a Grand Prix of cogitation. Nothing I did would stop it. There was no start or end; it just went on and on, round and round. Breathtaking and endless. Boring.

I stopped for a break, taking a banana from the bowl in the kitchen. Easing myself onto a high stool, I bit into the soft flesh, mashing it up in my mouth and feeling it slide down to be embraced by my stomach. I was concentrating on how far down I could actually follow the progress of the banana pulp before I lost sensation of it, when I was startled by the fruit in my hand.

Something otherworldly had taken hold of my banana. I held it up and moved it around, looking at it from every angle, not sure what I was seeing. From the end I had bitten came an ice blue light, shooting out in jagged sparks. I rubbed my eyes and held the banana up to the light. There it was, as clear as the fruit itself; I wasn't imagining it. The aura of a banana.

I watched the light fade in amazement and wondered what Linda would make of this development. No I can't read your aura, Linda, but give us a look at your fruit bowl. I finished eating the fruit, pushing away a thought that the banana might know what I was doing on some deep unconscious level. *Now, that really is a mad thought.* Perhaps my eyes were playing up, as well as my brain.

Adam chuckled as he listened to my report on my meditation practice. I was shocked and amazed at the repetition, the negativity, and the running commentary in my head, but he found it all highly amusing.

'I mean, why do I have to tell myself what I'm doing? I'll put the kettle on, I need the milk, where's the spoons, oh no, they're all dirty, I'll have to wash up. On and on. It's mad. Is everyone like that, or is it just me?'

'Don't worry. It's quite normal.' His eyes twinkled with laughter, but I knew he wasn't laughing at me. Nothing I said ever surprised him.

'So you've discovered how little control you have over your own mind,' he said. 'Self-mastery is the beginning of freedom. We have much to do.' He leaned forward and fixed me in his depthless gaze.

'Tell me, Zoe. Who are you?'

I opened my mouth to say the first thing that came to mind, then stopped, goldfish-like. It was a trick question; one of those Zen things. I closed my mouth and waited for inspiration. Nothing happened. Adam was waiting for a response.

'Well... I suppose... starting with the physical: you could say I'm a woman, small, possibly a pixie, wayward hair, hazel eyes, the requisite limbs, 33 years old. In terms of how I relate to others: I'm daughter of Rebecca, twin sister to Danny, girlfriend of Jonah. I'm a cleaner, so there's my customers. You could say I'm managing director of my own company.' I grinned proudly at Adam and, receiving no response, ploughed on.

'Emotionally: there's all the usual human stuff, happiness, sadness, anger, fear, confusion, love and so on. Mentally, well, we've kind of covered that. All the usual thoughts about what's going on, what's been going on, and what I would like to be going on at some point in the future or in another universe.'

I took a deep breath, trying to work out if I'd missed anything and wondering if Adam had fallen asleep; his eyes were starting to glaze over. I pressed on.

'Then there's all the weird stuff, the trances and visions, but aside from that I'm, for want of a better word, normal. I want to live and love and be someone, to matter, and for my life to mean something. I want to be happy and not be in pain or suffering. Everyone wants that. I'm a human being, a person.'

There was a pause. I waited. Was he still breathing? Finally...

'No.'

I spluttered an incoherent response: not a woman? Not a human being? Not a person? What planet was he on?

'All those things change,' he said.

'A human being is a human being, a woman is a woman, that doesn't change.'

'Those are ideas, Zoe. Are you an idea?'

'No, but then... who am I?'

'An excellent question. Your homework for this week.'

I shrugged. 'Okay, I'll explore.'

Adam laughed. 'Very good. You can tell me what you discover next week.'

It was the end of our session, but there was one more thing I needed to clear up and I didn't know how to approach it. His strangeness had been bugging me and I wanted to reassure myself. It wasn't that I didn't trust him; I was just curious.

'Is there some way I can contact you before next week, if I need to. I mean, a phone number? Where do you live? Is it nearby?'

'I'm afraid I don't have a telephone. Is there something else on your mind, Zoe?'

'Well... it's just the lights, when I'm meditating. Dozing off I can handle, but the lights are annoying. Is there something wrong with me? Should I get my eyes tested? A brain scan?'

'Are you really so determined to be ill?'

Adam oozed compassion from every pore. I looked at my feet and felt guilty for doubting him.

'Ignore the side effects, the lights, psychic disturbances, and so on,' he said. 'They're distractions. Remember, we're interested in discovering the nature of reality and to do that, first you must understand the nature of your mind. Have you had any more trances since starting meditation practice?'

'No. I'm just seeing things.'

'Perhaps now you're cooperating with the process, the unconscious doesn't need to shout to get your attention. Monitor it. Stay grounded.'

I nodded. It was reasonable enough. 'Until next week then.'

Adam waved me off and I walked away from the seats towards the footbridge. Once out of sight, I stopped and waited. I wanted to see him leave, to find out which way he went. It occurred to me to follow him, but I dismissed that as over the top and possibly paranoid. If he came this way, I would run into him. If he went the other way, I would see him heading up the path into Byker. I sneaked back and peered around the corner.

The seats were empty. He was gone.

Metaphysical Flimflam

I walked back to the flat in a daze, mind on a loop trying to work out how I'd missed Adam and how fast you would have to walk to disappear that quickly, *unless he was going round behind the farm along the river, perhaps that was it, I'd have to check*, when I nearly ran into Jonah. He was hanging about on the corner opposite The Ship, wrapped up in his duffel coat and evidently waiting for me.

'Took your time,' he said.

'It was a long one today. Lots to talk about.'

He took my hand and started walking up the street, pulling me along behind him. This narked me a little, then I remembered we'd made a date, and I'd been late, and now he was annoyed.

'Sorry,' I said, and caught up with him. 'I forgot you were waiting.'

He kissed the side of my head and we ambled into town, my concerns over Adam still ferreting around in my head. I felt Jonah squeeze my hand so I glanced up at him.

'You look worried,' he said.

'It's just Adam.'

'What d'you talk about?'

'How things are going. Mainly, he just keeps showing me how little I actually know about anything. All the stuff you take for granted, like who you think you are. But that's not the problem.'

'So, what is?'

'He keeps disappearing. Well, I can't work out where he goes when we're done. It's nothing really.' I felt silly saying it out loud.

'Just ask him.' He put his arm around my shoulders. 'I'm sure there's a logical explanation.'

We had lunch at the Tyneside Cinema, getting lucky with a corner table so we could spread out on the softer seats and make a plan. Jonah had been saving what he could from his stingy public sector pay packet over many years, inching his way toward fulfilling a dream he'd had since he was a child. He wanted to go home and visit the city where his mum was born, walk the streets and smell the air.

Grace Nelson had lived in San Fernando in Trinidad, along with her three sisters. She fell pregnant and came to England with her boyfriend to get married and start a new life. But the boyfriend vanished within months, leaving Grace to cope alone in an alien country with a growing bump. Her sisters soon arrived in solidarity, celebrated the birth of Jonah, and then stayed.

Jonah never knew his dad's name. His mum refused to discuss it and his aunts pretended they didn't know. He had never even seen a photograph.

'And now Mum's gone,' said Jonah, 'and I want something solid, something real, something I can touch, to connect me to them.'

He looked so forlorn and lost surrounded by the bold art deco furnishings, I didn't have the heart to ask what had happened to his mother. He'd never mentioned her before and it obviously cost him to think about it. I guessed an illness, probably cancer, and didn't want to spoil our veggie burgers and chocolate cake by bringing that up.

We left the café and trawled the travel agencies to pick up brochures. None of them had what Jonah was looking for. While he wandered off to speak to an ultra helpful woman with a huge cloth bow tied around her neck, I flicked through the holidays on offer. Superficially, they were all the same. Page after page of ultramarine sea and sapphire sky, immaculate beaches and palm trees. And no people. The resorts were deserted. It didn't seem to matter where you went, wherever you were, you got the same stuff. Rows of loungers in regimented blocks on the sand or in lines around sculpted swimming pools, overlooked by great slabs of hotels. It was paradise tamed, rendered safe and stylish. I'd expected to feel drawn to the tropics, the heat and the sunshine, but I was repulsed. It was too fake.

I couldn't imagine Jonah in any of these places. He reappeared at my side and I slung the fraudulent brochure back on the stand.

'I'm gonna need to grow my own,' he said.

We walked through the Sunday shoppers burdened with bags crammed with late January sales, and ducked into Trailfinders. These brochures didn't freak me out quite so much. I sat in a bucket seat and waited, while Jonah grabbed all the information he needed to build his own holiday – island hopping between Trinidad and Tobago.

Walking back down Northumberland Street, he looked over the collection of printouts listing hotels, flights and prices, doing calculations in his head, his lips moving with the effort.

'Have you got a passport?' he said.

'Of course.'

I stopped walking and stared at him, mouth hanging open like someone had removed my brain.

'I'm not going on my own,' he said. 'What? Are you having another-'

'Jonah, I can't afford to go somewhere like that. I can barely afford to go to Scarborough.'

'Don't matter,' he said, and kissed me. 'You make me happy. God knows why.'

I punched him playfully on the arm, and we carried on down the street.

'Who would you've taken if you hadn't met me?' I said.

'Nisha.'

'Oh.'

'She didn't know I was planning this, it was going to be a surprise, and I reckoned she would've changed her mind about-'

'About dumping you.' I could feel a massive sulk coming on and knew I was being childish, but what the hell. 'So it doesn't matter that much who you go with, so long as they've got a pair of tits.'

'Zoe, I didn't mean... that's just what I thought before I fell...'

He stopped walking and gave me a sidelong glance. I knew what he was about to say but I wasn't going to make it easy for him by leaping to the rescue. We stood there in the middle of the busiest street in Newcastle, creating a blockage on the pavement, bodies swerving to avoid walking into us. The swirling crowds faded to a blur; we were the eye of the storm.

'Before I fell in love with you,' he said.

Monday was a quiet day, cleaning wise, so as soon as I was done I made for the posh new library in the city centre. I often came in to read the paper or find a good story to distract myself from the dull tedium of my existence, although there had been less of that soul-destroying boredom since I'd met Jonah. I was happier now, but didn't know if that was down to him or the meditation.

The sheer glass walls diffused light through the building. It was more like a church than a library. I zigzagged between lines of bookshelves searching for religion and suppressing a grin. Something very peculiar was happening to me: here I was, the ultimate atheist, looking for religion. It was all I could do to stop myself erupting into giggles.

I was flicking through a book about beginner's mind by a man who sounded like a motorbike, when I felt a light tap on my shoulder. Standing behind me was Professor Harrison, smiling like he had Alzheimer's but was dimly aware somebody somewhere may have offended him.

'Hello Charles,' I said. 'Did you have a good Christmas? Doctor Felix wasn't too much of a handful, I hope.'

'Yes, yes, he can be rather...' His eyes kept wandering to the book in my hands and a small frown was gathering strength on his forehead. 'Listen, Zoe. Good to see you again, by the way. I just wanted to say, you don't need to avoid me.'

I tried to look as innocent as possible. 'What makes you think I'm avoiding you?'

'Yes, of course... well... What is that you're reading?'

'Zen. It's a classic, apparently.'

He nodded, a deep furrow carving itself between his eyes. 'About Felix. Have you called him yet?'

I shook my head. I could tell from the look on his face he was about to warn me off but I was in fighting mood. Since met Adam and started meditating I'd found a new sense of purpose: I was taking control of my life, of my mind. I was no longer the passive victim of an unfortunate genetic inheritance and I wasn't about to have my experience rebuffed.

'You don't think I should get involved,' I said.

'It's up to you, of course, Zoe. I just think you should be careful. All this...' He indicated not just the book I was holding but the whole shelving section before us.

'Mystical eyewash,' I said.

Charles cleared his throat and looked at me steadily. 'Felix can be very persuasive. He is blessed with great charisma and energy but that doesn't make him right.'

'I am capable of independent thought, professor.'

He frowned at the Zen book again and nodded. 'Of course. I just don't want you chasing off after metaphysical flimflam when you could be making real world contributions.'

'You wouldn't say that if you'd seen what I've seen,' I said, sticking my chin out in defiance. 'Do you really want to get into a debate about what constitutes the real world with a mystic?'

The M word was out of my mouth before I'd realised. Charles looked as surprised as I felt.

'It was you who compared me to Jung,' I continued before I lost my nerve. 'He was a mystic. I assume that's what you meant by it. You can't deny the truth of something just because you haven't experienced it. It would be like me denying the existence of quarks or the Higgs boson because I haven't seen them and can't understand the maths.'

'Interesting point,' he said, nodding as if he was thinking about it, even though we both knew he thought I was talking nonsense. 'Just be careful, Zoe. You know where I am if you ever need to talk.'

Charles eventually wandered off and left me to my flimflam. I had come armed with a robust shopping bag, and filled it with every book I could find on Buddhism, practically cleaned them out. The short walk back to the flat seemed to take twice as long, laden as I was with a ton of books and my backpack full of sprays. I collapsed onto the sofa with a cup of coffee, and dove into the first book.

By the time Jonah got back from work, I was at the desk in the corner surfing the internet and downloading every pearl on Zen I could unearth. I was so engrossed I didn't hear him come in. The desk was disappearing under reams of scattered paper, the books stacked up beside me, while the printer clattered, firing out pages like bullets. I was peering at the computer screen, pen clenched in my teeth, trying to decipher a series of Japanese line drawings of a man befriending an ox, when he appeared beside me.

'Hey, babe.'

I spun round in the chair, clumps of paper in each hand, surprise turning to pleasure as fast as ice cream melting on your tongue. I grinned at him and the pen in my teeth stuck out like a cigar. Jonah scrunched his fingers into my messy hair. I had been yanking at it while I worked, so it was probably in a right old state, jutting from my head in mad tufts. His eyes twinkled with amusement, then shifted abruptly into an intense smoulder, and I knew what was on his mind. I pulled the pen from my mouth.

'Don't you ever think about anything else?'

'No.' He leaned over and kissed me, then reluctantly pulled back, a tiny moan sounding at the back of his throat. He ruffled my gravity defying hair and straightened up, turning towards the kitchen.

'I'll put the kettle on,' I said, leaping out of the chair and planting another kiss on his dumbfounded lips. I sashayed into the kitchen.

'I know I said it was cool when you did that, but babe, have some mercy.'

I poked my head back round the corner. 'Come off it, Joe, that's not psychic. You always have a cuppa when you get in. And I like making it for you. There's you, slaving away all day, unappreciated. It's the least I can do.'

I ducked back into the kitchen and poured his tea. Jonah worked at the big civic building in Gateshead. Open plan hell, he called it. Every office and corridor looked the same, and he'd spent his first months getting lost, wandering up and down the lurid green carpets holding important looking documents so people would think he was working. I could imagine him prowling the corridors like a wild animal, or when he wore his bright orange or red shirts, like a caged bird of paradise searching for an open window and freedom.

I brought his tea through and plonked it on the coffee table, then returned to the desk and burrowed deep into the mound of information I'd accumulated.

'So, how's the research going?' he said.

'Dunno. It's all a bit baffling, to be honest. I think I should be meditating, but I don't know what I'm looking for.'

Jonah sank onto the sofa and kicked off his shoes, plopping his feet onto the table. He warmed his hands on the mug cradled against his belly.

'Fancy a takeaway?' he said. 'I can't be arsed.'

'You love cooking,' I said, feeling disappointed.

I loved watching Jonah cook. He had a reverence for the ingredients and the process of transmogrifying them into feasts. I threw stuff together and slapped it on a plate. It was edible and it did the job, but I didn't have inspiration. Jonah's mum had taught him, standing him on a chair at the stove when he was six. She sang as she cooked, and so did he, following her recipes, her melodies; the flavours nothing to do with the spices and everything to do with home. The home he had never visited. Limes and mangoes fattened by sunshine, steel pans rattling the windows loose, and deeper than deep sub-bass dissolving the foundations of the house. I couldn't wait to see him come alive in Trinidad.

'I'll cook,' I said.

'Oh yeah?'

'Beans on toast?'

Jonah rested his head on the wall behind the sofa and closed his eyes. His stomach growled.

'Food of kings,' he said.

I arrived at Ella's house early and found it deserted. I wandered through to the large, designer kitchen and switched on the coffee maker: a ludicrous contraption covered in esoteric buttons, lights and nozzles, bought for Ella by her errant husband. Of the three of us, I was the only one who knew how it worked, achieved by randomly pressing buttons until something resembling coffee materialised.

While the apparatus sputtered and coughed, I began loading the dishwasher. Lying on the breakfast bar I discovered a note addressed to me. Ella, it seemed, was out getting her nails done and didn't want the bedroom cleaned. It was a week since I'd given this house a thorough scrub and I felt sure the bedroom would be in a desperate need of one by now.

I dropped the note into the bin, then froze, hand extended, as a thought I actively didn't want shouldered its way to the front of my mind. The certainty of it hit me like a migraine, screaming through my brain as I ran up the stairs. I threw open the bedroom door to see my worst fear made flesh.

'Jesus, Zoe. Fuck,' shouted Danny. He was lying on the bed, naked save for a pair of silky boxers covered in pink lipstick prints, his hands cuffed behind his head to the bedposts, eyes wide with terror.

I leaned on the doorframe. I expected to feel angry, but all I could muster was mild amusement. Danny squirmed and yanked at his handcuffs, embarrassment seeping in to replace the fear. I suppressed a giggle, my eyes alighting on his swanky, if cheesy, underwear.

'Are those new?'

'What the fuck, Zo? I thought you were Martin.'

The giggle escaped and shot out of my mouth before I could catch it. Danny relaxed and grinned at me. I gazed back at him: my beautiful, hopeless, impossible brother. We had been closer to each other than anyone else; how had we ended up so far apart?

'Let me go, sis. The key's up there.' He nodded at the chest of drawers.

I decided to milk the moment, slowly considering my options, eyes flitting from key to Danny and back again, index finger tapping my chin. The air in the room was toasty; Ella had obviously left the heating turned up – she didn't want her plaything to freeze. Danny looked healthier than usual; his pallor banished in favour of a rosy glow, and he had definitely put on weight, in a good way. I made up my mind.

'Ella would be terribly disappointed if she came home to find you'd escaped, and besides, I don't want to spoil your fun.'

I chortled and closed the door. I could hear Danny shouting all the way down the stairs. He didn't give up until I'd finished cleaning the kitchen and poured myself a second cup of coffee.

Jonah put down his chopsticks and rested his chin on his hand, elbow jammed against the tabletop. Ray, Linda and Robin were shovelling rice into their mouths as if in a race, while Henrik helped himself to more crispy seaweed. Morgan had returned to Oslo to await the birth of his first child, so the Village had decided to celebrate in advance with a gargantuan Chinese feast.

I sat opposite Jonah chasing a battered prawn round and round my plate with my chopsticks. I could sense everyone around me as my mind spun, turning in on itself, as crazed as the poor prawn. Jonah watched me, his eyes drilling into my skull. All week I had worried about my question, my koan. Tomorrow was Sunday and I was going to have to give Adam an answer and I didn't know what to say.

'What's up, babe?' said Jonah.

'Darling, I thought you simply didn't care,' said Robin.

Jonah slung a mini spring roll at his drummer, then went back to staring at me. I glanced up and smiled at him.

'I wish I could climb inside your head,' he said.

'Be careful what you wish for. It's carnage in here.' I tapped my head with my chopsticks, then went back to tormenting the prawn, getting more exasperated by the second. 'I'm going to starve to death at this rate.'

'You're squeezing too tight,' said Henrik. 'Here...' He leaned across and took my hand. His was so large it made mine look like a child's. He guided my fingers into the right position. 'Relax your grip, like so, yes?'

I scooped up some rice.

'You worried about tomorrow?' said Jonah.

I nodded, rice balanced precariously over my plate. 'He's going to ask me again and I don't understand it.'

'Just be honest,' he said.

'I know, but it seems like it should be obvious and I feel like an idiot, like I'm missing something right in front of my face.' I froze and stared at the rice poised on the end of my chopsticks. 'Relax your grip,' I said to myself.

Jonah watched and waited. The room was hushed, all eyes on me as I sat, seemingly transfixed by a nugget of sticky rice.

Linda nudged Jonah's arm and whispered: 'Is this to do with the strange gentleman?'

He nodded, his eyes never leaving my face.

'Relax your...' The rice fell and I looked up, acutely aware everyone was watching me. My face flushed hot. 'Um...'

'I love it when an epiphany comes together,' said Robin.

'So?' said Jonah. 'Have you figured it out?'

I shook my head. 'I can feel it, it's right there, hovering on the edge of my mind. Like when there's a word on the tip of your tongue.'

'Maybe we can help,' said Ray. 'What was the question?'

'Apparently, it's the ultimate koan,' I said. 'If you can crack this, you're sorted, your troubles are over.' All faces were turned expectantly in my direction. I doubted they'd be able to help. The answer to this question was the goal of enlightenment, and there were no Buddhas at this table.

'Who am I?' I said.

A burble of chuckles travelled around the table. I could feel everyone falling into the same trap I had, thinking it's an obvious question, thinking they know who they are, thinking it's obvious so why would you even think about it.

'I'm a drummer when I'm drumming, an engineer when I'm recording, an eater when I'm eating.' Robin bit a chunk from a spring roll. 'And a lover when I'm loving.' He waved the remaining roll. 'Like an army of me's, a self for every occasion. Am I wrong?'

Yes, I thought. Yes, you are. But I don't know why.

'I'm a process,' said Linda. 'A process of being. An evolving soul on a journey to self-knowledge.'

Better, I thought. But what's a soul?

'Yeah, but what's a soul?' said Ray, and I beamed at him. 'Is it the same thing as a self? You got to define your terms, Lindy. Am I a bass player when I'm at the office, listening to Hairy Margaret telling me about her verrucas? I would say I am.'

'The music never leaves me,' said Jonah. 'It's in my soul.'

'Right,' said Ray.

Hang on, I thought. We still haven't defined soul.

'So I'm a musician, even when I'm not playing,' continued Ray. 'It's what I do. Even when I'm not doing it.'

'What?' said Robin.

What? I agreed, and beamed at Robin.

'I like what Daylight says,' said Henrik. 'I am a scientist in the lab, a father with my children, a lover with my wife. But then, Cosmic has some truth, I think. I am thinking like a scientist even at home, on the bus, in the shop buying Chinese food.'

Are you really a scientist while making love to your wife? I thought. I doubted it, but Henrik hadn't finished.

'So some things are the same and some things are changing, so it is also as Linda says, a process.'

I couldn't take anymore.

'Okay, okay. This is all fascinating, but here's the thing,' I said. '*What* is a process? *What* is the self? That's what I'm trying to get a hold of. When you say: I'm a musician, who is saying it? We say: I think such and such, I feel happy, sad, whatever, I do this, I don't do that, but what exactly is this I? The thing doing and feeling and thinking. I remember doing things yesterday so that must've been me doing it, but what happens if you lose your memory? Are you still you if you go senile? Or insane? If half your memories from childhood are false, where does that leave you? Something is giving you that sense of continuity. What is it? I mean, I still feel like me from one day to the next, even when everything else changes.'

Everyone nodded thoughtfully.

'It's your self, surely?' said Linda. 'The self feels and thinks and does things. Who else?'

'That's just it, though,' I said. 'Every time I look for it, try to catch it in the act, so to speak, I can't find it. There is no self. There's nothing there.'

Dionysus Wept

I walked carefully down the cobbled path under the giant archways of the Byker Bridge. I had started to think of them as Mindfulness Cobbles, since I always had to concentrate when walking on them. It was good practise, brought me right into the moment. My stomach lurched as I rounded the corner and the seats came into view. I was late and Adam was waiting for me.

I still had no answer to his question. The books and endless pages from the internet hadn't helped. There was all this talk about Buddha nature, original mind, and luminous emptiness, but I had no idea what any of those terms really meant. They were just words. I could tell Adam I was my original mind, but suspected he would know I didn't know what I was talking about. Bullshit never worked with him.

'So, Zoe. Who are you?'

'I'm a bit confused.'

Adam chuckled. 'Confusion is good.'

'I'm not my body or my feelings or my thoughts because they change and I can observe them, watch them changing. So I must be something that doesn't change, the thing that observes all this change – the I or self.' I knew what was coming...

'What is the I?'

'I don't know. It's me observing, I suppose, but I can't get outside of me to look at me to see what's going on. I would need another self to look at that self, and on and on and on. Where does it end?'

'An infinite regress.'

'Yes.' I shrugged.

'We've stripped back the body, the emotions, and thoughts,' said Adam. 'These are the contents of our consciousness. What is left?'

'Consciousness itself?'

'Yes, but let's call it Awareness,' he said. 'It's less confusing.'

I was still confused.

'So, I am Awareness?' I couldn't see why this was such a big deal. 'But what is it? What is Consciousness or Awareness?'

'This is why we meditate,' said Adam. 'To discover the true nature of Mind.'

'Is it the same thing as original mind?'

'You've been studying.'

I shrugged. 'I didn't understand most of it. Are they being deliberately obscure? Is it some kind of elitist thing, where only the initiated get the keys to the kingdom, or whatever?'

'It's not obscure. You just think it is.'

'That's helpful.'

'Look, Zoe, this is the bottom line. Awareness is all you need to know, it all comes back to this one thing. And you have it, right here.' He tapped his forehead, then the centre of his chest. 'How does it feel when you meditate?'

I lowered my eyes and breathed deeply, letting my thoughts fall away into nothing. The sting of frozen air pressed against my skin, the river babbled softly over the rocks, and the wind seemed to hold its breath. Even the traffic on the bridge, flying over our heads, had stopped. All was still.

'Hard to say,' I said, my voice almost a whisper. 'It's kind of peaceful, spacious. When I'm moving around, doing things, it's like I'm not really trying, things flow and seem to happen on their own. It's weird.'

'It's Awareness.'

I looked at Adam. 'Can it really be that simple? I mean, life is so complicated. How can you possibly solve all your problems with Awareness?'

'It's where you start. Everything arises from Awareness.' Adam twinkled and opened his arms wide. He looked pleased with me, although I couldn't think why.

'Keep practising,' he said.

The throb of the sub-bass hit me in the guts before I even got to the pub. The whole building vibrated, sending shockwaves into the surrounding air. I eased open the door and pushed into the crush of bodies. A sticky fug of compound clashing aftershaves and sweat hit my throat and, trying not to breathe, I squeezed towards the bar.

A low stage had been set at the far end of the room. Jonah's pride and joy sat on its stand, basking in a spotlight: a gleaming custom Les Paul, red orange wood flaming under the lights. Ray was standing at the bar near the stage, towering over everyone. He saw me and waved. I retrieved my wine from the barman and inched my way down the bar towards him; a Cosmic lighthouse in a storm.

Jonah appeared from behind Ray and wrapped himself around me. He was wearing his favourite purple silk shirt, which made his skin glow deeper than usual, and his dreads were adorned with multi-coloured beads and silver amulets. He was beaming and wired, his head full of music, and I knew I'd get no sense out of him until after the show. I let myself be vigorously hugged. Robin was beside us, bouncing on the spot, eyes fixed on the stage, like a dog desperate for his ball to be thrown.

Sitting at a table across from the bar was Linda with a queen's view of the stage. She was surrounded by a gaggle of friends, all squawking with excitement. Linda, for once, was serene, calmly awaiting the arrival of Dionysus Wept, as she had many times before. I had listened to the band rehearse for weeks and couldn't wait to see the songs performed for real. Aside from the boys themselves, only Linda and I knew the audience were in for a treat. I caught Linda's eye and grinned. She gave me a regal wave, followed by a cheeky wink.

My breath was coming in shallow bursts. I was letting the tension in the room get to me. I needed to calm down. I gulped at my wine and straightened my spine, planting my feet and raising my chin. Jonah still had one arm around me and I could feel his exhilaration shooting through my body, running around inside me like I'd eaten too much sugar. I hated that feeling, especially when I couldn't do anything about it. Maybe I should start jumping about and screeching, maybe it would help. Or maybe it would be plain undignified. I took another deep breath.

The pulsating jukebox and incoherent noise from the crowd swirled through my brain. This kind of sensory assault always left me feeling ragged and I longed for peace, for some space. Niggling at the back of my mind I knew I should meditate. It was Adam's answer to everything. But there were times when the meditation gave rise to something else.

Maybe I was doing it wrong, but beyond the peace and clarity a storm was menacing on the horizon, and I knew I couldn't out run it.

I tried to focus on my awareness of what was happening, the space around the stuff in my mind, to not get caught in the battles erupting around me, but the racket was too intrusive. A shout at the bar for three shots of vodka, the wail of a rising guitar as it morphed into a shriek from a girl, followed by the lascivious laughter of the man who had finally succeeded in throwing a peanut into the shrieking girl's cleavage.

It would be all right when the band started; order would be restored.

An image flashed into my mind. A memory of a room in uproar, chaos triumphant. But the only person in this room had been me. I was seven or eight and looking for washing up. The room was my dad's work room, his artist's den. Normally I avoided going in there; it was just too crazy, and Dad too unpredictable. I picked my way into the middle of the room, hands clutched to my chest, and stood, awed by the mess. There were stacks of paintings turned to face the walls and a long bench running below the windows piled with brushes, pastels and paints. Dirty rags, old jam jars spattered with explosions of colour, heaps of magazines, photographs and sketches strewn over the floor and every surface. Dad was a magpie, hoarding trinkets and curios; a squirrel storing inspiration and revelation. You never knew what you would find in this room; it contained the whole world.

I didn't want to touch anything, as if the clutter was sacred, a jumble sale of holy relics. Turning on the spot, I scanned with my eyes, not looking for anything in particular, just resting my gaze on whatever was there, and the domestic objects would jump out. A plate of crumbs or a scummy mug didn't really belong, so I saw them without trying.

'I see you got a new one.'

My attention snapped back to the bar. A tall and dazzlingly beautiful Asian woman was looking down her nose at me. She transferred her attention to Jonah, who had a look of utter panic spreading across his face.

'Nisha,' he said, trying to sound unruffled. 'This is Zoe.'

'I meant the shirt,' said Nisha, running her fingers down Jonah's silky torso.

'Zoe found it in Oxfam,' he said. 'Where you left it.'

Nisha flashed her teeth at me; it wasn't what you could call a smile. I wondered what Jonah had seen in this woman, apart from the obvious. This was where thinking with your gonads got you. Men could be such fools, at times. As if on cue, Nisha was joined by an enormous, rippling hunk of a guy who was undoubtedly cute, but his eyes were too close together, and his collar size probably exceeded my thigh.

'What are you doing here, Nisha?' said Jonah. 'Come to gloat?'

'Darren wanted to see you,' she said, hooking her long scarlet nails around her boyfriend's tree trunk arm. Darren smiled meekly at everyone. I was starting to feel sorry for him.

'I'm glad you've moved on,' said Nisha, looking me up and down. 'She's... cute.'

Jonah's jaw was clenched. I could see the muscles working down the side of his face. He still had his arm around my shoulder, but now it was rigid with tension as he fought to control his temper. It was all I could do to stop myself throwing what was left of my wine in the stupid cow's face. But then, I didn't want to waste it.

Nisha's clawed hand came up and cupped Jonah's cheek. He jerked his head back, a fierce scowl flashing over his face. My heart rate tripled – he was going to rip her head off. I needed to act, do something to diffuse the situation, but what? It was obvious Nisha still fancied the pants off Jonah, and frankly, I couldn't blame her.

'Oh, Joe, don't be like that,' said the bitch. 'We can be friends. Can't we?'

'That's not what you want though, is it?' I said.

'Huh...' said Nisha, all fake surprise, 'she speaks.'

'Zoe don't,' said Jonah. 'You'll encourage her.'

'I know how this works,' I continued, slipping Jonah's arm from my shoulders so I could square up for the fight. 'I know what you do and I know why.'

Nisha stood up straight and glowered over me. That rictus smile must be giving her lockjaw by now.

'Zoe...' warned Jonah.

'No, no, Joe,' said Nisha, through her teeth. 'I want to hear what the opinionated little elf has to say.'

'When I saw the way you dumped Jonah, I thought you were passive aggressive. But you're not, are you?' I said. 'There's nothing passive about you.'

'You're flattering me.' She flicked her hair and fluttered her eyes at poor lust-struck Darren.

'You think if you give them a hard time, play the bitch, make them crazy, they'll keep coming back. Because no matter what you do, no matter how far you push them, even if you dump them, they can't resist you. Look at you. Half the women in here probably fancy you. The question is, why do you do it?'

Nisha bent her head close to mine and looked into my eyes. 'Why does a dog lick its bollocks?' She stood straight again, triumphant, and beamed at Darren, who gave her a blank look, waiting for the punch line. She shrugged. 'Because it can.'

Darren chortled, rather sweetly, and gazed at her like a devoted puppy. Jonah rolled his eyes and glanced at his watch, desperate to start the gig.

'I do it because I can,' said Nisha. 'You got yourself a jealous one, Joe. Your perfect match.'

Jonah took a step forward, and I thought he was going to slap her, so I grabbed his arm and elbowed him aside.

'Oh, I'm not jealous of you Nisha. After all, I have what you want. You had your chance. He invited you to move in with him. You dumped him, expecting him to come begging, grovelling on his knees. But he didn't. He went off and met someone else. You lost him because you were too busy trying to prove how irresistible you are. And now, the man you want is living with someone else.'

Nisha's eyes darted back and forth between me and Jonah as she fought to keep her cool. 'You moved in with him?' Her voice froze the air between us.

'Nisha, will you please fuck off,' said Jonah. 'We're about to start.'

'Well,' said Nisha, staring at me with naked contempt, 'you're a braver woman than me. I hope you realise what you're letting yourself in for.'

'You know what?' I said. 'I am braver than you. I'm also less lonely.'

She took a step back with a look on her face that said she'd been punched. She fiddled with her dress and draped herself on Darren's substantial shoulder. I was just warming up, ready to hit her with everything I had, but felt Jonah's hand slip into mine, pulling me back towards him. He would have to do more than that to stop me now.

'I actually feel sorry for you, Nisha. It's a tragedy that someone as beautiful as you on the outside can be so ugly on the inside. But you only have yourself to blame. Perhaps you should spend less time looking in the mirror.'

Nisha turned away and pushed against the bodies crammed into the bar. There was no escape.

'Zoe, stop,' said Jonah, but I wasn't listening.

'No amount of adoration will ever be enough for you, no amount of attention will fill the black hole in your heart. You keep clawing at them until you destroy them, until they feel as wretched as you.'

Nisha pulled Darren's arm and tried to use him as a battering ram to break through the crowds, but no-one would move. Her face began to crumple into tears. With my victim trapped, I continued my tirade.

'Relationships built on insecurity and self-hatred will never give you the love you're so desperate to feel, and compensating for that by getting yourself fucked silly by some hunk of meat with more neck than brains is just going to make it worse.'

Jonah yanked me round and encased me in his arms, holding on tight until I shut the hell up. I felt his mouth warm and wet on my ear.

'I love you, you crazy, beautiful freak.'

'Was that too much?' I said.

'Little bit.' He kissed me, long and deep, then pulled back. 'Gotta get to work.'

I turned round to face the stage. There was no sign of Nisha or her sex slave. I realised I'd over done it, but refused to feel guilty. Someone had to tell her the truth.

The rage was still burning my blood. Where had it come from? The distant tempest was closing in. I took a deep breath and willed myself to calm down. The band were taking the stage, the jukebox was silenced, the audience hushed. I allowed my mind to relax, feeling my way into the spaces between the sounds. The clink of glasses, a cough, the buzz of the guitar switching on. I closed my eyes.

A still, eternal pause.

A beatific voice sliced through the silence. The melody carried every heart skywards, hope sprouting wings, Jonah's joy transmuting all grief into grace. I knew it was coming but the crack from the snare still hit me like a gunshot to the head, the music igniting around me like the flames of a furnace consuming the air. I stood transfixed as Jonah, Daylight and Cosmic turned every member of the audience inside out, showing them how to live. This is what you do with your rage, this is what you do with your pain, this is what you do with your joy.

Magicians birthing a new world.

Calcified Cake

Kayleigh stood in the store room, clipboard crooked in one arm, and waggled her pen at me. She had been talking non-stop for an hour. I had lost track of the subjects covered; they ranged from art history to sandwich fillings, boys to TV theme tunes to the sociological impact of the Wii. It was like watching a human version of hypertext unfurling itself before my eyes. I marvelled at the way her mind worked, finding connections between the most unlikely subjects and then expanding on them exponentially, seemingly into infinity. How did the girl ever sleep?

I was sitting on a folding chair eating my lunch surrounded by cardboard boxes. Popper Originals had just taken delivery of a collection from Gilroy, one of Mum's favourite artists; favoured because he sold well. The boxes filled the tiny store room which was lined with metal shelves and lit by a single naked bulb. Kayleigh was unpacking and cataloguing the pieces without any let up in her rambling monologue.

I was content to let her talk, as it meant I could concentrate on my awareness of what was going on. Adam had told me to give it a try on and off throughout the day, so whenever I remembered, I would let my mind open and let go. The result surprised me: instant calm and a feeling that I could handle anything. I had been more productive and less stressed out. It was a miracle cure for the mind.

I slurped my tea, enjoying the spreading warmth in my throat. I ripped open the plastic wrapper on a cereal bar and watched the light reflect off the honey glaze on the oats. The door opened behind me and I heard it bang shut before a cool breeze wafted around my ankles. I felt an arm slide around my shoulders and squeeze, then my mother planted an unexpected kiss on my cheek.

She straightened up and ran a tender hand through my hair. I was so stunned I sat frozen with the oat bar halfway to my open mouth; open now in surprise, rather than in anticipation of food. The room had fallen silent, Kayleigh's stream of consciousness dammed by the uncharacteristic display of affection.

'Thanks love,' said Mum.

I shot her a sidelong glance, almost frightened of what I would see. She was smiling at me. I was baffled. I made an effort to close my mouth.

'I don't know what you said to him, but it worked,' she said.

'Mum, I don't know what you're talking about.'

'Danny. He's stopped stealing, and look.' She took her mobile from a pocket, pressed a few buttons and handed it to me, beaming. The text message read simply, 'Sorry Mum Xx'

'I wish I had it on paper, I'd get it framed,' she said, taking back her phone and smiling at the screen.

I knew Danny's good behaviour wasn't down to me. I'd been trying to get through to him for years and nothing I said had made any impact. Responsibility for this new, considerate version of Dan could be laid at the feet, or in the bed of Ella Richmond.

'He's got a new, erm... girlfriend. So someone else is feeding him now.'

Mum looked up sharply. 'Oh no, Zoe, it wasn't just food he was taking.'

My Tuna Surprise churned in my stomach. Not only had Danny been stealing from Mum, he'd been lying to me.

'But it doesn't matter now,' Mum continued. 'He's stopped, that's the most important thing.'

'You're just going to let it drop?' I was starting to wonder if my mother had been replaced by an imposter. She never lost an opportunity for reinforcing her own self-importance. She must be up to something.

She shrugged. 'I'm not going to prosecute him, if that's what you're driving at. Besides, I can't prove it.'

I nodded; order was restored. My pragmatic mother was still in there after all. I decided it was time to come clean and give her my news. 'Since you're in such a good mood, would you like my new address?'

'You moved? Why didn't you tell me?'

'I'm telling you now.' I got out one of my business cards and scribbled the address on the back. 'I'm living with Jonah. My boyfriend.' I handed over the card.

Mum's eyebrows shot up. 'Ouseburn. Gilroy has his studio there, how marvellous.' Typical of her to focus on the one piece of information pertinent to her world, her business.

'Does he make you happy?' she said.

'Gilroy?'

'Don't be silly. Jonas.'

'It's Jonah, and yes. He does make me very happy.'

'Good.'

She patted me on the head and swept towards the door, letting in another blast of cool air as she returned to the shop floor. I sat motionless for a moment. Where was the lecture on men and how you can't trust them? Where were the endless questions about this man I had chosen to live with? Did she not care? No, that wasn't it. If she didn't care she wouldn't go on the way she did. It was down to Dan. One little text and our mother was a different person.

A polite cough reminded me of Kayleigh's presence. She was still diligently logging Gilroy's artwork, a faint smile playing about her lips.

'If I didn't know better, and I do, cos she's out the other side of it by now, but I'd say she was menopausal,' she said.

I mentally shook myself and noticed the neglected cereal bar still clutched in my hand. I took a thoughtful bite.

'Or maybe she's got a secret lover,' said Kayleigh, twirling her pen.

'Don't,' I said, suppressing a giggle.

'Maybe it's Gilroy.'

We exploded in laughter, and I sprayed oats over my knees. From the shop floor came a shout: 'I hope you girls aren't laughing at my expense,' which made us cackle even harder, like a pair of stoned witches.

I calmed myself down and shoved the remaining snack into my mouth. As I crunched, I gathered together my things and prepared to leave. My mind was still spinning from Mum's unusual behaviour, so when the crack resounded through my skull it was such a shock it made me drop my bag.

'Ouch,' said Kayleigh. 'I heard that.'

Something was wrong in my mouth. I tried to swallow as much of the mashed up oats as I could before sticking my finger in to investigate. In amongst the gunk was something rock solid and definitely not oats. I had broken a tooth.

A tiny wedge of dentine, a slice of calcified cake, nestled in my palm.

'Bugger,' I said.

I scuttled down Northumberland Street, weaving through the shoppers, my tongue worrying at the cracked molar. I hadn't been to a dentist in years, not because I'd avoided it, I told myself, but because I hadn't needed it. The broken tooth wasn't causing any pain so maybe I could ignore it, buy some toothpicks and put up with it.

I reached the end of the street and was about to turn left towards Ouseburn when I saw Danny heading the other way. His hands were buried deep in his pockets and a fierce frown twisted his face. Worried something bad had happened, I hurried after him.

'Danny,' I shouted.

He didn't hear, continuing his lurch towards the Monument. I ran and caught up with him just as he mounted the steps at the base of Earl Grey's column to cut across into Grainger Street.

'Hey you,' I said, getting my breath back.

'There you are,' he said.

A smile wiped the frown from Danny's face as I joined him at the top of the steps. He threw his arms around me, giving me a long, affectionate cuddle. This was the day for hugs, I thought as I snuggled into the warmth of my brother's coat. I couldn't remember the last time he had been so loving, and felt my eyes stinging hot. I pulled back as one tear escaped, wriggling its way into my mouth.

'Hey, what's up, sis?'

He smoothed away the tear with his fingers and gave me a look so filled with compassion I felt I could burst into inconsolable weeping at any moment. First Mum, and now this. *Who are you and what have you done with my brother?* I chuckled to myself, sniffing back the remaining tears.

'I broke my tooth,' I said, pouting like a two year old.

'Awww.' He enveloped me in another hug. 'Does it hurt?'

I shook my head and released myself from his grip again.

'When I saw you just now, you looked fierce,' I said. 'Is something wrong?'

'Did I?' He looked mystified. 'Just my normal face, I guess. I always look like I want to kill someone when I'm walking in town. Stops the nutters bothering you.'

'Or makes them think *you're* one of the nutters.'

Danny gave me a manic grin and took my hand, leading me to the edge of the steps where he sat down. I joined him, hugging my knees in my arms.

'I was looking for you,' he said. 'Came over to your place, but no-one was in.'

'I'm out.' I smirked at him. 'What did you want?'

Danny shrugged. 'Nothing really. Haven't seen you in a while. Thought I'd come over, say hi, y'know.'

'Hi!'

'Howdy!'

We bumped shoulders and beamed at each other. I liked this new improved version of Dan. He was more himself, more like he was when we were kids. Fun and happy. We sat companionably together and watched people scurrying back and forth laden with shopping bags.

'Do none of these people have jobs?' I said. 'I mean, here we are, it's the middle of the week, and it's heaving. Where do they all come from?'

'You going to go all philosophical on me?'

'Is shopping the only thing that means anything to anyone anymore?'

'And she's off...'

'It's so passive, all this consumption. Running around like this, hunting for bargains, gives you the illusion you're doing something, but you're just mindlessly following what everyone else is doing. You sit there, cramming... stuff into every orifice, desperate for entertainment, for distraction, anything to stop you actually thinking about anything. Fear of life, disguised as conformity. Cowardice as a lifestyle choice.'

Danny put his arm around my shoulder and kissed my cheek. 'You think way too much, sis.'

'Yeah, well, somebody has to.'

'Maybe that's your job, Zo. Keep the rest of us right.'

'Only works if you listen, and anyway... bollocks, Dan, you should think for yourself, right? You don't want someone else telling you what to do all the time.'

'Damn right.'

I shot him a guilty look. I was always bossing him around and I really had no right. There had to be a better way.

'Thanks,' I said, taking his hand and giving it a squeeze.

'For what?' He squeezed back.

'For growing up.'

Danny hooted with laughter, throwing his head back and kicking his feet out. When he laughed like that he looked like a joyful little boy. I smiled and giggled along with him. Ella was right; he really was quite handsome.

'What did I do?' he said, once he'd calmed down.

'The text you sent Mum. She's doolally with happiness.'

'Oh, that.' He looked away and fiddled with his shoe laces, tightening the knots. 'Ella said I should be nicer to her, to Mum. Give her a break, she said.'

I hooked my hands round Danny's arm and snuggled in close, resting my chin on his shoulder and inhaling the musky smell of his aftershave.

'How's that going? With Ella, I mean?'

'She's good for me. I know, I know what you're going to say. She's married, and all that, but she says I make her happy. She even stopped taking the pills. I never made anyone happy before.'

'You make me happy. You just made Mum happy.'

'Yeah, I know but, don't get me wrong, it's just, you don't count.' Danny twisted his head round so he could look at me. 'You and Mum love me cos I'm yours, it's in our blood. Ella loves me cos-'

'Cos you shag her brains out.'

Danny chuckled softly. 'Maybe.'

I straightened up. My tongue found its way back into the hole in my tooth and I frowned. I hoped Danny knew what he was doing. I wasn't going to lecture at him or tell him to be careful. I'd had enough of that. No doubt, he had too.

'You know she can't have kids?' he said, concern making his handsome face beautiful. 'That's why she gets the way she does. Martin doesn't care. He gave up on their marriage, and her, a long time ago. She's been going out of her mind with loneliness ever since.'

'And then in walks you,' I said.

Danny beamed. 'I don't see the harm in loving someone. All this crap about adultery and cheating on people, sneaking around, keeping secrets.'

'Isn't that part of the fun? Or does part of you want to get caught?'

'I hate it.' He was suddenly serious. 'I want her to tell him, to get a divorce. She'd be free. She could feed me up on cake and we could get on with making each other happy.'

'And live on love, presumably. You're a hopeless romantic, Dan.'

'You are too.'

'You reckon?'

'Underneath all that cynicism and psychobabble, lies the beating heart of a desperate idealist.'

'Mmmm, well, maybe.'

Like a switch had been thrown somewhere in the recesses of my brain, I felt my mood spiral down. My tongue jammed itself into my broken molar and a frown tugged my face towards the filthy pavement.

Danny looked at me. 'What's wrong with wanting to be happy?'

'Nothing. Never said there was. It just seems so bloody hard sometimes.'

What had happened? I was practising and staying focused, and I should be getting better. I *was* getting better, and happier, but that damn cyclone kept circling at the edge of my awareness. I realised I'd been inching out over a frozen lake, oblivious of the consequences. The ice had appeared solid and thick, but now I was at the centre, cracks were sprouting at my feet, spreading like lightning to the shore, moving with such force they could blast through the ice then continue into the earth, splitting the ground into a million pieces.

Something deep inside was breaking apart, and not just my teeth. I was worried about Dan, but there was nothing I could do. His happiness was so fragile and he clung to it like a raft in the Pacific, hoping against all the evidence that he'll wash up on the beach of a lost paradise and live happily ever after. What would he do when his raft sank? How quickly would the peace between Danny and Mum be corrupted when reality reared its ugly little head again? I knew I couldn't hold us together; bind us to each other through the force of my will. Even the thought of it left me exhausted.

And then there was Jonah. He had made his choice and I didn't doubt his devotion, but I wasn't about to underestimate the devious beauty of Nisha, no matter how twisted she was. The rage that flashed through me and tore into her soul hadn't really left since the gig. Weeks later and I was still broiling and spoiling for a fight. It came in spurts, even while meditating: mild irritation or full-blooded fury erupting from nowhere then vanishing again, leaving scorch marks of shame.

I trudged down Stepney Bank, dodging dollops of horseshit. It had been a long day already, but I'd promised Jonah I'd visit the studio. Dionysus Wept were recording a demo to send to venues in London, in the hope of getting some gigs in the capital to spread the word of their imminent world domination.

I decided to dump the backpack at the flat and grab a sandwich before heading down to the ESP studio. As I approached the front door, I noticed a small brown hump lying on the tarmac right outside the door. Thinking it was more manure, I was trying to work out why a horse had been that close to the flats, when I realised it wasn't what I thought it was. It was a dead rat. A car must have squished the poor thing. The rat's head was swathed in a halo of blood so red I had to blink several times to be sure that was what I was seeing.

I ran up to the flat, grabbed a plastic bag, then returned to deal with the unfortunate rodent. The limp body was still warm as I scooped it into the bag. I slung it into one of the wheelie bins, feeling absurdly sorry for the rat and musing about the perils of being in the wrong place at the wrong time. There he was minding his own business, foraging for food, when BANG. You never knew what was just around the corner. You had your dreams and hopes for the future, your schemes and plans, and then life creeps up on you when you're not looking and crushes you to death. Fate had so many hidden tendrils, the unconscious and ancient origins of every situation were so vast and tangled, how could you ever hope to break free? How could I believe I could gain mastery over my life, like Adam? Would I end up crushed, like the rat?

My appetite thoroughly ruined, I walked down to the footbridge outside the Cluny and crossed the river. The Epsilon Sound Palace was in one of the warehouses on the other side of the Ouse, its blacked out windows giving no clues to the activity within. I leaned on the doorbell and waited. The door swung open and Jonah's grin appeared on the other side. He stepped back to let me in, hooking his arms around me, kissing my neck and growling. I felt myself stiffen involuntarily, and he let go.

'What?' he said.

'Sorry. Long day.' I wasn't in the mood. I just wanted to sit quietly and think, or perhaps better still, not think. Then again, maybe that was a bad idea too.

Jonah took my hand and led me into the control room sealed behind two doors back to back. The sound of drums and bass filled the air, and on the other side of a huge glass window I could see Daylight hammering like a Fury at his drum kit. Behind him was an acoustic screen above which was bobbing the head of Cosmic, headphones wobbling as he rocked out. I ambled towards the window and stood at the mixing desk, lights dancing in lines as the music pumped through from the other room. A computer screen scrolled blocks of coloured lines, laying down the tracks.

'I thought Robin was the engineer,' I said. 'How can he record himself play?'

'He's put me in charge,' said Jonah, plopping into the comfortable swivel chair and rolling himself up to the desk wearing a crazed grin. 'He set it all up, then all I had to do was press record. Easy.'

Seeing all the knobs and faders and flashing lights made me want to start pressing things to see what would happen, but I guessed that would get me in trouble, so I retreated to the sofa on the other side of the room. The music stopped and Jonah pressed a button on the desk so he could talk to the boys.

'She's here,' he said.

Daylight stood up and saluted from behind his kit, and Cosmic peeped over the top of the baffle and waved. 'Hiya, Zoe.'

'Put the kettle on, love,' said Daylight, sitting down again.

'Cheeky bastard,' said Jonah. 'You promised to behave.'

Robin performed a piercing snare roll, cymbal crash combo and twirled his sticks. I wasn't sure I could cope with this level of testosterone and exuberance, so I stood and went to the door.

'S'okay. I don't mind,' I said, opening the doors and disappearing down the hallway as fast as I could.

I found the kitchen at the end of the hall, and filled the kettle, searching round for a tray and some mugs. It looked like the mugs had never been washed. Ever. So I filled the sink with suds and gave them a proper clean.

'You don't have to do that, babe.'

Jonah was leaning on the doorframe watching me, and holding several more dirty mugs. He brought them over and dropped them into the hot water with a plop, kissing the side of my head as he did so.

'I honestly think men would live smeared in their own excrement if they could get away with it,' I said.

'I'd do it, even if I couldn't get away with it,' said Robin, bouncing through the door and slapping Jonah on the back.

'He often does,' said Ray from the doorway, grinning like a loon.

I made the coffee while the boys fooled around, behaving like they were back in school. Perhaps this was what men were like when we weren't looking. I retreated into a corner and watched, sometimes mortified, mostly baffled by what I saw. They were all in their thirties and yet, left to themselves, they reverted to adolescent or even prepubescent antics. My function seemed to involve keeping them clean, feeding them and stopping them from killing each other. It was a bit like having a pet.

I knew they were just letting off steam after working so hard, and they were going to get back to it as soon as the coffee had been drunk, but there was a bug in my brain and it wouldn't let me be. Everything was getting under my skin, even my shirt felt uncomfortable all of a sudden. My tongue worked away at the hole in my tooth and I fidgeted in the corner, desperate for the noise to stop. Not just the noise of the boys dicking about, but the stupid noise in my mind.

I felt a hand gently touch my face and I looked up. Jonah was standing over me, looking concerned.

'All right?'

I nodded. 'Why did you want me to come?'

'Thought you might like it, find it interesting. I can show you how it all works, well, Robin could.'

'You gotta see Jone the Bone in action,' said Robin. 'He's a fiend.'

'Jone the Bone?' I said. 'Is that your alias?'

Jonah nodded and shrugged. 'What can I say? They're jealous.'

'Sometimes I wish the Bonester was gay,' said Robin, a wistful look in his eyes. 'Then again, I'd probably be crippled for life.' He took my hand in his. 'You are a very lucky woman.'

'Right, that's it,' I said, pouring my coffee down the sink. 'I'm going home.'

A chorus of disapproval and supplication rose all around me as I fought my way to the door. Jonah gave me puppy dog eyes and held onto my hand as I stepped into the street.

'What's wrong, babe?'

'Nothing, I'm just... I don't know... I need to be on my own.'

I let go of his hand and turned away.

'Later, babe,' he said, and closed the door.

The front door banging shut woke me from turbid dreams. I rolled over into a ball, burrowing into the duvet like a mole, and dissolved into the murky depths. A warm hand found its way over my hip and down between my legs, pulling me back into woozy consciousness, and I felt Jonah press himself against me from behind. He tugged at my knickers, kissing my neck and breathing heavily into my ear, as he pushed my legs apart with his.

I turned my shoulder, rolling back to face him, and gave him a shove in the centre of his chest.

'Not now. Sleepy.'

He wasn't listening and yanked my knickers down, plunging eager fingers where I didn't want them. I moved away and grabbed his hand, pulling it free.

'I'm tired. Go to sleep.'

Jonah ran his hand over my belly and up to my breasts, massaging and squeezing, while scattering delicate kisses over my lips and neck.

'Sunday tomorrow,' he said, between kisses. 'Lie in. Come on, babe.'

'Will you stop calling me that.' I sat up, livid. 'I have a fucking name.'

'Sorry, ba... Zoe.'

'Please just go to sleep.'

I threw myself onto the pillows and turned my back on him. I was now thoroughly awake and may as well have had sex with him, but I wasn't going to give him the satisfaction. I lay there, pretending to sleep, while a righteous fury burnt through my veins. After a moment, Jonah disappeared to the bathroom. I didn't want to think about what he was doing in there, but couldn't stop myself, and it fuelled the flames of my indignation.

In a little while, he returned and promptly fell asleep. I lay beside him and listened as his breathing slowed and deepened. I was now so awake it felt like I was plugged into the mains. A line of drool escaped from Jonah's open mouth and slid over my shoulder.

I was incandescent.

'So, how's it going?' said Adam.

'Well, Danny's in love, so he's being nice to Mum, which is making her dead happy, she even hugged me, which was bizarre. Jonah's band is selling out every gig and he's writing songs constantly, he's on fire.' Even if he is annoying, I thought, rather ungraciously.

Adam gave me one of his penetrating looks and a crooked smile. 'I meant you.'

I wriggled in my seat. I knew very well what he meant. It was all so complicated, I didn't know where to start.

'Start anywhere,' said Adam.

I froze and stared at him. That must be what it was like for Jonah when I apparently read his mind. Last night I'd wished he could read my mind, but I knew it wasn't that simple. It was never what it appeared.

'Can I ask you about that? I mean, did you know I was thinking I didn't know where to start? Or was it just psychology, y'know? An educated guess based on my body language and the look in my eyes.'

'Yes.'

'Cos when I do it, I never really know, y'know? If you stopped time and asked me, what am I thinking? I couldn't tell you. It's just, I don't know, like you sense the flow of the conversation, or pick up the emotion, and most people say the same sort of stuff all the time anyway so it's not that difficult to guess what's coming next. It's just intuition, isn't it?'

Finally, I paused, realising I'd missed something. 'Hang on. Did you say yes? To which one?'

Adam chuckled. 'You think too much, Zoe.'

'Danny said that too.'

'He's right.'

'So which was it? Can you read my mind?'

'Where is your mind?'

Adam had succeeded in dragging me back to the point, and I fought the urge to get up and run. I took a deep breath.

'My mind is a mess. It was going well before, but now... Sometimes the meditation kind of works and I feel peaceful, my thinking slows down, just ambles along, and I can focus on Awareness, on the space. But sometimes the space is too big.'

I rubbed my hands over my face and felt my chest tighten in panic.

'I get scared of it. I'm trying to be cool and calm and Zen-like, but then there's these surges of fear and rage. Jesus, Adam, the rage is immense. Where the hell is that coming from?'

'It's okay,' he said.

'No it isn't.' I fought against the tears I could feel pressing against my eyeballs. 'It is not fucking okay.'

'When I was at Hosen-ji,' said Adam, 'I struggled with the routine. It was strict, almost like being in the army or in prison. Everything personal is stripped back. You have a bowl, robes and sandals. Nothing else. I had to learn the chants and sutras, all in Japanese, and observe the ritual offerings to the temple deities. Any mistake or transgression and you'd be beaten. One monk was stripped and made to burn his robes just for sleeping late and missing the early morning meditation. At four a.m.

'I sat every day in the sodo practising zazen. If you dozed off, you got whacked, and I got countless cuts and bruises, still have a scar on my left shoulder. Every day you must present yourself to the Roshi for sanzen. He waits for you to be honest, to be true, spontaneous. But how can you be spontaneous if you're trying to be spontaneous? So I would panic, just like you.

'There were days when I wanted to tear off my robes and set fire to the temple. I wanted to gouge out the eyes of my teacher, he terrified me so. I would sit on my mat and vibrate with rage. I could barely move when it was time to get up and walk around the sodo. I wanted to run and scream, but I couldn't. I had to hold it in. I had to work with it.'

Adam folded his hands together in his lap and looked at me with such kindness and joy I found it hard to believe he could ever feel as angry as I felt. I was glad I wasn't in a Zen monastery, it sounded like torture.

'Don't try to be calm, Zoe. The purpose of meditation isn't to be peaceful. It is to be awake. Sit with your rage. Sit with your fear.

Investigate. What is it? Who is feeling the fear? Who is feeling the rage? Find the source. Penetrate the causes and conditions.'

'But that's the problem,' I said. 'The fear and rage are primal. They're scary because they're not really personal. Yes, there's personal stuff irritating me, but the rage is so out of proportion, it's magnificent, mythical. It's like the fear and rage were always there. I can't get to where they're coming from. I hit a brick wall.'

I searched his face for a sign. I knew he understood, but sometimes I felt so alone. I was systematically cutting myself free of everything I had ever taken for granted, everything I had ever known. The terror swirled through me, leaving no space for anything else, catching all in its wake. If I surrendered to it, let it take me, it would tear me apart.

'I just want to be happy,' I said, desperation making my voice squeaky. 'I want to be at peace with myself, not this incessant war. I mean, if I'm awareness, then I'm, well... nothing. Awareness isn't anything, is it? It's empty. Unless you're conscious of something, it's just unconsciousness, blackness. This process, this investigation into causes and conditions, feels like annihilation, like death. I mean, do I even exist, Adam? Do you? Do the seats we're sitting on? What am I breathing? Is it air? Is it nothing? What the hell is going on?'

I wanted to grab Adam by the throat and force him to tell me the truth. But he sat serene, smiling at me in the most infuriating way.

'Nagarjuna was an Indian master living around the year 200,' he said.

'Please, no more stories or obscure utterances. I can't take it. I just want the bloody truth.' I regretted my irritable outburst immediately and lowered my eyes. Adam went on as if I hadn't spoken.

'He wrote verses that point towards reality, to truth. Works of prajna-paramita, or wisdom for crossing to the other shore. The main one is called Sunyavada or the Doctrine of the Void. See if you can track it down, Zoe, it'll blow your mind.'

He twinkled at me and I felt myself unwind. He had been here. There was a way through and he was going to show me.

'Nagarjuna demonstrated four perspectives, or logical refutations, which you were to apply to everything,' he continued. 'Have you ever looked at a photo of yourself as a baby and wondered if it really is you?'

I nodded.

'Is the baby in the picture you or not?' he said.

'Is this a trick question?'

Adam smiled and waited for me to answer.

'Well, it kind of is me,' I said, 'but then, it isn't because I've grown, I have more hair and teeth, and back then I didn't even know I was born. But then, I can't say it isn't me because it was me, well, sort of...'

I trailed off and stared into space. I'd never thought about this before. When did I become me? There was no moment I could pinpoint where I could say – there, that's me. As soon as you think it, the moment has gone and a whole new me is being formed. Calling it 'me', or 'I', made it sound static and fixed, but it wasn't.

'There are four ways of looking at this,' said Adam, and counted them off on one hand. 'Yes, the baby is you. No, the baby is not you. The baby is both you and not you. And finally, the baby is neither you nor not you. Which one is true?'

'None of them? All of them? But they negate each other,' I said, confusion pushing the fear out of my mind.

'It's a great tool for breaking through to reality,' he said. 'Apply it to objects, thoughts, feelings, everything. Another example: you can ask, does this concrete seat exist? And you have four answers. The concrete seat exists – here I am sitting on it. The concrete seat doesn't exist – it can't exist, in fact, because it is a compound thing and so does not inherently exist. Third, the concrete seat both exists and doesn't exist, and then it neither exists nor doesn't exist.'

'Is that supposed to be helpful?' I said, feeling mutinous.

'Listen, Zoe. The point is to see through the nature of appearance and emptiness. The blackness or void that you feel you are hitting, is really a glimpse of the nature of reality. It's just that you're conceptualising it, thinking it's something you can get a hold of. It can't be understood with the intellect. This is what Nagarjuna demonstrates. The process, the deconstruction, is designed to push you beyond concepts, beyond thought.'

He beamed at me, his smile dazzling and terrifying in equal measure.

'You've reached the limits of rationality,' he said. 'This is a good thing.'

He made it sound like a fantastic achievement. I was far from convinced. I had set off to explore reality, sailed to the horizon, and was about to drop off the edge of the world. *Here be dragons.*

'Just remember,' said Adam, with what looked like a crazed twinkle in his eyes, 'the four perspectives apply to everything. Emptiness is also empty of emptiness.'

I pushed the front door open to find Jonah waiting for me. Well, he was pretending not to be waiting for me, sitting on the sofa and flicking through a magazine full of pictures of guitars and hairy men with tattoos. But I could tell. His attention was on me the minute I walked through the door, even if his eyes never left the glossy pages in his lap.

My head was still unravelling after my philosophy marathon with Adam. I didn't want to talk about what happened last night. I didn't want to talk about anything, I could barely think straight. Ideas were uncoiling and whipping about like loose cables in a gale. I wished I'd never started on this liberation process thing. All I wanted to do was crawl upstairs and hide. I hovered in the doorway watching Jonah pretend to ignore me.

'How was it?' he said.

'D'you mean my meeting with Adam or you groping me while I was asleep last night? Because, since you ask, neither was much fun.'

He turned to look at me, his face blank. 'I said sorry. And I meant Adam.'

I shrugged. 'I have to keep practising.'

'That's all you ever say now. What exactly is it that you're practising?'

'You've never asked before. Why are you bothered now?'

'I didn't have to ask, Zoe. You used to fucking talk to me.' He slung the magazine to one side.

'I see, so the one time I refuse to have sex, you go into a sulk. Maybe you're used to more compliant women. Maybe Nisha was a slag as well as a bitch, maybe you had unfettered access, or maybe it doesn't matter what I'm feeling or how much shit I have going on in my head, it shouldn't stop me fucking you.'

Jonah rose from the sofa, his face scoured with sadness. 'I just want you to talk to me. Tell me what's going on.'

'I can't.'

How was I supposed to explain it to him when I couldn't even understand it myself? Where would I start? Nothing exists, but it does, but not really, well, sort of. I didn't understand how Adam could be so joyful about what he called the facts of existence and non-existence. It just confused and scared me.

Jonah came to me and gently brushed his fingers against my cheek. The sadness in his eyes sent a stab of pain through my chest. I knew I was making him unhappy, but I didn't know how to stop.

'Just try,' he said.

'It's complicated.'

I stepped back and bolted for the door and up the stairs. At the top, I looked back to see Jonah watching me from the bottom. He turned away, resigned, and disappeared into the living room. Moments later, guitar chords pushed through the floor and into my ears. I sat heavily on the bed and wept.

Toast and Marmalade

The middle-aged man sloped along the pavement, head bowed, shoulders up to his ears. In his left hand was a dog lead and beside him trotted a perky white and tan Jack Russell.

I walked along behind them marvelling at the differences between this odd couple. The man appeared defeated. He was trapped in his own world, eyes fixed on the ground in front of his feet as he ploughed unconsciously into his future. He had no idea where he was or what was going on around him. I could run naked and screaming right past him and he wouldn't see me.

The dog would. The little terrier bounced along the pavement on tiny spring-loaded paws. His tail stood straight, his ears twitched, scanning and alert. The dog was undoubtedly alive: fully present and here in the world. Where was his owner? He was thinking, conjuring another world inside his head. Did he prefer his make-believe world? Did he think it was more real than this world, the dog's world? He didn't look like he preferred it; he looked positively miserable. The dog was as happy as a dog ever was.

The spirited dog pulled his zombie master round the next corner and they disappeared from my view, leaving me wondering: could the man learn something from the dog? Could I? Millions of years of evolution, of pain and suffering, trial and error, have brought us to the point where we can exist without even knowing it. Our minds are supposed to make it possible for us to be more awake, more conscious, but we spend most of our time asleep, oblivious to the world. Perhaps we prefer unconsciousness.

I arrived at Dorothy's house to be greeted by squeals of joy and the thundering of baby feet careening up and down the hallway. Charlotte must be here. She was Dorothy's youngest daughter, and unlike her mother, had left it late to have kids, spending a fortune on fertility treatments and nearly destroying herself emotionally in the process. The little boy standing open mouthed, staring up at me like I was a wonder of the ancient world, must be Thomas. He was only 18 months old but already intent on taking over the world.

I crouched down so I was eye level to this budding Napoleon, and put out a steadying hand. Thomas was a little wobbly and he leaned against my arm, mouth still hanging open in awe.

'Hey there, Thomas. I've been hearing all about you. I'm Zoe.'

His pointed finger came out of nowhere, thrust towards my eye, accompanied by the loudest yelp of glee I'd ever heard, especially from someone so small. I dodged my head back just in time.

'Hello, Zoe.' Charlotte bundled Thomas into her arms and stood. 'Sorry about that. He's full of himself today, aren't you Tommy?'

'That's okay. I never use that eye much anyway.'

Charlotte was a slightly taller version of her mother: same curve to the nose, same thin lips, same attitude, but without the wisdom. The lips were now pulled into a feeble smile at my pathetic attempt at humour, but her grey-blue eyes were miles away. She was worried about something.

'Listen, Zoe. I'm ever so grateful for all the help you give Mum. I really appreciate it. Things have been so hectic lately, what with everything.'

'It's not a problem,' I said. 'I like coming round. We have fun.'

Charlotte looked perplexed, which was an achievement with Tommy's hand clamped to her nose. She pulled it free and gently slid the wriggly octopus down to the floor.

'Go and find Grandma,' she said.

Thomas rampaged off down the hallway, hooting like an owl. His exhausted mother watched him with pride. 'I don't know where he gets his energy. He's my little miracle.' Charlotte was in her forties, but at this moment, looked older. Something was wearing her down. Perhaps it was just the sleepless nights and long days. I sensed it was something else.

Before I could figure it out, Charlotte wrapped her arms around me and held on with such force I started to wonder if someone had died, or was dying, or something equally awful.

'Thank you, Zoe. Thank you so much.'

I eased back so I could look at her face. 'Is everything okay? I mean, are you all right?'

'Oh yes. I'm just tired. You know.' She smiled as the sound of frenzied giggling came from the living room down the hall. Then her smile vanished. 'It's Mum. Will you help me?'

I was confused. I thought I already was helping.

'She had another fall,' said Charlotte. 'She's all right, but I'm worried about her. I want her to go into a home.'

'She won't like that,' I said.

'Won't like what?' Dorothy was watching us from the living room doorway, an aquamarine teddy bear held against her bosom. 'Anyone fancy making a cuppa?'

'I'll do it,' I said. 'You two go and sit down.' I turned to Charlotte. 'Shall I take Thomas so you can, um... have a chat?'

She squeezed my arm in reply and took Dorothy back into the living room. Thomas appeared, his tiny hands clenched around two colourful plastic bricks.

'Come and help me make tea, Thomas,' I said, in that overly bright voice people use when talking to children. He dropped the bricks and followed me into the kitchen.

I filled the kettle and got the tea things out of the cupboard, all the while giving Thomas a running commentary on what I was doing and why. He stood, swaying like a drunk in the centre of the room, watching with round eyes, interjecting his own incomprehensible comments on how he felt things were proceeding.

I could hear raised voices coming from the next room. It wasn't going well. I couldn't imagine Dorothy leaving this house, except in a box. Thomas finally surrendered to gravity and sat on the flagstones with a bump. He had lost interest in the finer points of how to make tea, and was now investigating the floor. I leant against the counter waiting for the kettle to boil, and watched Thomas explore.

He gingerly ran his hand back and forth over the uneven stone surface transfixed by the sensation, looking as if it were the most incredible thing he had ever touched. His exploding brain must be processing all this fresh information, creating templates, maps of experience, truths to live by.

I hunkered down beside him and put my hand on the floor. It was cold, hard and rough. It was stone. It was exactly what I expected it to be.

I ran my fingers across it, imitating Thomas, the master. How could I recapture that joy and openness? Watching him, I felt jaded and ancient, worn down by life and expectation. To me, a stone floor was always going to be just a stone floor, unless I could break through the invisible wall standing between me and the real world. It was a wall built of words and assumption, memory and laziness. And fear.

In that moment, I knew it was all over. I had to be free. Nothing else mattered. Whatever it took, no matter how long; the fear couldn't last, it was just emotion, it would change.

'What are you doing down there?'

I jerked my head up in surprise. Charlotte was standing over us, hands on hips, lips pursed.

'Sorry.' I jumped up. *Why was I apologising?* 'I'll sort the tea.' I busied myself with the tray. 'I heard shouting. I'm guessing she didn't go for it.'

'I'll keep trying,' she said.

I smiled to myself. They were as pigheaded as each other. 'I don't mind popping in more often. Now I live just down the road, it's easy.'

'Could you? That would be such a weight off. I'll give you my number too, just in case.'

I washed my hands and grabbed the biscuit tin. 'I think we're in need of a little something, don't you?'

'Zoe?'

'Mmmm?' I arranged an assortment of digestives and shortcake on a plate and plopped it next to the pot. I picked up the tray and turned around. Charlotte held Thomas in her arms – he was now investigating her necklace.

'Do you think you could have a go?' she said. I must have looked completely lost (because I was), so she continued, 'I mean, ask Mum to reconsider the home option. It would be safer for her and she wouldn't be on her own so much. She says she doesn't get lonely, but, well... I don't know.'

'She likes it here and her arthritis only plays up every once in a while.'

'Yes, but it'll only get worse.'

'Not necessarily.' My arms were starting to protest about the weight they were carrying.

'She listens to you. She seems to have a lot of respect for you.' Charlotte had really struggled to say those last words. I was used to this: I was a cleaner, I was nobody. What could I possibly know about anything?

My phone beeped into the awkward silence hanging between us, so I took the opportunity to put the tray back on the counter and rest my screaming arms. Charlotte was waiting for me to agree with her, so I decided to be honest.

'Listen, I don't think this is any of my business, but I'll say what I think anyway. Dorothy isn't stupid. She knows her situation. Yes, she's stubborn, but she's independent and that means something to her. If you put her in a home it would be like putting her in a prison.'

Charlotte didn't look pleased. She frowned at me, so I continued. 'It also occurred to me, while I was grovelling down on the floor, that it might make sense to rip up these flagstones.'

'They're an original feature,' she said. 'It would bring down the value of the house if you took them out.'

'But if you had lino or something in here, your mum wouldn't fall over so much.'

'But then she wouldn't need to go into a home,' she turned away and wandered off down the hallway, looking thoroughly defeated.

I slipped my phone out of my jeans and checked it. There was a text from Jonah. It read: 'Where r u?' I fired back with: 'Dots', shoved my phone back in my pocket and carried the tea tray through to the living room.

After my little epiphany on Dorothy's kitchen floor, I threw myself into my meditation practice with fanatical dedication, becoming increasingly calm and detached. It was as if nothing could touch me. Over the following weeks, Jonah continued to text every so often, asking where I was, and I would reply. I was feeling so impersonal about everything that I did it without thinking. Having completely forgotten Nisha's veiled warning, it never occurred to me to question why he was doing it. Maybe if I had, things wouldn't have turned out the way they did. If I had a time machine, maybe this was the moment to which I should return. But I didn't know and I didn't think. The unceasing movement of life churned around my still centre. I was the eye of the coming storm.

The tranquillity reminded me of a summer holiday somewhere on the south coast, possibly Devon, although it could have been the end of the earth. We must have been seven or eight because Dad was there, in his own way, which is to say that he wasn't really there. He was bodily present, but mentally looping the loop. We buried him in the sand, right up to his head. He didn't seem to notice.

I wandered off on my own along a spit of sand jutting into the sea. The tides had created a kind of island linked to the mainland. Between my thin strip of land and the beach, the waves rippled and the light bounced and danced. I looked back and saw the beach, and beyond that, the road, shimmering in the heat haze. Cars and buses undulated silently along the road. Even the crowds on the beach were mute in the mirage. I was alone in my bubble of serenity. With the cool breeze at my back, all I could hear were the mournful cry of seagulls circling overhead and the ocean lapping and widening behind me. I thought: it should always be like this. If only it could always be this peaceful.

Crashing through the illusion came Danny, splashing across the shallows, kicking up spray in his wake, a grin on his face and a crab in his hand.

'Look what I found, look what I found.' He stood, dripping and smiling, until the crab pinched him and he flung it back into the sea with a hollow plop.

I smiled to myself and pulled my mind back to the present, standing in the kitchen at home. Jonah was watching me. He didn't look happy.

'Who were you thinking about?' he said, a knife clenched in his hand.

'Danny.'

'Huh.' He turned back to the workbench and grabbed a chilli, gutting it and expunging the seeds in one deft move. His shoulders were tense, his movements not as fluid as usual.

'Are you all right?'

'Nothing wrong with me, Zoe,' he said, his back turned.

He continued to cook, chopping, frying and tasting, and he must have made an effort to relax or else the cooking did it for him, because he transformed into a wild dancing Shiva armed with a knife and a wooden spoon, spinning his preordained eternal movements into manna.

I always enjoyed watching Jonah cook because of the way he shimmied around the kitchen, but now it felt less sensual, more dispassionate. Like I was conducting an experiment or doing a field study. He dished up dinner with half an eye on me, in fact, he seemed to be watching me as closely as I watched him. We sat side by side on the sofa to eat, our spicy chicken curry balanced on our knees.

I put my fork down for what felt like the hundredth time, and hooked a finger into my mouth to dislodge a grain of rice from the hole in my tooth. I was carefully chewing on the other side, but the food kept migrating across and getting stuck. I pulled out another tiny chip of tooth and balanced it on the edge of my plate. My concentration was wavering, the disintegrating tooth eating into my peace of mind.

'You okay?' Jonah had cleared his plate already. He leaned back and unbuttoned his jeans, breathing out in relief. 'That tooth giving you jip?'

I nodded and continued to eat. I could feel Jonah's eyes on me and knew he was brooding, but I must concentrate.

'Worried about the dentist, babe?'

I shook my head, then thought perhaps it did worry me a little, so shrugged too. I took another mouthful, sighing as more rice filled the hole. Jonah gently ran his hand over my back and I felt myself bristle. *What was wrong with me?*

'D'you want me to call them?' he said. 'My guy is dead nice-'

'I'm fine.'

He took his hand away and sat very still while I ate. I had snapped at him for no reason. I just wanted to be left alone.

'I'm sorry if I keep calling you babe, Zoe. I'm sorry if you don't like it. It's a habit, I don't mean nothing by it, s'just affection, y'know. I mean... I... I miss you. You're right here, but you may as well be a million miles away. I miss our talks. I miss my friend.'

He spoke so quietly I had to strain to hear him over the noise of chewing in my ears. I knew what he meant and he was right, but I couldn't focus, not on him. Not at the moment. He would have to wait. I knew I should explain it to him but didn't know how, couldn't find the words. I knew I should apologise, but as the rice compacted into my crumbling tooth, my frustration with myself and the limitations of my own mind and character, bubbled up and filled my mouth with spite.

'I can't eat and talk at the same time, can I?'

I swallowed a couple of ibuprofen and headed down to the river to meet Adam. My broken tooth was a constant niggle but I didn't want to deal with it. I wished it would just go away. The weeks were flying by now that my mindfulness practice was running smoothly. I must be on the cusp of some sort of breakthrough. I could feel excitement rising, the imaginary brick wall surrounding me was about to shatter and reality would stand revealed in all its glory.

'What did you have for breakfast?' said Adam.

I looked at him in surprise. I couldn't imagine what breakfast had to do with awakening.

'Marmalade on toast,' I said.

'No marg?'

I chuckled. 'No, just marmalade. Erm... how is this relevant?'

'How is it not relevant?'

'I know, I know, everything's interdependent, but I still don't get what this has to do with toast.'

'Imagine I'm an alien,' he said.

'Not difficult.'

Adam grinned. 'I've just arrived on your wonderful planet and you are feeding me toast. With marmalade.'

'Why?'

'Why what?'

'Why am I feeding an alien marmalade on toast? What if you can't eat wheat, perhaps you'll have a catastrophic reaction to citrus fruit.'

Adam exploded into a fit of contagious giggling and the pair of us sat vibrating with glee, while the breeze bristled through the branches of the white willow above us, teasing the budding catkins, daring spring to arrive.

Adam recovered first. 'Never mind all that, Zoe. This is just a story. So... Explain to me: what is marmalade on toast? How is it made?'

'From bread and oranges and sugar and probably some other stuff like preservatives,' I said.

'Remember I'm an alien. You have to explain everything.'

'Right. So, the bread is made from flour which is made from wheat, and yeast, which is a kind of fermented fungus. Eurgh, that sounds disgusting. And water and butter, which is made from cream. The marmalade is made from oranges and sugar.'

'And how are all of those things made?'

I started to get an inkling of what Adam was leading me by the nose into realising, but I ploughed onwards. 'The wheat, sugar and oranges grow in the ground, well, the oranges are on trees that grow in the ground. The cream comes from cows who eat grass which grows in the ground. Fungus, don't know. They probably grow it in a factory somewhere. Yeast R Us, or something.'

'How do all these things grow?'

'They need soil, sunlight and rain,' I said, getting a bit bored.

'Go on.'

I frowned at him. He really wanted to push this all the way. We could be here for hours. I took a deep breath and continued. 'In order for there to be soil, sunlight and rain you need to have... well, the planet, an ecosystem, weather. And for that the planet must be a certain distance from the sun and have all the right elements, like oxygen, nitrogen, etcetera, in the right combinations, not to mention all the laws of physics, like gravity, entropy, and... well, time. And space.'

'And how did the bread and marmalade come to be in your possession?'

'I bought it from a shop. Do you really want me to do this? All of it?'

Adam nodded, not even a hint of twinkle.

I stood up and stepped onto one of the seats, looking down at the top of Adam's head as he sat waiting for me to continue. I paced the semi-circle, hopping from EYES to OPEN to WITH and back again, counting everything off on my fingers.

'You need, in no particular order, farmers, bakers, shop assistants, delivery drivers, managers, orange pickers, people to build all the machinery involved, people to maintain the machinery, oil to run the machinery and power the delivery vans, unless they're electric, people to drill for oil and distribute it, factories to make jam jars and lids, and the plastic wrapper the bread comes in, designers and printers for the labels. You need an economic system, money, banks, and so on.

'For me to be able to walk into a supermarket and buy a loaf of wholemeal bread and a jar of thick-cut marmalade, endless other people are necessary, doing things that each rely on the next step in the chain. But it's more like a network: it criss-crosses and weaves, like a web. And I'm tangled up in the middle of it.'

'What about the people in this web?' said Adam. 'We know where the bread comes from. Where do the people come from?'

'From other people,' I said. 'I'm here because of my parents, and their parents before that. Same for everyone else in the web. It takes in billions of people. It's not just the farmer you rely on to grow the wheat, it's his wife who cooks his breakfast at five in the morning, his parents and their parents, back and back and back. All the way back to where? The first hominid? The first ape that thought, hang about, why don't I try walking around instead of swinging? The first fish to crawl out of the sea? The first single-celled organism to feel lonely and get together with another cell? Where do you stop? The big bang?'

'All so you can have marmalade on toast for breakfast,' said Adam, smiling at last. 'Pretty amazing, wouldn't you say? Truly miraculous.'

I jumped down and sat. All the talking was making my jaw ache. My tongue found its way into the distressed molar and recoiled as a red hot icicle shot across my skull. Adam was still talking, but I hadn't heard. I pulled my attention back and focused.

'What I'm saying is, this experience of oneness isn't a philosophical theory,' he said, 'and it's not wishful thinking. We are, quite literally, bound up with one another, entangled, enriched at the points we intersect.'

I nodded and tried to look like I was following. 'We're all stardust.'

'How big is the human race?'

Adam's eyes were blazing; he was up to something. I forced myself to concentrate. He raised one hand and held his thumb and forefinger a centimetre apart.

'If you remove all the space between the sub-atomic particles that make up seven billion people,' he said, 'the matter remaining is that big. Tiny. And yet, you have more connections in your brain than there are stars in the sky. We all have atoms in our bodies that were once in Buddha, or Shakespeare, or anyone, everyone. The entire universe is continually recycling itself. Nothing is separate from anything.'

'Hang on.' My broken tooth throbbed and I pressed my hand against my jaw, as if that would help. It didn't. 'How does awareness fit into all this?'

Adam beamed at me. 'Good question.'

'And?' The pain was making me peevish.

'I can't *tell* you, Zoe.'

'Why not? No wait, I know. I need to practise, right?'

'You're in pain,' he said, oozing compassion. 'Got a dicky tooth?'

I nodded and worked my jaw, willing the ache to stop.

'You should get that seen to,' he said.

'Thank you, doctor.'

'Everything changes. The pain will pass. It couldn't be any other way.'

'Why not?'

'Impermanence.'

Adam fixed me with one of his penetrating looks. It was like he'd climbed inside my head, grabbed hold of my brain and squeezed. Or perhaps that was just the toothache. I looked away and focused on the cobbles at my feet. He was willing me to figure it out, to understand. He wanted me to be free as much as I did, but I couldn't think past the pain. I shut my eyes so I could concentrate.

When he spoke again, his voice was gentle, a whisper on the breeze. With my eyes closed it felt as if he were speaking directly into my mind.

'Nothing inherently exists,' he said. 'An object which has its own existence, separate and self-contained, simply cannot be. Nothing can exist without everything else. This is the nature of reality. Impermanent, interdependent co-origination. We depend on each other. We breathe each other. We are each other. I can't tell you the truth. I can't tell you what the nature of reality is, because you are it. You are the truth. You are reality. All of it. Nothing and everything. This is what waits for you on the other side of your brick wall. Only, Zoe... look at me.'

I opened my eyes. One look at Adam's ecstatic face and my heart stopped.

'There is no other side,' he continued. 'You are already free. I can't tell you anything you don't already know. Even if I gathered together all the atoms in my brain that once lived in Shakespeare, I couldn't tell you. Shakespeare himself would be struck dumb.'

I could feel it now. The bricks were wafer thin, chinks of light seeped through the gaps. My heart started to pound sending a surge of pain into my jaw, leaving me gasping.

Adam had flinched, I was certain of it. When the pain sliced through my skull, he had recoiled. I stared at him in disbelief. Empathising with someone's emotions was one thing, but this...

'You actually felt that,' I said.

'Please see a dentist, Zoe. There's no need to suffer.'

Over the following days the toothache crouched like a parasite in my consciousness. I had called Jonah's dentist first thing Monday morning, but they didn't have any space until the end of the week, and the ibuprofen wasn't working. I was literally counting the hours between doses, and found eating practically impossible, resorting to a soup and yoghurt diet.

Sticking to my cleaning schedule became increasingly difficult, especially with the occasional interruptions from Jonah, either calling or texting to ask where I was and if I was all right. I knew he was just concerned about me, but it was still annoying. The ferocity of the electrical storm in my skull grew steadily, and by Friday I was exhausted. So I abandoned the cleaning, sending apologies to everyone and promising to make it up to them next week.

I huddled in the corner of the sofa and lay my head on the armrest as another explosion crackled, shooting down my neck and arcing across my brain. The tooth had it in for me. I told myself it was just an agitated nerve ending. It was completely impersonal. The nerve didn't want anything. It was just there. But as my tears soaked the sofa, I felt victimised, persecuted. My body was plotting against me, determined to stop me being free.

My phone beeped and I snatched it up. Another text from Jonah. I groaned. He wanted to know where I was, again. I texted back: 'With the queen of pissing sheba' and tossed my phone across the room.

Adam had said there was no need to suffer, but how could I not suffer with a toothache like this? Was there a difference between pain and suffering? I didn't see how I could stop suffering right now. I was supposed to be using everything that happened to wake myself up. Perhaps meditation would be worth a try. It couldn't make the situation any worse.

I straightened up and blew my nose, wiping away the trails of salt lining my cheeks. The pain had subsided briefly. It tended to come in waves, and I guessed I had about five minutes before the next onslaught. Breathing deeply, I consciously relaxed every part of my body, letting my thoughts settle to a gentle hubbub in the background. My eyes kept flicking to the clock on the digital recorder under the TV, anxiety mounting as I waited for the torture to start.

A ticklish fizzing buzzed in my jaw. A wasp caught in a thimble. I breathed into it and the pain increased. I fought with myself not to take it personally. *Don't label it, don't think about it, just let it be.* I breathed hard, hyperventilating; the pain scorched, flames enveloping my head. I ran through everything I could think of: the pain is empty, the pain doesn't inherently exist, it's all happening in awareness – flinging words and hope at the fire, as if that would put it out. Tears leapt from my eyes to escape the blaze.

As it had begun, it ended, simmering down to a flicker, and I marvelled at the intensity of the pain. It pushed every other thought from my mind; there was no space left, not even for me. At the end, there had been nothing but the inferno; it consumed everything in its wake. The pain was miraculous, unfathomable, glorious.

When the next wave hit I was ready for it. I held at my centre, in awareness, and the pain became fascinating. I watched its progress, rising and falling. I was one with the pain. Awareness didn't make the pain stop, it still hurt like hell, but it was okay. I could handle it. Awareness dissolved the suffering.

I continued my mediation at the dentist. I watched with curiosity as the anaesthetic turned my jaw to mush, and was delighted when it disappeared altogether. I lay in the chair, eyes fixed just to the left of the blinding light hovering over my head, and mused about interdependence. Here we all were: my unruly tooth, the dentist and his assistant, locked in a dance, a pattern of engagement, each utterly dependent on the others. As the drill rattled my skull, whirring and screaming in my ear, I sensed an ancient ritual being enacted; just as with Jonah cooking or playing guitar. But now I was connected. I was part of the dance.

The dentist's light seemed to fill the room. It swarmed into a halo around my head and I felt a giggle bubble forming in my belly. I couldn't start laughing now, not with my jaw clamped open and the dentist's fingers jammed inside. The absurdity of the situation fed into the bubble and it expanded, rising to my chest. I must keep it together.

I breathed slowly, dropping all thoughts. I focused my attention on the movement of the air through my lungs and the sensation of the chair supporting my body. Calmness descended and the joy diffused into peace.

I wafted from the dentist surgery, light-headed and woozy, wearing a lopsided smile.

The Gateless Gate

On Sunday I bounced over the Mindfulness Cobbles to my meeting with Adam excited by what I had learned and ready to share my new insights. Adam was in an odd mood. I couldn't work him out at the best of times, but today he was stern – not unkind, but uncompromising and a bit scary. However, that didn't stop me prattling on.

'It was incredible. As soon as I stopped taking it personally it completely transformed. None of this has anything to do with me, not really. It's just there, just happening. Then I come along and get my knickers in a twist and make life harder for myself. Why? Why do we do that?'

'I'm glad you're feeling better,' he said, his face a blank wall.

'Is it self-importance? I mean, life has a way of making you realise how small you are. There are so many things you can't control. You want to be the centre of the universe, everything must revolve around you. Our whole culture is set up to reinforce this idea that we can have whatever we want, when we want, whatever the cost. Convenience is king. We're all petty tyrants, children really, throwing tantrums when things don't go our way.

'So along comes something you can't control, something you can't buy your way out of – illness, death, love, toothache, whatever, and to maintain the illusion that you are the centre, you are the most important thing ever, you try to control it. And the only way you can do that, since you're powerless in the face of it, is to victimise yourself. You bitch and moan. Poor me. Poor little old me, look how I'm suffering, isn't it just the worst. Don't you feel sorry for me. Isn't life just so unfair.

'But – now here's the tragic part – all it does it make the pain worse. What's wrong with us? Are human beings insane? Why, when you find yourself in a hole, do you try to dig yourself out by digging a deeper trench? It's bonkers.'

Finally, I stopped talking and looked at Adam sitting there in his spruce suit, hands resting in his lap. He appeared subdued. Was I boring him? Last week, despite my grumpiness, he had been playful. Now he was blank, unreadable. I was pleased with my breakthrough and thought he might congratulate me, or something, but he was behaving as if nothing had changed.

'So anyway,' I decided to plough on regardless, 'I thought, if it works on toothache, it'll work on anything, right? All I have to do is stop taking everything personally. It's so close now, I can practically taste it. If I can just stay focused on awareness and stop identifying with stuff, I'll be free. I'll be able to see properly and I'll be happy.'

'So you know what to do,' said Adam.

'Yes. It's like you keep saying. I have to practise. It makes sense now. I was sceptical at first – seemed like hard work and I didn't really get why I had to do it. But now I can see it's just a matter of time. If I keep going the way I am, I'll have satori in no time. That's what it's called, isn't it? Satori?'

'You've been reading again.'

I nodded. Surely that was the point. I had to re-educate myself. I was training my mind to think differently and that included finding new concepts, new perspectives.

'What's wrong with reading?' I said.

'There's nothing wrong with studying the dharma, Zoe. But remember, it's just words.'

'Oh, I know that. That's the point of meditation practice. You have to do it, not just read about it. Well, I'm doing it.'

'I have known individuals,' said Adam, 'who spent 20 years meditating, or more, and while they may have achieved a certain calmness and focus, they have most emphatically not attained satori. The one does not necessarily follow the other. There is no guarantee.'

'You can have satori without meditating?'

'Absolutely.'

'Then... what...' I was mystified.

'When the fruit is ripe, it falls from the tree,' said Adam.

'And how do you know when it's ripe?'

'When it falls.'

I laughed. 'I see.'

'No, you don't.'

I wanted to slap him. How did he know? I was working my arse off learning all this stuff and it wasn't easy. He was supposed to be helping me and now he said it made no difference.

'Meditation is preparation,' he said. 'For the fruit to grow at all, the seed must be planted and the soil tended, watered, cared for. By training your mind you are preparing the ground. Your desire to awaken is the seed. Mindfulness is husbandry. You are working diligently.'

'So I'm not wasting my time with this stuff?'

'Please understand, Zoe, when I say there is no guarantee, it's because we never quite know how it will work itself out. Everybody is different. We are working towards something absolutely impersonal, and yet it unfolds uniquely, conditioned by the structure of your character and the circumstances of your life. Imagine you want to learn a new skill like the guitar. Your Jonah plays guitar, does he not?'

I nodded, and he continued. 'There are things you can do, steps you can take that will bring you closer to your goal of playing the guitar. You buy an instrument and some chord books, maybe get a few lessons, and you practise. You learn songs, and if you have any talent, before long you're-'

'Rocking,' I interrupted. 'But there's a difference between someone who just plays a bit and someone really good. I mean, I know nothing about music, but even I can tell Jonah's dead good. There's something special in how he plays. I don't know what it is. It transcends the playing somehow. It's soulful, it means something, it connects with people.'

'Exactly, Zoe. That's my point. Soul can't be practised. You'll not find it in a book. It's hidden in plain sight. It's who you are. With a basic skill you have steps, a path and a clear goal. With awakening, or satori, there is no path and the goal isn't a goal because you're already there. It's the pathless path. No doubt you've read about that.'

I nodded. 'The gateless gate, too.'

'This is why books won't help you in the end. It seems like a puzzle, a riddle to solve with the intellect. But the more you try, the more confused you become. You end up chasing your tail. You may succeed briefly in tearing down a section of your brick wall, then in the next breath, in the next thought, you rebuild it.

'Ultimately, there is nothing you can do,' he said. 'Freedom lies in the willingness to recognise you are unable to free yourself.'

I frowned. 'Um… right. Well…' I stood up feeling disoriented and turned on the spot, trying to remember what I was supposed to be doing next. Adam watched, patiently. 'Um… I'm going up to the shop now. Do you go that way?' I pointed up the path running beneath the curved metro bridge.

'Not today,' he said. 'Same again next week?'

'Yeah. Um… thanks, Adam. See you next time.'

I wandered up the path, my mind feeling fuzzy. I still hadn't worked out where Adam went at the end of our lessons. I knew if I ducked back round the corner now, he'd be gone. I rubbed my head in frustration and plodded up the path towards Byker. The tangle of bushes either side of the path were beginning to show signs of life. Snowdrops and daffodils had pushed their heads through the ground, and blackberry buds clung to their stalks, praying for sunshine and rain.

I was completely confused. I had to keep practising at the same time as realising it wasn't going to do me any good. But it was doing me good because I needed to ripen my fruit, or something. That made no sense whatsoever. But I trusted Adam. He knew what he was talking about and he wanted me to understand.

I picked up a basket and squeezed through the open doors of Morrisons. It seemed as if everyone in Byker and Heaton had come shopping together, the aisles were crammed with trolleys and bodies. I found myself stuck behind a man carrying a baby over his shoulder, and unable to get past, followed him up and down, filling my basket as we went. The baby was about 8 months old and the colour of fudge. Huge brown eyes fixed on my face as we passed biscuits and cereals, soup and beans.

I smiled at the baby and said hello. The baby continued its impassive stare. I crossed my eyes, stuck out my tongue, pulled my face into ludicrous shapes, anything to get a reaction.

I got nothing. The baby would not respond.

I peered into those enormous eyes, deep with intelligence and blank as a desert. It was unnerving. I looked away and focused on my shopping, but something compelled me to look back. The baby remained unmoved. It was a still point, the centre of the universe, a black hole.

With my basket clasped in two hands, I felt the ground lurch beneath my feet and my heart started to pound. I closed my eyes. This was the way Adam looked at me. No matter what I did, no matter what games or roles I tried to play, he would just sit, giving nothing away, refusing to fall into the usual patterns of engagement. It forced me inward and demanded absolute presence.

I was stood with my feet welded to the floor, taking long calming breaths, when a trolley rammed into me from behind. I jumped and opened my eyes. The baby was gone. I breathed out in relief and completed my shopping.

The lines at the checkouts snaked down the aisles and I resigned myself to waiting. I put my basket on the floor, nudging it along with my toes as the queue crept forward. The encounter with the Zen-like baby had shaken me, the clamour rising from the shop floor assaulting my ears and eyes. My usual reaction would have been panic. On the worst days of my breakdown all those years ago, I would abandon my basket and run from the shop, fighting to get outside into the fresh air and space, and away from all the people, the noise, the pushing and shoving and grasping. It was all so ugly, so uncivilised.

Now I realised I could stand it. I let my mind relax and spread out. All around were voices, talking, hectoring, whining, none of it loud enough to drown out the background music, the songs you end up singing along with in your head, despite yourself. The tills whirred and beeped and clattered, plastic bags rustled, coins jangled.

I found myself amused by the din. It was like a vast animal, wriggling and stretching, breathing and alive. From my centre of meditative poise, I could see how it all interconnected, the umbilical lines drawing everyone together into a ballet of consumption. I felt my way into the spaces, into awareness, and something gave way in my mind. It was like stepping off the edge of a cliff, but instead of falling, I was flying.

One thought filled my mind. All these people, all this noise, this life, was one consciousness. We were all different manifestations of one awareness. I wasn't only thinking it, I could feel it and knew it to be true. The supermarket was a wonder filled with miracles. I felt the umbilical connection tugging at my heart as a searing love spread through my body, making me vibrate with joy. I wanted to jump up and down and laugh.

I didn't, though. Obviously. We are British, after all. That kind of behaviour would get you arrested. I beamed at the people around me. Some returned my smile, some a little wary. Others turned away and ignored me. This made me want to laugh even harder, and I fought the urge to hug the hunched old lady in the queue in front of me. The dear woman would probably keel over from surprise. How could I have missed how marvellous everything is? Even something as apparently soulless as an identikit super shop with its corporate branding and pretend homeliness. It was all fantastic and throbbing with life, no matter how dead it appeared on the outside. How was that possible?

I packed up my shopping bags and paid the glorious assistant, with three warts on her face. *Three!* She had the most luscious golden brown hair. I wanted to run my fingers through it, but settled for the receipt instead. I left Morrisons giggling to myself, drawing baffled glances from the other shoppers, and for once in my life, didn't care what anybody else thought.

I waltzed back down to the Ouseburn valley, smiling up into the trees. They waved back in the breeze and sang to me through the beaks of birds as I passed.

The sound of beautiful guitar music filtered through the front door as I put the key into the lock. Jonah stopped playing abruptly when I lurched into the living room carrying two bulging shopping bags and wearing a big stupid grin all over my face. He looked unsettled, but I had something to cheer him up.

'Hey, babe,' he said.

I giggled and walked past him, plonking the bags on the floor in the kitchen. I whipped out my surprise and slung them in a vase, returning to stand in front of him, lilies and carnations held aloft.

'I bought flowers,' I said, kind of stating the obvious. 'To say sorry. And to cheer you up.'

He sat with his guitar held in his lap, staring up at me like I'd gone mad.

'What's the matter? You look worried,' I said.

He shrugged. 'I never know what to expect with you these days.'

I put the vase on the window sill and returned to the kitchen, rivulets of joy still buzzing through my bloodstream. I unpacked the shopping and put everything away, then stuck the kettle on.

'Tea, Joe?'

'Erm... okay.'

I brought our tea through and put it on the coffee table. Jonah was still sitting exactly as I'd left him: guitar in his lap, perched on the edge of the sofa like he was about to launch off it any second. I stood and looked at him, trying to read his mind, but couldn't work out what was going on.

'How's that tooth?' he said.

'Much better, thanks.'

'How's Adam?'

'Fine. Did my head in today, but then I had a breakthrough. I think maybe he deliberately pushes me towards the edge, y'know?'

He nodded and ran his hand up and down the neck of his guitar. He was sad about something. I was going to have to try harder to make up with him.

In one fluid movement, I stepped forward, took his guitar from his hands, tossed it aside on the sofa, and straddled him. I slid my arms around his neck and snuggled in close, kissing him, taking my time, feeling the warmth of his skin on my fingers and lips. Slowly, his hands came up to embrace me, and soon it felt as it always had. I wanted to wipe away the past month or so, pretend it had never happened. I sat up and gazed into those dark, sorrowful eyes.

'I'm sorry, Joe. I know I've been an arse lately.'

He smirked, and some light re-entered his eyes. 'An arse?'

I nodded, mock serious. 'An emphatic arse.'

We both laughed and something deep inside me relaxed. It was going to be all right. I gave him another lingering kiss, then reluctantly shimmied backwards and stood up. Jonah reached out and grabbed one of my hands, trying to pull me back to him. I smiled and winked.

'Later, babe,' I said, and disengaged my hand. 'Got to meditate.'

His eyes clouded. I picked up my tea and made for the door, turning to see Jonah staring at the lilies on the window sill as if they were responsible for some grave personal injury for which he would never forgive them.

I pushed and dragged the monstrous Dyson around Mum's bedroom, full of specially designed and handcrafted furnishings. I loved to watch the lost hairs, discarded skin and plain old dirt spin in the plastic chamber, even if the high pitched scream of the machine made me want to rip off my ears. You would think something designed to mop up dust would enjoy cleaning, humming instead of whining, but the poor thing sounded like it was being tortured.

I manoeuvred the beast into the hallway and trundled it along the landing. As I rounded the corner at the top of the stairs, I thought I heard a voice rising above the racket and hit the off switch. Mum was marching up the stairs, arms flapping a ferocious semaphore to get my attention.

'Zoe. Zo... Oh, thank goodness. What a ruckus.' She leant on the banister to get her breath back.

'Good day?' I said. 'Sell lots of art?'

'Yes, yes. Listen, Zoe. I need to talk to you. Are you done with that thing?'

'As good as.' I pulled the plug from the wall. 'I'll pack up. I need to wait for Joe anyway, he's picking me up.'

'Coming here? You can introduce us.' She trotted back down the stairs and peeled off her coat. 'Now, come down. We need to talk.'

That sounded ominous. I packed up my stuff and went downstairs, replacing the dirt eating demon in its cubbyhole under the stairs. I stood in the kitchen doorway watching Mum throw a frozen steak in the microwave to defrost.

'You're welcome to stay for dinner,' she said.

'No thanks, Mum. Jonah's cooking.'

She gave me a lingering look full of questions, then went to the fridge and poured two glasses of orange juice, handing one to me.

'A cook, huh?' she said.

I accepted the juice and sat at the tiny kitchen table. It looked bonsai compared to the great slab they had at The Village. Mum sat down beside me.

'Is he any good?' she said.

'Very.' I grinned. 'He's a good cook too.'

Mum smiled faintly and turned her glass round and round on the table, making damp intersecting rings in the wood. When she spoke, her voice seemed to come from a long way off, a distant and dimming past.

'Never underestimate the power of sex to addle the mind,' she said, without looking up.

I searched my mother's face, looking for signs of the men-based rant I had no doubt was about to spurt from her lips.

'It's no basis for a relationship,' she said.

'Yes, Mum. I know that. You've only told me a gazillion times.'

'Your father was spectacular...'

'Mum!' I did not want to hear this, but it didn't look like I was going to get my wish. She was just warming up.

'...he was rabid and passionate and... oh, I don't know, Zoe, he swept me up and I melted. He ate me alive and I loved it, and loved him for it. If I'd had my wits about me I'd have noticed he was clinically insane, but...'

'I wouldn't exist.'

'It has its compensations.' She patted my hand, her eyes still captured by regrets.

'What did you want to talk about?' I said. 'I'm guessing it wasn't to confess your youthful lust and how it led you astray.'

Mum dragged her memories free of her hungry ovaries and frowned. 'Danny.'

My stomach tightened. The frown told me everything. Something had gone wrong with Ella, and now Danny was back to his old self.

'He's stealing again,' she said. 'I noticed it last week. Last time it was the DAB radio, which I can, frankly, live without, but this time... You know that beautiful opal necklace? I can't imagine where he's going to sell it. I've checked eBay and it hasn't appeared yet. If he wants money, why doesn't he just ask, or get a bloody job?'

I sat back heavily in my chair. I had been wrong. Danny hadn't split up with Ella. He was stealing her presents.

Dad had given Mum the necklace to celebrate our birth. He said we were the best thing he'd ever created, mainly because he hadn't had much to do, except enjoy himself. From that day, he made a promise: he would take his medication, he would be there for us. It had worked, for a while.

'I think I know what he's done with it,' I said, an aching sadness filling me up like flood water, my mind weeping at the thought of what I would have to do. 'I know how much it means to you. I'll get it back.'

I downed my juice, took the glass to the sink and gave it a rinse, leaving it to drain on the side. Mum watched from her seat at the table, looking wistful.

'You're such a good girl, Zoe.'

I leant against the sink and smiled down at her. I wanted to tell her Danny wasn't all bad, he hadn't taken the necklace for nefarious reasons, and it wasn't like he was my evil twin, he was just in love – foolishly, hopelessly and insanely – but the doorbell rang.

Mum shot out of her chair and bolted for the door, excitement buzzing about her hair like a gang of delinquent butterflies. I followed, picking up my backpack on the way.

Jonah stood on the doorstep looking surprised. 'Oh, hello Mrs Popper.'

'Rebecca. Nice to meet you at last, Jonah,' she stuck out her hand and Jonah shook it, smiling but wary. I'd told him so many stories about my mother, the poor guy probably didn't know what to think. I smiled and rolled my eyes at him, then squeezed past Mum who was blocking the doorstep.

'Oh, Zoe. You didn't tell me he was one of those,' she said lightly.

Jonah took a step back. Just for a second, it looked like he'd been knifed in the chest. My mouth was hanging open, mind blank.

'Mum... you... what the fuck is that supposed to mean?'

Jonah retreated to the van parked at the kerb, his eyes fixed on the pavement. I couldn't imagine what was going through his head. How was I going to fix this?

'It was just an observation,' said Mum. 'I didn't...'

'Observation? Jesus, Mum, I never had you pegged as a fucking fascist.'

'Racist, dear. Fascism is a different thing.'

'What? It's the same difference. Fascism is inherently racist, anyway that's beside the fucking point...'

'Do you have to swear quite so much, love?'

'Yes, I fucking do. I'll stop swearing when you stop discriminating against people because they look different to you.'

'I wasn't... I'm not-'

'Whatever.' I turned and stormed towards the van.

Jonah was leaning against the passenger door at the front, rolling a stone around on the ground under one of his feet. I stood before him and he looked up.

'I'm sorry, Joe. I had no idea she was going to say something like that.'

He shrugged. 'It's fine.'

'What? It's not fine.' I dropped my backpack on the pavement. 'Okay then, tell me. Why did you wince?'

He turned away, walked around to the driver's side and climbed into the van. I snatched up my bag and wrenched open the door. I was about to launch myself into the passenger seat without looking, but Jonah held out his arm.

'Watch it.'

There was a casserole dish on the seat. I clambered up and placed it on my lap.

'So?' I said.

Jonah started the engine and pulled away. 'What?'

'It hurt you. I saw it.'

He sighed the saddest sigh I'd ever heard; a sigh thick with grief as ancient as life. I should've known better than to dive into the heart of it. I should've left it alone.

'Joe, you have to defend yourself. How else will things change?'

'You can't talk people out of their prejudice,' he said. 'It's a waste of oxygen. You gotta prove them wrong by your actions, by living, by being who you are. Besides, I don't think your mum's racist. She's just clumsy.'

'Clumsy? That's a charitable way of putting it.'

'And what the fuck do you know about it?' Jonah stopped at a traffic light and turned to face me, his eyes tormented with rage and anguish. 'I'll tell you what racism is, Zoe. It's being stopped every week by police, for years, because they think you've stolen the guitar you're carrying. I had to get Steve to write me a certificate of ownership for it. He did it in the police station, in front of the police and showed it to them and told them. And they still fucking stopped me.'

'That's horrible,' I said, sinking into my seat and wishing I could climb into the casserole dish and hide.

Jonah lurched the van forward into the moving traffic, his hands gripping the steering wheel like he was holding onto a life raft.

'You want more?' he said. 'Here's a real classic for you. When I was ten my mum got breast cancer. Our landlord had seemed decent, he was always pleasant, used to pat me on the head and shit like that. She told him she was dying and you know what he said?'

I shook my head, ashamed I'd pushed him into this, wanting to take it back, rewrite history, free him from his heartache.

'He said, she'd got cancer because she shouldn't have come here. Quote: it wouldn't have happened if you'd stayed where you belong. *That* is racism.'

'I'm so sorry.'

The words felt inadequate and I felt stupid. I reached across and put my hand on Jonah's leg. His face had turned in on itself, as if he were barely seeing the road ahead of us. A single tear trickled down his cheek. He didn't wipe it away, just kept driving, staring straight ahead.

'Why didn't you tell me about your mum?' I said.

Silence.

We pulled up outside The Village. Jonah sat, hands on the wheel, still strapped into his seat. I could feel the heat from the casserole warming through my legs and belly. I wanted to toss it aside and take him in my arms, wrap myself around him and protect him from the world. Instead we sat, motionless, in silence.

Fat raindrops began to patter over the windscreen, drumming an eclectic rhythm on the roof of the van. Slowly, Jonah unwound and sat back, releasing his seat belt. He ran a hand over his face and stared, unseeing, into the rain.

'On my eleventh birthday I opened my presents sitting on her bed so she could see my face,' he said. 'The cancer had eaten its way into every part of her and she was shrinking. She said she was getting smaller so I could get bigger. She was surrounded by cushions and pillows and agony. Most of the time she didn't even know I was there. I would sit with her and play guitar, and she would mumble to herself and pluck at the bedclothes. I can't even remember what I got that year. It didn't matter. She was in too much pain.'

He stopped and looked at his hands lying open in his lap. Another lone tear splashed onto his fingers.

'She held onto my hands so tight I thought she would crush my fingers. I was scared I'd never play guitar again. But she wouldn't let go. She hung onto me and pleaded over and over with me to kill her.' He wiped a hand over his nose to mop up the tears. 'Or maybe she was talking to God, I never did work that out.'

I reached across and took his hand, threading my fingers with his, turning it over and kissing his palm.

'She died two days later,' he said, almost in a whisper.

I pressed his hand to my cheek and he felt my tears, turning look at me, an unfathomable sadness in his eyes.

'The hot pot's getting cold,' he said.

Jonah remained quiet all through dinner at The Village, but no-one else noticed. He answered when spoken to, but otherwise kept his head down. Dionysus Wept were preparing for an important gig at the Cluny. A scout for The NonLocal was coming to see them and it had to be perfect. If they could convince him to give them a gig at one of the funkiest places to play in London, they were laughing. Cosmic and Daylight buzzed back and forth, running through their pre-gig checklist. Occasionally, Jonah would nod or interject.

I watched him, feeling an unhappy mix of compassion, sadness and remorse. I nudged my stool closer to his and snuggled against his arm.

'You okay?' I said.

He nodded, and I ran my hand over his back. He stood abruptly and took his plate to the sink.

'Zoe, you're coming aren't you?' said Ray.

'Course she is,' said Robin. 'The Bone'll kill her if she don't. Right?'

Jonah sat back at the table and looked at me expectantly. 'You will come, won't you?'

I nodded. 'Course.'

'Promise?'

'I promise. I wouldn't miss it for anything,' I said.

A Mountain Made of Sand

Ella was in danger of being swamped by the cushions stuffed around her on the sofa. I watched from the doorway as she raked one hand through her long hair while the other flicked absently through the latest Cosmo. She was due to pay for a month's cleaning. I could see the cash on the coffee table next to a half eaten blueberry muffin.

I was hovering on the threshold like a vampire waiting to be invited in, knowing what I was about to do was going to be messy and painful, and would have consequences I couldn't bear to think about. Danny might never forgive me, and I could lose one of my best customers. To make matters worse, Ella was actually wearing the necklace.

I coughed gently and squared up to the razor's edge, stepping treacherously into the room. The teardrop opal nestled in Ella's considerable bosom, glinting in the afternoon sunshine. I found myself staring at it, unable to shift my gaze. I felt dizzy.

'Beautiful, isn't it?' said Ella, her fingers stroking the gem.

I was paralysed. I willed myself to move, to say something. Ella glanced up and gave me a quizzical look.

'Money's on the table, Zoe. Are you all right? You look a bit peaky.'

I shook myself and picked up the cash without bothering to count it. Ella would never try to short change me. I could easily believe her affair with my brother was the first and only time in her life she had transgressed.

'Yeah, um... thanks. Listen, Ella...' I couldn't stop my hands from shaking. 'I need to have a word.'

'Sit down. Join me. I'll put the kettle on, shall I?' Ella was trying to extricate herself from the cushion monster on the sofa, and losing the battle.

'No. Thanks.' I sank into the armchair before my legs gave out and pressed my hands against my knees to keep them still. I took a couple of deep breaths, desperately searching for the right words. My mind had gone blank. All this time practising meditation and my head had been teeming with words. Now, when I needed them, it was empty. I stared into the abyss, and looked Ella in the eye.

She was now perched like a meerkat on the edge of the sofa, panic flashing across her face. 'Oh, lord. You're leaving me, aren't you? You do such a good job. Do you know how hard it is to find a cleaner you can trust these days? Please tell me you're not leaving.'

'I'm not leaving, but you might not want me to stay when you've heard what I have to say.'

Ella swallowed hard and blinked, her eyes fixed on me like I was a policewoman about to deliver bad news. And in a way, I was.

'It's Danny,' she said. 'Oh, God. It's Danny.'

I nodded.

'He wouldn't... not after...' Her hand shot to the opal and clutched at it like the safety line on a parachute. 'He can't leave me.'

'Oh, no. No Ella, he's not leaving you,' I said in a rush. 'He loves you. It's... That necklace. He gave it to you, didn't he?'

Ella nodded, totally lost.

'It wasn't his to give,' I said sadly.

Ella's mouth formed a perfect oh. She looked down at the stone in her fingers, then with great effort, looked back at me. When she spoke, her voice came out in a rasp, as if she couldn't believe what she was saying.

'He stole it?'

'From our mum. It was a gift from our dad.'

Ella's hands shook and a single tear ran down her cheek. 'Of course.'

'I'm sure Danny didn't mean any harm by it. I mean, he just doesn't think sometimes. Probably thought it was romantic and got carried away...' I could feel myself rambling, the words pouring back into my head.

Ella unfastened the clasp on the necklace and held it out to me, her eyes averted. The stone's iridescence reflected in the light as it hung, suspended in the air between us. I stood and gently took the pendant from her fingers, slipping it into my pocket.

'Thanks, Ella. I'm really very sorry.'

I went to the door and turned to look at her. She was hunched on the sofa, a half deflated balloon.

'Um... do you still want me to clean for you next week? I mean, if it's too awkward or whatever, I'd understand.'

Ella looked up and pulled her face into a tight smile. 'This wasn't your fault, Zoe. I'm sorry you had to get involved. See you next week, as usual.'

I nodded, picked up my backpack and left.

On my way home I called Danny's mobile but couldn't get a response. He was probably out of credit and had it switched off. Part of me wanted to march over there right away, but I was tired and couldn't face another confrontation today. I dropped the opal off at Mum's and thought I was going to have to call the fire brigade to free myself from her effusive grasp. Harder still was persuading her not to call Danny. I didn't want their moral fisticuffs to escalate any further. In the end, I left him a text asking him to call me.

By the end of the week he still hadn't been in touch, so I decided it was time to see what had happened. I raced through my cleaning schedule and arrived at his flat by mid-afternoon, letting myself in as surreptitiously as possible. There was a good chance he wouldn't even be up yet, so I crept into the living room holding the keys in my palm so they wouldn't jangle.

My mobile beeped and I froze, straining to hear if the noise had woken Danny. Then I thought: what if that was him, so I fished it out and had a look. It was Jonah wanting to know where I was. He had band rehearsal tonight and I'd promised to be back before he left. I still had time, so I ignored the text and shoved my phone back into my pocket.

I edged around the coffee table and perched on the sofa. The flat was a tip, as usual, although this looked like only a few days worth of disarray to my skilled eye. The sound of running water drifted through the open door behind me. Danny was in the shower.

I decided to make a pre-emptive peace offering, so while waiting for him to finish getting up, I went into the kitchen to make tea and toast. Reaching for a couple of mugs from the cupboard, I did a double take. There was a bottle of pills sitting on the shelf. I picked it up to read the label.

'What are you doing here?'

I spun round, the pill bottle clutched in my hand. Danny was barefoot in his dressing gown, hair dripping down his neck. He looked like he wanted to kill me.

'You can't help yourself, can you?' he said.

'Why didn't you call me?'

'Why the fuck would I call you?'

'Danny-'

'Fuck off.'

He turned and stalked into the living room. I followed, still holding the pills.

'Danny, tell me what happened.'

He sat on the sofa and started to roll a joint. 'Like you don't know.'

'It wasn't yours.'

'Why did you have to interfere? We were happy. You fucked everything.'

'No,' I said. 'You did that by stealing from Mum.'

'She never wears it. It's just sitting there.'

'You could've asked her first.'

A lifeless laugh shot from Danny's mouth. He stuck the spliff between his lips and searched the cluttered coffee table for his lighter.

'You don't know a fucking thing,' he said, finding his Zippo under a pile of empty crisp packets. He lit up, sucking the smoke deep into his lungs.

'What about these?' I rattled the pills.

Danny looked at me through a haze of smoke, narrowing his eyes and looking more murderous than ever.

'I took them,' he said. 'Without asking first.'

'But Ella needs these.'

He shrugged. 'Fuck her.'

'I thought you loved her.'

'Yeah, and I thought she loved me. She kicked me out. Martin's back, apparently. Cunt.'

'Did you just call me-'

'Fuck Zoe. Listen to yourself. The world doesn't revolve around you. Little Miss fucking Perfect. Always knows what to do. Always in everybody's business. The puppet mistress, always in control.' He stood and held out his hand. 'Give me those pills.'

I took a step back. 'No.'

He lunged at me over the table, grabbing at the bottle. I snatched it away and flung it across the room. It bounced off the far wall and skittered under the sofa.

'Bitch,' said Danny.

'Right. That's it. I've had enough.' I stormed towards the door.

'Fantastic.'

I spun on my heel to glare at him. Danny sunk back onto the sofa, retrieved his spliff from the four leaf clover ashtray I gave him for Christmas, and took another long drag. I was so infuriated by his wilful stupidity my mind burned as hot as the end of his cigarette.

'If you thought Ella was ever going to leave Martin for you,' I said, 'you're more stupid than I thought. She likes security. How were you ever going to give her that? She was using you to make herself feel better. You can call that love if it makes you feel better.'

'See, that's you all over, that is. You can't resist twisting the knife, can you sis?'

'It's the truth, Dan. When are you going to start living in the real world?'

'When the real world is worth living in.'

'That's ridiculous,' I said. 'I'm trying to get away from this bullshit. I can't deal with it anymore. Or you. I don't want to see you.'

I turned away from my brother, unable to watch his heart shattering. It was too late to take it back, truth or not. I didn't know if I was doing the right thing. I couldn't think straight about anything anymore. I wanted to understand what was real, and I wanted to be free, and I couldn't do that if I kept getting dragged into other people's dramas. But then, what was I supposed to do? Leave them to fight it out between them, rise above it and drift off on a self-righteous cloud like I didn't care about them. I couldn't win either way. I was trapped in a nightmare of my own making.

I went to the front door as Danny shouted after me. 'S'okay, Zoe. I'll add you to the list. Dad, Mum, Ella, and now you. No-one wants me. Story of my fucking life.'

I closed the door.

By the time I arrived home I'd convinced myself not to feel guilty about Danny. He had made a series of choices and this was where he had ended up. Even without my interference, Ella would've dumped him eventually anyway. He was going to have to move on. Actually, I reasoned, I had done him a favour by bringing it to a head. I had freed him from a situation that would have choked the life out of him given enough time. He didn't see it that way now, but he'd come round.

I opened the front door and found Jonah sitting on his amp in the hallway looking at his watch. *Shit.* I'd forgotten he was waiting for me to come home.

'Sorry I'm a bit late,' I said.

'Where've you been?'

'Danny's. What's wrong?'

'It's Friday evening.'

'I know,' I said, mind running double time trying to work out what was going on.

'Wouldn't he be seeing that woman?'

'They split up. Seriously, Joe, what's going on?' I stared at him, utterly baffled. He was sitting with his arms folded and clearly didn't believe a word I was saying. I didn't know what I was supposed to say.

'Looking forward to Sunday?' he said.

He wasn't even trying to conceal the cynicism in his voice, or the frozen look in his eyes. I decided to try for appeasement, even though I'd done nothing wrong. At least, not as far as I could tell. Who knew these days?

'I thought your gig was tomorrow.' I smiled too brightly. 'Looking forward to that. I expect you'll be wanting to get off to rehearsal. I'm sorry if you were waiting for me, I had a bit of a crisis with Danny, and didn't realise the time. I don't want to make you late, Joe.'

He was unmoved. I didn't know what else I could do so tried to squeeze past him to the living room, but there wasn't enough space and I got wedged between the wall and Jonah's unyielding body.

'What do you do with him?' he said.

I looked down at his sullen face. He was looking straight ahead at the door and seemed to be holding his breath. I thought for a second he was talking about Danny, but knew that wasn't right.

'Do you mean Adam?' I said cautiously.

'You know very well I mean Adam.'

I managed to wriggle out of my backpack and took a step back so I could look into Jonah's eyes. He looked up at me, waiting for a response. I knew he wouldn't believe the truth, but what else could I say?

'We talk. Well, he asks me questions and I talk.'

'What do you talk about?'

'All sorts of things. Zen. Life. The universe. Everything. Y'know.'

'Specifically.'

'Come off it, Jonah. What do you expect? D'you want me to give you a detailed breakdown of every conversation I've ever had with him?'

He simply sat there, looking at me. I didn't know whether to laugh or cry. The situation was preposterous. I knew I should try to reassure him, but he was determined not to believe me, no matter what I said. I took a deep breath and tried to calm down.

'I'm sorry you feel this way Joe, I really am. I don't know what you want to hear. Adam and I talk about complicated stuff. I don't really know how to explain it to you. I'm not sure I understand it most of the time.'

He nodded, like I'd confirmed his suspicions. 'Isn't it incredible? Merely talking about complicated stuff can make you so happy. You come back from your little get-togethers bouncing around all over the place, grinning like a maniac.'

He stood and glowered over me. 'Talking doesn't have that effect on anyone. No-one I know.'

'What are you saying? You think we're...' An incredulous laugh bubbled up and hit him in the face before I could stop it. I placed my hand on his arm. 'You're being absurd.'

He pushed my arm away and picked up his amp, shouldering past me to the door.

'Is that right?' he said, wrenching open the door. He stomped into the corridor, the door slamming shut behind him.

'What about your guitar?' I shouted at the closed door. I ran into the living room. The guitar was lying in its case in the middle of the room. I shut the lid and bolted out of the flat and down the stairs. The van engine growled as I burst through the door.

I ran out in front of the van just as Jonah was about to pull out. My blood froze and for a moment I thought he would run me down, but he slammed on the brakes and glared at me through the windscreen instead. I held up the guitar case, then walked round to the passenger door. Jonah leaned across and flung it open.

'Jonah, I didn't mean to call you absurd.' I put the guitar on the passenger seat.

'What did you mean then?'

'Adam is... If you saw him, you'd understand. He's old enough to be my dad. Honestly, please believe me. There's nothing like that going on.'

He pulled the door shut without a word and drove away. I stood shivering as I watched the van disappear up the street.

Jonah came home late that night. I waited up for him, determined to prove I cared about his feelings, but he went straight to bed and ignored me. He slept late on Saturday and I woke him with breakfast at lunch time, slipping back into bed and snuggling while he ate his scrambled eggs. But when I slithered under the duvet, working my fingers into his boxers, he leapt out of bed like he'd had an electric shock.

'Nice try,' he said, and disappeared into the bathroom, locking the door behind him.

I wasn't about to give up that easily. I found a two pence coin and flipped the lock, slipping out of my T-shirt and into the shower. He let himself be washed and enticed out of his sulk. By the time he was ready to leave for soundcheck, I had cajoled a smile or two from his lips, and saw him off at the door with a lingering kiss.

'Eight o'clock, remember?' he said, his fingers clamped around my jaw. 'We won't be on 'til later, but I don't want you to miss it. Okay?'

He gave me a quick peck on the lips and stepped out the door.

I diligently watched the clock all evening, rustled up some fish fingers for dinner, then ran upstairs to get ready for the gig of the century. By the time I was spruced, plucked and coiffed (as much as I ever am), it was only seven thirty, so I stood at the window watching people arrive at The Cluny across the street. The lilies and carnations I had bought Jonah were starting to wilt in their vase on the sill so I pinched off a couple of shrivelled pink heads, dropping them into the bin under the desk.

When I turned back to the window I saw Jonah emerge from a side door, followed by Ray. They were deep in conversation: Jonah was upset about something and Ray was trying to calm him down.

I flipped off the light and opened the window, leaning out slightly so I could hear more clearly. Their voices echoed up in fragments as Jonah paced a wild, erratic circle and Ray followed him with his head.

'I have to say… over-reacting,' said Ray.

'Why else… if she didn't… guilty?' said Jonah.

'I've seen… she looks at you, Joe. Why… cheat?'

'… talked about him… then stopped… avoids discussing… can't look me in the eye. What am I supposed to think?'

'You… going to drive her away if… just like the others… trust her,' said Ray.

'Trust… won't even talk…'

My guts lurched and my fingers tightened on the window ledge. I had made this happen. Nisha warned me and I didn't listen. Jonah was just a scared little boy, insecure over losing his mother all over again, and I had pushed him away in my own ignorance and fear. If only I had explained things to him, even if it was just to share my confusion, but I didn't know how. I didn't understand what was happening. Everything was changing on the inside and yet it all looked the same on the outside. How could I explain that without coming across like I was hiding something?

The deep throb of a helicopter filled the air, drowning out their voices and making them look up. I stepped back from the window, worried Jonah would see I'd been listening. The police searchlight scanned over the warehouses opposite then whipped across to the flats.

The living room was illuminated in a brilliant flash of intrusive light. The transparent heart-shaped crystal hanging in the window, dangling over the dying flowers, caught the beam as it passed, firing out dozens of rainbows, scattering them over the walls of the room.

Suddenly my head was buzzing and liquefying. My knees weakened but I managed to stay upright. The helicopter beam had gone but the room was still lit. I stumbled over my own feet, looking around in amazement. I hadn't switched the light back on, the bulbs were off. So where was the light coming from?

I wasn't sure I could move, my whole body was vibrating. Carefully, I turned on the spot, keeping my breath even, searching for the source of the light. It seemed to be everywhere and nowhere. My eyes were dazzled, as if I were looking directly into the sun, only it didn't hurt. I blinked over and over, trying to shift the illusion. *It has to be an illusion.*

It reminded me of the ice blue aura I had seen around the banana. This light was similar, but appeared to come from inanimate objects too. I ran my eyes along the book shelves and over the furniture. Everything pulsed with energy and light, similar to the way I'd seen things years before during the breakdown, only now it was more intense. I could see details in objects on the far side of the room without even trying: a tiny crumb nestled in the fuzz of the carpet, the scuffs and creasing on the book spines, the tightly packed weft and warp of the sofa fabric. My eyes had been transformed into Super Eyes.

I lifted my hands and looked down on them as if from a great distance. I was a giant and my reach extended across the world. Colours pulsed around my hands, bands of light chasing each other round and round, swirling in tendrils reaching out into the space beyond. The air was filled with showers of light, raining down. I laughed with joy. This was the best show on earth.

I turned back to the window. The drooping lilies were ablaze, as if as the life left them they burned brighter, releasing their light into the world. Astonished, I watched as the vibrant tentacles of my own light reached out to the flowers, before I had even moved my arms. I took a step towards the window sill but my aura got there first, wrapping itself around the vase. The lilies responded, their light merging with mine in a dance of celebration.

I picked up the pulsating flowers and sat down with them on the floor, gazing at them in utter amazement and delight. I had no idea how long it had been since the helicopter flew by. It felt like seconds and eons. I let myself be carried into rapture, my mind fuzzy with warmth from an unseen fire.

A crashing sound sent shock waves through my being and I felt a surge of cold air. Another energy had penetrated the euphoria. I raised my eyes to search out the interloper. A dark mass hovered before me sending out tendrils of anger and bitter betrayal. It was Jonah.

'Where were you?' he said.

I smiled up at him, oblivious to his mood, the ecstasy refusing to leave me. He scowled and looked about him, as if he didn't recognise where he was.

'What are you doing sitting in the dark?' he said.

I pointed dumbly at the flowers and beamed at him. I couldn't speak. I didn't seem to know any words.

He lunged at me, grabbing my arms and yanking me to my feet. The vase of lilies tipped onto its side and rolled away, the water spilling into a puddle on the carpet. Jonah's hands gripped my arms, holding me in a vice, but I continued to smile, the light pulsing erratically. Something about the situation seemed funny, the joy making me light-headed with glee.

'What's wrong with you?' he said.

I giggled. He was so angry, it was hilarious. I could feel the magma of rage boiling through his veins, his face contorted in fury, as if he were about to rip open his mouth as wide as he could and bite off my head in one chunk. I chuckled at the image.

He started to shake me, back and forth. 'I should never have bought you that fucking drink.'

The violent movement sent my mood crashing through the floor. I found myself in the dark, held in a furious clinch by Jonah, who was looking at me like I was evil. He stopped shaking me and let go. His hands trembled as he raised them to clutch at his head, an animal whine rising from his throat. In a rush, I realised what had happened and felt myself hollow out in dismay.

'Oh, Joe. I... What's the time?'

He glared at me, his face shut down, jaws clenched. I could tell he was fighting to stop himself hitting me, and my heart started hammering through my chest in fright.

'You were with him.' He hissed the words through his teeth.

A chill poured over me. There was nothing I could say to convince him. I should have been there. I was about to leave when the trance took me. It was the truth, but he wouldn't accept it.

'Jonah. Please. I wasn't. I don't even know where he lives.'

He turned away and stormed out the flat, slamming the door behind him. His guitar case lay on the sofa where he must have thrown it when he came in. I stood for a moment, suspended in shock. Finally, the spell of fear broken, my knees gave way beneath me and I hit the floor, sobbing and shaking with remorse.

After a little while the storm subsided and I sat, hunched and drained, staring at the bedraggled lilies and carnations strewn over the carpet. I snatched them up and slung them in the bin. I knew Jonah wasn't coming home tonight, it was pointless to wait up for him, but I couldn't face going upstairs to bed. So I curled up on the sofa using Jonah's duffel coat as a blanket, and sunk into fitful dreams.

The mountain rose forever into the clouds, steep and rugged, pitted with gullies and outcrops of rock. Clumps of bushes and grasses sprung from the ground and tightly clustered pines lined the path. I was climbing with a group and we were strung along the trail like raindrops on a spider web. Jonah helped me over a boulder, taking my hand and pulling me up.

A mist descended, blocking our vision as we penetrated the clouds. We stumbled onwards and upwards, coming out the other side to find ourselves at the summit. Exhausted, we watched as the cloud miraculously evaporated, revealing spectacular views across the terrain we had travelled. We stood in awe of the glorious beauty, silenced by the space.

After absorbing all we could, we decided to head back down the mountain. It was important to leave before the weather changed. The others were ahead of me. I took a step and the ground shifted beneath my feet. It didn't seem stable and I became frightened. The others moved off down the trail.

I tried again.

Again, the ground moved. It was as if the mountain were made of sand. Every time I placed a foot on the ground it dissolved into granules and slipped away. If I moved, the whole mountain would crumble from under me. Panic gripped my heart. The others had left. Only Jonah waited for me, but I couldn't move. He gave me one last mournful look over his shoulder, and was gone.

Alone now, I pressed my body to the ground, clinging to it in desperation, terrified to move. Paralysed.

The sound of helicopter rotor blades beating against the sky grew louder and louder, until it became deafening, throbbing through my skull and threatening to slice it into a million pieces. I looked up from the disintegrating ground to see a man dangling from the helicopter by a rope, flying straight at me.

It was Adam.

He lowered himself down and bound himself to me. We were winched up into the sky as the helicopter flew over the awesome peaks.

I clung to him, too scared to enjoy the view. I was pleased someone came back for me, that I wasn't abandoned to the mountain, but a terrible feeling encircled my mind. Something wasn't right. As we climbed higher, the light became brighter, more dazzling. I couldn't bring myself to look at it. I buried my head in Adam's chest as the tears poured down my cheeks, and I cried out in anguish.

'No. It's all wrong. I have to go back down.'

Resistance is Futile

Jonah still hadn't come home by the time I set off to meet Adam the next morning. The dream had shaken me, confirming my fears. Things were getting out of control. I half expected the Mindfulness Cobbles to dissolve under my feet, just like the mountain, as I made my precarious way down the path to the river.

Adam was waiting patiently in the spring sunshine. Instead of joining him in the stone circle, I went to the fence running along the river bank and stood watching the river tumble by. The sound of quacking drew my attention, and I noticed a mother duck leading her line of offspring upstream, the fluffy ducklings bobbing in the current, getting snarled up in the rocks and fighting with the water, determined and relentless. Adam joined me at the fence.

'I count thirteen,' he said, with a chuckle. 'Although it's difficult to tell with them whirling like that.'

'Why is waking up so hard?' I kept my eyes on the spiralling ducklings, but could feel him looking at me.

'Ah,' he said.

The silence that followed was so long I thought he had gone. I turned around and he was sitting in his usual spot on the DREAM seat.

'Tell me what has happened,' he said gently.

I sat on the OPEN seat opposite, feeling sick and mumbled into my lap.

'It's getting too... I'm getting worse. I mean, I'm scared.' I looked up and fixed him with what I hoped was a determined stare. 'I want to stop.'

'You have no choice,' he said.

'You always have a choice. Why do I have to do this? Why can't I be like a normal person, and do normal things, and have normal bog standard happiness? Never mind bliss or nirvana or whatever. Why can't I just live my life?'

'You think what you call normal people are living their lives, Zoe? You think they're happy?'

'I don't know,' I said. 'They're not going nuts and driving people away who love them.'

'Aren't they?'

I knew Adam was speaking the truth, even if it was over-simplified to make a point. I knew that what passed for happiness in many people was a disguise, a way of distracting yourself for as long as possible from dealing with reality (whatever the hell that was), but I was feeling rebellious and petulant. I shrugged and felt my age spiral backwards a couple of decades. I knew I was being stupid but I didn't care.

'Zoe, once you have begun, the process carries you along. You must finish what you started.'

'I didn't start this, okay? I didn't ask for an overactive brain or whatever the fuck it is that's wrong with me. I didn't ask to start seeing shit all over the place. I'm a nutcase, Adam. Maybe I *should* be locked up. All I do is mess things up and hurt the people I care about.'

'What happened?'

'I had another trance. I lost it completely. I wasn't even... I didn't know where I was. Jonah was... I'm losing him. He looked at me like he hated me. What am I supposed to do? I couldn't stop it. I should've stayed grounded but, I don't know, I just got caught up in it, in the light, and I couldn't stop it and Jonah's gone.'

'Deep breaths, Zoe.' Adam was an oasis of calm. 'This is why you must practise.'

'I know that, I am, but...' I wanted to scream. I felt trapped in my own stupid head and in a wild fit of madness imagined ripping open my skull, tearing out my brain and flinging it as far as I could throw it.

'I can't control it,' I said. 'I can't do anything. I just want it to stop.'

'That's good, Zoe. Do that. Stop.'

'Stop what? I just said I wanted to stop the process. You say I can't. Then you tell me to stop. What is *wrong* with you?'

'Just let go,' he said.

'I'm too fucking scared to let go, Adam. That's the point.' I leapt to my feet and started pacing the circle, fear and anger fighting it out for supremacy. 'If I could let go, I'd be all right, but I can't. And you sitting there smiling at me doesn't help. I'm falling apart. My life is a mess.

Danny hates me. Jonah hates me. And all you can do is... is, what? Nothing?'

My voice was bouncing around the valley, echoing off the brick arches of the road bridge. I stood glowering over Adam. Part of me wanted to stalk off, run away, just as I had at our first meeting. I should never have come back that day. I allowed myself to be persuaded this path was worth pursuing and now I was too far gone to return. I was paralysed with rage and dread. Adam's smile vanished and he shot me a look full of fierce emptiness.

'What do you think will happen if you stop trying to control everything?' he said.

My knees buckled and I staggered back to my seat. My whole body was vibrating violently, although I could barely move. I sucked down great gulps of air, willing myself to be still. Did he expect me to answer his question? I wasn't even sure I understood English anymore.

'You breathe, your heart beats, your guts digest,' he said. 'How? Do *you* do it?'

He had me locked in his gaze. My head gave a tiny shake to confirm the negative.

'Do I breathe for you?' he went on. 'Do I digest your breakfast? Do I think for you? Live for you? Who lives your life, Zoe? How can you live your life if you keep trying to control it? Will the sun not rise if you let go? Will your heart not beat? Will life not go on? Is it you creating supernovas or turning the earth on its axis? No wonder your head hurts. You can't even control your own thoughts, how can you possibly believe you could control anything else?

'Just stop,' he said. 'There is nothing else to do.'

I fought the tears filling my eyes. I felt so tired of banging my head against this impenetrable wall. I wanted to curl up, crawl away and hide.

'I don't know how,' I said in a whisper.

'You are transcending your ego,' he said. 'Your ego is resisting. You can't beat it by facing it head on, that only makes it stronger. Practise will wear it down. The daily humiliations of life will wear it down. Stop resisting. Stop trying to hold on.'

Adam's voice was gentle again, and I relaxed. A bit. A single tear escaped and ran down my cheek.

'Will I lose everything?' I said. 'Will I lose my mind?'

'There is always a price to pay for freedom, Zoe. I'd be lying if I said there was no risk. But what is the price of continuing as you are?'

For all my protestations, I knew I could never settle for normal happiness. I'd seen too far and too deep to be satisfied living on the surface of life. I had run out of options. The way I was wired, the choices I had made, the circumstances of my life, and who knows, maybe my karma, were all pushing me down this path. My ego was doomed, whether I liked the idea or not. I wiped my cheek with my fingers. I still felt sick but understood what I had to do. I just had to figure out how to do it.

'How long will it take?'

'A lifetime, or a second. It's up to you, Zoe.'

I nodded and stood. 'Um... thanks Adam. Sorry for shouting, it's... y'know.'

Adam smiled and his eyes twinkled, but there was a hint of sadness at the edges, and I knew he understood. And I thought, if he can free himself – an ex-stockbroker, one of the most stressed out and controlling occupations ever – then so can I.

I walked slowly over the cobbles, eyes on my feet, creating a new mantra for myself. *I will be free. I will be free.* I wanted to plant the roots of my determination so deep that nothing could pull them out, not even my own stupid, deluded ego.

I turned the corner and stopped in surprise. Jonah was standing in the middle of the footbridge. My heart leapt with joy – he'd come back. I rushed to him, beaming with happiness.

'Joe. Quick.' I grabbed his arm. 'Come and meet Adam.'

I pulled him towards the seats in a frenzy. I could prove it to him. I could show him the truth. But the seats were deserted, as I knew, deep down, they would be.

'He's gone. He does that.' I looked down the various paths leading from the seats. 'I've never been able to work out which way he goes. He moves so fast.'

It was then that I noticed the look on Jonah's face. The anger of the past few weeks had vanished. Now he was sad and perhaps a little sorry for me. He must have overheard our conversation and realised the truth after all. There may even have been a smidgen of guilt in there. He was staring at the moss growing thick between the cobbles, a deep frown carving ridges into his forehead.

'I'm sorry, Zo,' he said, looking up suddenly.

His dark eyes were wells overflowing with compassion and I thought he might start to cry, so I stepped forward and slipped my arms around his waist.

'Let's not talk about it,' I said. 'Let's just pretend it never happened and start again.'

He held me tight, almost too tight, and I rested my head against his chest. He pressed his lips to the top of my head and breathed in deep.

'Fancy going out tonight?' he said. 'There's a band on at The Sage I'd like to check out. The guys are going too.'

I nodded and raised my face to his. He brushed a gentle kiss against my lips and closed his eyes. When he spoke, it sounded like he was making a solemn promise, and my heart ached with joy.

'I'll never abandon you again, Zoe.'

It was approaching midnight by the time Jonah and I parted company with Ray, Linda and Robin outside The Sage. We had conducted our post-gig appreciation and deconstruction as a viscous fog wrapped itself about us, disguising distances and muting the harsh edges of the world. The glass curves of The Sage dissolved into the misty darkness. We could have been transported anywhere in the world and wouldn't have known it.

I held tight to Jonah's hand as we descended the steps to the Millennium Bridge. I couldn't see the other side of the river. Points of light hung in the murk, marking the line of the Tyne as it curved away from us. The great steel arc of the bridge rose out of the fog, its edges blurred, the rainbow of lights playing over the archway, pulsing and swirling as if under water. The Tyne as painted by Monet.

'D'you think that pipe was an affectation?' I said. 'I mean, who smokes a pipe these days?'

'Probably.'

I looked at Jonah through the haze. He seemed preoccupied and distant, but in a different way to before. Drizzle sprinkled over our faces as we stepped onto the shrouded bridge. I raised my face to the sky and gazed at the coloured beams cutting through the fog over our heads.

'It's beautiful, Joe.'

'Mmmm.'

'You okay? You seem-'

'I'm fine.'

The drizzle found some purpose and started coming down harder. I wrinkled my nose against the wet, then caught myself laughing.

'Why do we do that?' I said. 'Wrinkling my face and hunching up against the rain isn't going to keep me dry, is it?'

I grinned up at Jonah. His eyes were focused on something internal and obscure.

'What's wrong? It's not still Adam, is it?'

Finally, he looked at me. His face glistening in the dark, grief and care swimming in his eyes. He seemed to be searching for the right words, his mouth working, stuttering for the truth. A chill ran through me, the rain on my skin solidifying into lines of ice, and I didn't want him to speak. I knew I couldn't bear to hear what he was about to say.

'I was there,' he said. 'I saw you.'

'I know you did, Joe. What is it?'

'He wasn't there.'

'He left. You can meet him next time, if you like. I'll ask him-'

'No Zoe.'

He stopped walking in the middle of the bridge, the high point of the arch invisible above him in the gloom. I was numb. I stood facing him, the look on his face making me nervous.

'He wasn't there at all,' he said. 'Before you saw me, I was watching.' He placed his hands on my shoulders. I had never seen him look so sad.

'You were on your own,' he said softly. 'There was no-one else there.'

He looked so serious and what he was saying was so bizarre, I felt giddy. A bubble of hysterical laughter burst from my mouth. I felt drunk, though I hadn't been drinking. The bridge lurched beneath our feet and Jonah's grip tightened.

'I'm serious. Please, Zoe-'

'My God, Jonah, would you do that? Would you do that to me? After what you promised. You're still jealous. I know I haven't been...

attentive,' I could feel anger burning through the hysterics, 'but I've been preoccupied. I know you may think I should only preoccupy myself with you and your happiness, but-'

'Would you stop?' he said. 'I don't want to hurt you. Why would I lie about this? I'm telling you what I saw. I'm not jealous. There's no-one to be jealous of.'

I yanked myself free of Jonah's hands and staggered backwards. The rain was pelting the bridge, zinging off the metal seats, the surface of the river dancing with countless exploding water bombs. I was soaked, my clothes sticking to my skin making it hard to move. I stared at Jonah as if I didn't recognise him. He shivered as the rain drenched his head and dripped from his chin in a fanatical baptism.

'Do you realise what you're saying?' I said.

Jonah reached out, tried to wrap his arms around me, but I spun away, my mind screaming with the effort of making sense of... of...

'You're saying I'm insane,' I said. 'I'm crazy. I imagined the whole thing. I just made it up. Tell me, why would I do that, Joe?'

He stumbled forward, blinded by rain.

'I'm sorry,' he said, his voice cracking.

I was crumbling. My mind thrashed, searching for solid ground. I clutched at the slippery handrail as the bridge reeled in the wind. Great ripples of fear flooded my veins making me tremble and hyperventilate, and I had to fight to stay on my feet. I felt Jonah's arm lock around my waist, trying to hold me up, but I didn't want him near me. I pushed at him and stumbled away, running for home, curtains of rain wrapping themselves around me like a shroud.

Jonah found me sitting in a puddle in the hallway just inside the door. I could feel his hands on me, trying to get me to stand, but I couldn't move. He wanted me to go upstairs with him, get out of my drenched clothes, but my body felt like liquid concrete. I thought I would never move from this spot again.

Jonah disappeared. I heard his feet fly up the stairs, then moments later, stumble back down, going so fast he nearly fell. He reappeared before me in his dressing gown holding a towel and my pyjamas. I was shivering now, eyes fixed on the floor. I had no idea what I was looking at. Jonah draped the towel over my head, gently rubbing my hair and wiping the rain from my face.

'Come on, babe. Let's get you out of these clothes. Get you nice and dry.'

I cooperated but kept my eyes averted. Did I feel ashamed? I didn't know if I would ever feel anything again. Jonah carried me into the living room, leaving the sodden clothes in a heap in the hall. He set me down on the sofa and ducked into the kitchen. I heard the kettle boil and click off and water being poured, then Jonah was beside me with two steaming mugs of hot chocolate. He put them on the coffee table and sat next to me, smoothing back the hair from my face.

'Hey, Zo. Talk to me, babe. I'm here for you.'

His words dissolved into the black void inside my head. Perhaps, somewhere buried in the recesses of my unconscious there was some appreciation for the sentiment, some gratitude for his kindness, but I couldn't feel it. I was empty. He started to speak again, gentle and cautious.

'Maybe there's a rational explanation for what I saw. Or didn't see. I mean, maybe you imagined him as a way to cope with what was happening, the trances and weird stuff. Maybe he was like an imaginary friend.'

I could feel cranks and levers being pulled, something in my mind started to whir into action. A rational explanation – that was what I needed. I blinked and turned to face him, searching his eyes for an answer.

A flash of pain ran across his face and he looked away, rubbing a hand over his fast drying hair.

'I had one,' he said, 'when I was a kid. An imaginary friend. She kept me company when I was little, and-'

'What was she called?'

Jonah screwed up his face in embarrassment. 'Isabella the Boat.'

'The Boat?'

He nodded. 'I don't think she was an actual boat. I can't remember. God knows why I called her that.'

Normally I would have laughed. It was a fantastic name for an imaginary friend, and probably an early sign of Jonah's poetic inventiveness. The mind was an amazing place, full of so many things we never see or understand. If I could just think clearly I could work out what had happened, but the words were getting jumbled up and slithering about. I needed to get a grip and be rational, make a list of all the likely explanations. Then I could go through the list and find my answer.

'Okay,' I said. 'So Adam could be an imaginary friend. What else?'

Jonah reached for the mugs and handed one to me. I held it in both hands and blew onto the hot chocolate, concentrating ferociously on keeping my wayward mind in check. Jonah leaned into me and sipped at his drink, eyes staring into space.

'Well, I'll say it, 'cos one of us has to,' I said. 'I could actually be mad. Adam could be a symptom of my encroaching psychosis.'

Jonah didn't say anything and didn't look at me. Every cell in my being was repelled by that possibility. I knew how it must look from the outside, and I knew society would stick me with the crazy label and throw away the key given half a chance. To look at it that way was too simplistic, too easy, and more about getting me to behave myself and conform to the consensus reality than about finding out the truth.

'What else?' said Jonah.

'He could be a projection of something in my psyche, something I find hard to accept,' I said. 'Like the mystical side of me. Or he could be my animus, my inner man, or a kind of father figure, like a compensation for losing my dad.'

'Why would you imagine him so vividly?'

I shrugged. 'Maybe that's the visionary thing at work. It's like you said, he was how I coped with the confusion. If you turn your conflict into dialogue, split it up and do like role play with it, you can face things you would normally deny or run away from. A kind of self-help therapy.'

Jonah nodded and gulped his hot chocolate. 'It makes sense. What else?'

'He could be a personification of my Higher Self, my inner Zen Master. Although why my Higher Self would look like an old-ish man in an expensive pinstripe, I don't know.'

Jonah smiled and put his empty mug on the table. 'Here's one. You'll like this. Maybe he's an angel.'

I gave him a lopsided grin and chuckled. 'Or a fairy.'

'Or a ghost.'

I snorted into my hot chocolate sending out a spray of brown water.

'Or an alien,' said Jonah.

This set me off giggling in earnest. He put his arms around me and held me as I vibrated against him. Maybe I was a tad hysterical but at least I was feeling something, and I was smiling. The laughter faded and a huge yawn sent a shiver through my body. Jonah took my mug and plonked it on the table, then slipped an arm under my legs and lifted me onto his lap. I nestled my head on his shoulder and ran my fingers over his beautiful face, tracing the lines of weary worry.

'There's only one problem with all this,' I said, my voice thick with drowsiness. 'Doesn't feel right. Where did it all come from? All those conversations. Adam knew things I could never know.'

'Sleep on it, babe.'

I nodded lazily and yawned again. Jonah carried me upstairs and by the time he slipped me into bed, I was asleep.

Sunshine woke me in the middle of the morning. I lay cocooned by the duvet and felt nothing but peace. Slowly, the revelations from the night before wormed their way back into my mind and I groaned. I'd had no dreams, no signs or indications as to what I should do about my predicament, so I dragged myself out of bed and wandered downstairs to find the kettle. I couldn't think until I had some caffeine whizzing around in my blood.

There was a note propped up on the coffee table from Jonah, reminding me he was at work and that he'd bring a Chinese takeaway on his return. I made a mug of coffee and a huge bowl of cereal, and took them to the desk in the corner. I stuffed muesli and crunchy oats into my mouth while I waited for the computer to sort itself out, then got to work.

In what felt like no time at all, I heard the key in the door and Jonah was beside me holding a plastic bag bulging with takeaway cartons. I looked at the clock. It was only five o'clock, so he must have sneaked out early, and here I was still in my jimjams. Jonah leant over and kissed the top of my head.

'What you doing?' he said.

'Looking for him.' I turned back to the computer. I had spent all day searching page after page on the internet, head propped in one hand. I couldn't believe how many entries there were for Adam Kadmon. My neck was starting to get sore. I clicked on another link, and Jonah rustled off to the kitchen.

'How long have you been up, babe?'

I shrugged. 'Couple of hours. Is that sweet and sour I can smell?'

'Hungry?'

'Starved.'

I spun in the chair to face the kitchen. Jonah was watching me from the doorway, looking worried. He probably thought I was losing it again.

'Here's what I think,' I said. 'He told me things about his life. Not much, but enough little details. I found the monastery he studied at, but there's no mention of him. Why would there be? I've tried Facebook. Again, nothing. Not a surprise. He said he wrote a book, didn't tell me what it was called, but I can't find it. It's not on Amazon, anyway. He must've used a pen name. So now I'm going through every reference to Adam Kadmon on Google.'

'Zoe, hold up. What happened to the idea of him being something from your imagination?'

'How could I come up with all the stuff he told me? How could I have guessed the name of the monastery? It's a real place. All that detail, the technical stuff-'

'You read those books, remember?' he said. 'Just after you met him. You must have read every book on Buddhism in the library. Maybe one of them mentioned the monastery, you could've picked it up anywhere.'

'Yeah, but...' I ran my fingers through my hair, sculpting it into a wild, impossible geometry. 'That just doesn't feel right.'

I stood and went to Jonah, hooking my arms around his neck. He pulled me to him and squeezed me tight.

'You didn't meet him Joe.' I pulled back and looked into his intense, earnest face. 'I know it sounds mad. I know it makes no sense, but he felt real.'

'You touched him? He felt solid?'

'Well, no actually, come to think of it.' I let go and stepped back. 'I tried to shake his hand a couple of times but he wouldn't go for it. He never let me get near him. I thought it was just some sort of teacher disciple protocol or something.'

I wandered back to the computer, searching my memory for anything unusual that happened between me and Adam, anything that could explain who or what he was. Of course, it all seemed pretty unusual now. I could hear Jonah clattering about in the kitchen, dishing up dinner.

'How many entries are there?' he said.

'Erm... Adam Kadmon. Tens of thousands, but that's just Google. I'll try Bing and Yahoo too. There's loads, mainly Kabbala – that's the mystical branch of Judaism. But there's a band and writers. There's a Guitar Grimoire full of chord progressions and stuff you'd know about. It's such an odd name, I didn't think I'd have any trouble finding him. Shows what I know.'

'You could be up all night,' said Jonah, placing a plate of steaming sweet 'n' sour noodles in front of me and handing over a fork. 'Several nights.'

'As long as it takes,' I said. 'Adam Kadmon means primordial man or prototypal man. Here, check this out, it says you become Adam Kadmon through activation of the divine nature. When enough of mankind has activated their divine nature we will evolve, blah, blah, blah... here we are, it's an archetype, the pattern for mankind. It connects God, Man and the World. Adam Kadmon was the first being to emerge from the infinite.'

I spun a knot of noodles onto my fork and cocked my head to look at Jonah, sitting on the sofa, his plate on his knees.

'So here's the thing, Joe. I'd never heard this name before. I know nothing about esoteric Jewish stuff. It's not mentioned in any of those Buddhist books, it's a whole different tradition. So how could I pick such a perfect name for my imaginary friend?'

I arrived at the circle of concrete seats early and walked around it, reading the words carved into the curved blocks. Dream With Open Eyes. Maybe that's what I'd been doing. It was another possible explanation. Dreaming while awake.

I sat in my usual spot and waited for Adam, determined to get real answers from him. I wasn't going to give up until I knew exactly who and what he was. And I was determined to touch him. I didn't care if it breached etiquette, or whatever, I had to know.

I checked my phone. It was quarter past. He was late. He was never late. I felt the flutter of panic around the fringes of my awareness and took a deep breath. I should meditate while I waited.

The sound of footsteps on cobbles approached from behind making me leap out of my seat with joy. He was here. Everything was going to be all right. I turned, a laugh rising in my throat.

It was Jonah.

He stood for a moment with his hands in his pockets looking solemn. The world appeared to tilt, my head spun.

Jonah ran forward and caught me in his arms. He sat me back down and joined me. The coldness of the concrete seeped into my bones making me feel unbearably old.

'He's not coming, Zo. He's not real.'

'Just wait. Just a little longer.'

I felt his hand move over my back and smooth my hair. His face was close to mine, his breath hot on my cheek as he whispered in my ear.

'Please, babe. You've got to let this go.'

I sprang off the seat like an attacking cobra and stormed away from the river, marching blindly up the cobbles, my eyes burning with tears.

I stumbled into the flat and stood trembling in the living room. Currents of panic scorched through me as I fought with myself to calm down, be reasonable. *Think Zoe*. But it felt like I was being shaken by a giant with a grudge. I scanned the room looking for reassurance, for something familiar and safe, but everything felt strange. I had been transported to an alien world.

Jonah barrelled through the door as my knees hit the carpet. He was speaking but the words made no sense. Part of my brain seemed to understand what he was saying, but the message wasn't getting across. It made sense and yet it didn't. My own thoughts were the same. They were coming slower now, as if from across a vast plain, winding towards me and crashing into my mind, then sliding away again.

All I knew was I couldn't stop crying. Breakers of grief pulled me down, pushing my head underwater and holding it there until I went limp from the effort of resurfacing. Too exhausted to lift my head, I slumped on the floor.

Jonah remained at my side throughout. I could feel his hands on me but couldn't understand what he was doing there. I daren't look at him, didn't want to see my fear reflected in his eyes. His fingers found my cheek, pressed against the carpet, and tenderly lifted my face.

'Zoe. Talk to me. Tell me what's happening. It's going to be okay, babe.'

A hurricane screamed through my mind. I dug my fingers into fists against the floor and when I opened my mouth to speak I was a dragon breathing fireballs, laying waste the world.

'You know nothing. You're nothing.'

I sat up abruptly, a deep growl forming at the back of my throat, layers of civilisation and humanity crumbling as I regressed. I wanted to shred the carpet with my fingers, tear down the bricks in the walls and smash through the floor. Jonah wrapped his arms around me and held on so tight I wanted to scream. I pushed at him, a savage growl seeping through bared teeth. It was all I could do to stop myself gouging at his terrified face, and with a final desperate thrust, I was free of him.

He sat back on his haunches watching me. He was crying and seemed lost. I looked at him and felt nothing. I was dead. There were no words. I looked at the world a blank slate.

Darkness crept across my mind, trailing terror and a crushing weight. My body was being squeezed and pressed down, like the dark had invisible mass. The horror of being asphyxiated by a ghostly boa constrictor forced me back to the floor, my breath coming in ragged bursts.

An expanse of green fuzz stretched away from my face as I lay there, empty, waiting. There was a foot and a knee. *Was someone sitting there?* I felt roughness under my fingers but couldn't name it; it was simply there. Somewhere in the back of my mind I knew it was the carpet, but my brain wouldn't connect the dots, everything was fragmenting and thinking about it exhausted me.

Despite being horizontal, my head spun, as if I could feel the world turning on its axis, hurtling through space. I clamped my eyes shut and felt a terrible inevitability blazing towards me. There was no use in fighting. It was coming for me, and it would take me.

Tendrils of white hot fire sparked through my body. Unseen spears lanced my flesh and tore my heart from my chest, over and over, in an orgy of death. I was being ripped apart, thrown to the pack and devoured. An army of invisible beings were dismantling everything I had been, tearing me to pieces so I could be put back together, reordered and renewed. I could take no more and cried out in wild desperation.

'Just stop. Please just stop.'

Jonah was beside me in a flash. I felt his arms around my shaking body and I clutched at his shirt, gazing into his face. Pity, horror and compassion chased each other around in his eyes.

I was a wreck. Life had become impossible. I could go no further. There was only one way out of this that I could see.

The End

Everything had receded, my mind was blank. I looked at the world as a visitor from a distant civilisation. I understood nothing. The key slid into the lock and I felt the serrated edge click into place, the mechanism turning, unlatching.

Danny was balled up on the sofa in his dressing gown, one hand buried in a packet of crunchy oat cereal, the television shouting in the corner. A pig snorted and insufferably twee music tumbled from the speakers. I watched as Danny dropped clusters of oats into his mouth, eyes following a pig driving a car.

With a jolt he saw me, freezing with his hand halfway to his mouth. For a moment it felt as if we would be stuck like this forever in an eternal face-off.

'You came back,' he said, voice heavy with reproach.

I looked away, shame spiralling in to fill the gaps opened out in last night's misery binge.

'What are you doing here?' He dropped the cereal box onto the table.

My throat was dry. I wasn't surprised. I must have cried out all the liquid from my body, and yet more was welling up. Another tidal wave was rising before me and it took every ounce of concentration to stay standing. I forced the words from my mouth as my eyes overflowed.

'I'm sorry, Dan. Please forgive me.'

I angrily swept the tears from my cheeks. I didn't want to keep crying like this. It was exhausting. Danny was looking at me like I'd died. He gave a tiny nod and rose from his seat in slow motion, his bewildered eyes fixed on my face.

'Can I stay for a bit?' I said. 'You won't even know I'm here.'

'What's happened? Jonah?' He was round the table and scooping me into his arms before I realised.

'Did he hurt you?'

'No, it's not Joe. He's... It's...' I pulled out of his clinch and made for the door on the other side of the room. 'I just need a bit of space. There's something... I need to do something.'

I left Danny standing in the living room looking confused, the aggressively upbeat clamour of kids TV filling the silence. I closed the door behind me and stood in the hallway. Everything looked exactly the same; it was as if I'd never left. The door to Danny's room at the end of the hall was open, revealing the usual carnage of clothes and rubbish, and the monstrous ticking from his alarm clock, so loud you could even hear it in the shower if you really concentrated.

I went into my old room. The sheets were still on the bed as I had left them four months ago, and a delicate fuzz of dust clung to the heart-shaped pebble sitting on the window sill. It hardly seemed possible that so much could have changed in such a short space of time. I piled pillows in the middle of the floor and sat on them, crossing my legs. I could only manage the half-lotus, and even that hurt, but it was the only way I could stop myself falling asleep while I meditated.

This was going to be the meditation to end all meditation. I was Gautama under the Bodhi tree and I wasn't going to move until I was free. I didn't know if Adam was real or not, and right now it didn't matter. All the wisdom I'd read was significant, I couldn't argue with it. Thousands of years of practice must count for something. There was a way through what I was feeling and I was going to find it.

Jonah's face swam into view and hung in my mind, his unhappiness taunting me. I couldn't imagine what he must think of me now. He had seen me crippled by terror and wrenched from sanity. How could I ever look him in the eye again?

I had crept from the flat before he awoke and wandered down to the quayside to watch the sky change colour as the sun came up. A strange emptiness had filled my mind and for a while I had been peaceful. I leant over the railings at the river's edge and watched the dark ripples passing through the water, the hypnotic movement lulling me into serenity. Kittiwakes circled, calling out as the sun roused them for another day.

I walked towards the Tyne Bridge, the monumental green steel girders dominated the surrounding buildings, drawing you towards it like a giant magnet. Maybe that was why so many people ended their lives there. The attraction was too great.

Out of the corner of my eye I noticed a man shuffling towards me. There was no-one else about, the city was still asleep, so whatever he wanted it probably wasn't good. At a quick glance he looked ravaged, clothes soiled from sleeping rough, hair matted and eyes wild with psychosis. I doubled my pace but he was on me in seconds, hands grabbing at me, pulling my clothes.

'Lend us twenty pence, pet. I'll pay you it back. I'll pay you it back.'

'I don't have anything.'

His toxic breath engulfed my head, making me gag. I pushed at him as hard as I could. He stumbled but hung on, so I tried again. With all my strength I hit him hard in the stomach and he fell backwards, tripping over his own feet to land, with a dull thud, on the pavement.

'Bitch,' he said, clambering to his feet.

I turned and fled. Looking over my shoulder, I saw him trying to run after me, arms beating the air with violent gestures of defiance, a torrent of invective screaming from his diseased mouth.

'I'll fucking kill you, you fucking bitch. Get back here and I'll fucking murder you, I'll do time for it, bitch, I'll rip your skull apart...'

By the time I reached Danny's my heart had returned to its usual steady beat. I sat on my pillows and concentrated on my breath. The old tumult was rising, laying siege my consciousness, battering at the walls of my self.

There was nowhere left to run.

My body shook but I stayed in my seat. Great sobs and spasms shimmied through me. I pressed my head down towards the floor, curling over, hands in my lap. I needed to be clear, I needed to think, but I couldn't with these convulsions ripping through my body.

A soft tap at the door penetrated the commotion in my head. Before I could pull myself together, Danny was standing in front of me holding a mug, a look of abject shock and terror on his face. He looked like he was about to drop the mug, so I quickly sat up and ran a hand over my face. I tried to smile.

'Um... I made coffee,' he said. 'There's no milk, but... well.' He put it on the floor beside me and straightened up, frowning. 'What's wrong?'

'I'm okay, really,' I said, rather unconvincingly. 'I'm just...'

Danny wobbled back towards the bed and sat, pulling his dressing gown tighter around himself. Something rattled in the pocket and he fished it out – Ella's pill bottle.

'I thought maybe you might, y'know,' he said. 'Just one. Take the edge off.'

'No thanks, Dan. Prozac isn't going to help.'

'This isn't you, Zo. What's going on?' He put the pills back in his pocket.

'What d'you want me to say?' I said, rubbing my knees.

'The truth.'

I wasn't sure Danny could take the truth. What I was doing went against everything we had been taught. I had always been the sensible one, the reliable one, the one with all the answers. As much as he complained about my incessant psychoanalysing, he still came to me for explanations, insight and perspective. Now here I was, falling apart in front of him. How could I explain that?

With the truth.

'I've been wrong about everything my whole life,' I said.

Danny stared at me like I'd just confessed to running a prostitutes and drugs cartel.

'Hang on,' he said, and left the room.

I stretched out my legs and waited. He returned with the clover leaf ashtray and a half-smoked joint. I didn't think getting stoned was going to help him understand, but I couldn't stop him, so kept quiet. His hands were shaking so much he almost set fire to his hair trying to get the thing lit.

'What you just said s'not true,' he said, taking a long toke. 'You're right about everything, Zoe. I saw Ella in town last week, arm in arm with Martin. You knew it would happen. You warned me. All the times I skipped school and got in trouble, you never shopped me. You backed me up against Mum, never told her I was living here, and I know you got a ton of shit for it and you never gave in. You hassled me for it, but you were right. I should get my life sorted, but I don't know what's wrong with me. I'm just a loser. Always end up at the bottom. Can't get any higher. And here's the thing, Zo. If you're wrong, then what the hell am I? Because I'm fucked.'

'You're not fucked, Dan. You're just sad. And so am I. So sad, and it's all got to come out before I can be free. All I'm doing is trying to find out who I really am, that's all.'

'Doesn't look much fun.'

'No, well, maybe it'll get better.' I tried to smile in a reassuring way. 'There's no guarantee what I'm doing will work.'

'What does that mean?'

'It means, Dan, and this is important, this is life and death important. I want you to promise me something.'

He nodded through a cloud of smoke.

'Promise that no matter what happens, you absolutely under no circumstances whatsoever call a doctor or a hospital. Or Mum.'

'Okay, sis.'

He stood unsteadily and wavered in front of me, then crouched down and hugged me, holding on with such fierce intensity I felt the tears return to my eyes.

'I love you, y'know,' he said.

He let go and I scrunched his hair in my fingers. 'Ditto.'

Finally, he left me alone and I gulped down the coffee, returning my legs to the half-lotus. I knew what I needed to do. Everything that stood between me and the truth had to go. Every thought, every emotion, everything I had ever identified with. It all had to be called back and destroyed. I was about to dig the ground out from under my own feet and leap into the void. Surely this was the definition of madness.

I smoothed the edges of my breath, focusing my gaze on the stained splodge on the carpet. I hadn't managed to get that stain out, no matter how hard I'd scrubbed and no matter how many toxic chemicals I'd thrown at it. I didn't even know what the stain was or how it got there. It appeared to be part of the carpet. Perhaps it had been there since the beginning of time.

Realising my concentration had wandered, I dropped the thought and let my mind loosen and spread out. I searched out the gaps, awareness opening into emptiness, the ticking of the clock in the next room giving architecture to the void. Each tick reverberated in my head, like water dripping into a pool in an underground cavern.

Tick, tick... tick... tick.

It seemed to be slowing, the gaps lengthening, eternity seeping into time, like water through rocks.

I was calm personified. A smile tweaked my lips. This was more like it. I relaxed into the space, carried by my breath. I knew this place well and had resided here for hours at a time, protected and safe, nourished by an invisible spring.

Something was tugging at the fringes of my awareness. A worm of doubt niggled and chewed at my contentment. I couldn't stay here forever. This wasn't reality. This was escapism.

But what *was* reality? How could I get past my own mind to find it? The soft trickle of the invisible spring was gaining momentum, the roar of the torrent cascading into my mind, smashing through every assumption, every concept, everything known and unknown in my being.

Panic gripped. I was willingly (stupidly?) going to my own death, hurling myself into the unknown. I could do nothing in the face of this fear, nothing but surrender. The horror tore through me. I wanted to scream and thrash, but didn't want to frighten Danny, so remained in my seat, vibrating, tears scorching my cheeks.

Was this suicide? Was I certifiable? I remembered reading that to attain satori you must be willing to risk everything: your sanity and your life. It sounded crazy to me at the time; the reality was worse.

A tornado ripped through my mind, hurling the debris of my life and personality at the walls, rupturing the foundations and flinging me into the chasm. Dark earth heaped over my head, blocking all light and air. I was lost underground, blind and despoiled, eyes and ears full of wriggly worms and bugs crawling over my skin, eating me alive. Like Inanna, I had been stripped of my clothing and jewels, and abandoned on a meat hook to rot.

I am not the body. I am not the emotions. I am not the thoughts. I am not Zoe. I am not your sister. I am not your daughter. I am not your lover. I am not your cleaner. I am not a woman. I am not a human being. I am not a person. I am not. I am not.

My head fell forward. I had no idea how long I'd been sat there and was exhausted. The effort of staying conscious was taking everything I had. It would be so much easier to get up and run, or let myself sink into unconsciousness. I wasn't sure I could take much more. Then for a brief, glorious moment I was gone. The haze of sleep pulled me under and I sank gratefully into nothingness.

A sharp ache in my chest brought me crashing into consciousness. The unending grief was back, squeezing out heaving sobs of guilt and regret. Every transgression seared through my mind, every act of wilful stupidity, every lie, every betrayal. My arrogance and my cowardice paraded before me until I cried out my repentance. Hollowed out by anguish, I reeled as another wave crashed over me, showering down centuries of tears.

I found myself moaning, a keening wail wrenched from the depths. My mind recoiled. I could feel my heart throbbing, sending the blood surging through my veins and filling my ears with a high rushing sound, like white noise, a scream in my mind.

'None of this is real. It's just your mind,' I whispered to myself, but it sure as shit felt real. I reminded myself to breathe and the phantom python returned, coiling around my abdomen and chest. Panic rose like a wall in the darkness.

I was trapped. The impenetrable brick wall against which I had been banging my head was back. I had been visualising it as one long straight wall, but now realised it surrounded me. I was encircled with impossibility and the wall was closing in. Entombed in a turret of my own making, I turned my mind this way and that, looking for a way out, a gap, a loophole or chink in the armour. I raced round and round inside the wall, tying my mind in linguistic knots, entrapping myself at every turn.

I couldn't go forward or back. I couldn't turn left or right. I couldn't stop and I couldn't not stop. Something had to give, there had to be a way through. My mind churned, throwing up bizarre and mundane images, thoughts that led nowhere, all in an attempt to distract from my chosen path. If I gave up now I would have to live with this bullshit for the rest of my life. I wanted rid of it. I wanted to be free.

'Is this it? Is this all there'll ever be?'

I didn't know to whom I was supposed to be talking. I just felt like calling out to something. Someone out there knew what to do. I felt so alone sitting there on my pillows, crashing my mind against the edge of the universe. Maybe I was crazy to think there was another way to live, another way to think and to be. But I knew that wasn't true. I could feel it, just beyond my grasp, hiding in the corner of my eye, on the tip of my tongue. I was so close. What was wrong with me?

'If I could just see it. Why can't I see?'

All resistance drained away. I was too exhausted to think or to push, or fight, or hold on. The impossibility of living with myself for a moment longer pressed against my mind and heart.

I was the problem.

I had done everything I was supposed to do. I had been good, learnt my lessons, prepared to enter the rat race, get on the treadmill, pay my taxes, breed and consume. An obedient soulless cog in the machine, squeaking and straining against the forced motion. But I'm not soulless, and that's why I squeak.

I was saved from that fate by my wayward brain and failure to conform. Normality felt like a pointless enactment of empty ritual designed to keep me incarcerated, eyes to the ground, nose to the wheel, mind dead, heart and spirit broken.

I had gone off in search of another way, a deeper truth, and here I was, smashed to pieces. Lost. I had failed anyway. I was good for nothing. I couldn't conform and be normal. I couldn't transcend and prove the system wrong. Perhaps I didn't have what it took to see. Perhaps I wasn't strong enough. Perhaps I had wandered down an evolutionary cul-de-sac because my brain was wired up all wrong and I would spend the rest of my life trying to look straight but only seeing round corners, a distorted version of reality. It was hopeless even trying to understand, I would never get it. I was incapable of understanding anything. It was probably staring me in the face right now and I couldn't see it.

Wretched tears sprinkled into my lap. All that work and practice so I could be torn apart, for what? So I could fail. Again. I wanted to give up and drag myself off like a wounded animal to find a quiet spot in the woods to die in peace.

A strange calm spread through me. I had reached the end. There was nothing left to do, nowhere left to turn, nothing left to lose. It no longer mattered. If I was driven insane, so be it. If I died, so be it. I could do nothing. I couldn't even let go.

Two thoughts collided in my mind:

Who is holding on?

Holding on to what?

My mind stopped.

A Cave of Shadows

I was not.

The water of life is a fire and it burnt me away. I never was. I always am. My life is not my life.

I believed I was broken. I was wrong. You cannot break that which is everything. I am the machine as much as I am the cog. I could breathe out and the entire system would shatter, a window exploded by a bomb, a heart exploded by love, a life exploded by truth. You can lock me up and make me walk blindfolded round and round, pushing a stone nowhere, but you will not break me.

I am unbreakable. I am indivisible.

A low thudding resonated through the universe, sending shockwaves cascading, tumbling over themselves in frantic entreaty. I was swimming in paradox, awed by complexity packed into simplicity packed into complexity, weaving a web of wonder with fire. Half-formed thoughts began to niggle, consciousness returning to its crystallised form, located in time and space. There was a banging...

'Who is that?'

Someone was hammering on the front door and ringing the bell at the same time. I stumbled to my feet and wobbled out to investigate. Amused by the urgency, I giggled as I opened the door.

'Jonah! Mum!'

I was overjoyed, and a little surprised, to find them standing together on the doorstep. I reached out a hand to touch Jonah's face, astonished by the sparks of light flying out all around his head. His halo was on fire. I giggled again.

He was looking at me with such seriousness I couldn't imagine what was wrong. One look at Mum and my heart flipped over, guts hollowing out in dread.

'Mum?'

'Where's Danny?' she said, pushing past me and lurching through the door.

Jonah took hold of my arms and looked deep into my eyes. 'Did he give you something?'

'What's all the hoo-ha?' I said.

He led me back into the flat where Mum was flapping from room to room, muttering an incantation under her breath. 'Please be all right, where are you, please be all right, where are you...'

'Maybe he went out,' I said, following her into the hall. The bathroom door was closed. It was never closed unless someone was in there.

'He's in here,' I said.

Mum flew at the door. 'Danny? Danny!' She yanked at the handle, but it was locked. She spun round and shot me a look of such raw intensity it made me step back in surprise.

'Open it,' she said.

The flimsy bolt shot from the frame as Jonah cracked his foot against the door, splintering the wood. He leaned into the door and heaved. Something was blocking it. As I was the smallest I squeezed through the gap Jonah had opened up. I slid one leg through and nearly stumbled as I stood on... *Don't think about it, Zoe.*

My mind had frozen. I wasn't thinking, just doing what was necessary. Finally I found myself on the other side of the door.

Danny was lying on his back, head lulling to one side, mouth open. His face was almost a mirror of Dad's face, without the rope or contusion, but the same slack absence. His legs were jammed against the door where he had slumped. Ella's bottle of Prozac lay open by the sink. It was empty.

I heaved Danny's legs away from the door. Jonah was speaking on the phone, giving instructions and details for the ambulance. I sat on the floor cradling Danny's head in my arms, smoothing his hair with my fingers. It seemed unreal. I was participating in a macabre play written by a sadist with no sense of humour. Any minute Dan would open his eyes and grin at me. 'Fooled you, sis.'

'No, no, no,' I said. 'Not now. Not like this, Dan. Not now I know the way home.'

There was a strangled cry and I looked up. Mum was standing in the shattered doorway staring at Danny, her face a sculpture of pure devastation. A single desolate tear traced a line of agony down her cheek.

'Is he… is he…' she said.

My heart was annihilated in a flood of compassion. All the miserable fights and reproaches were obliterated. I held her in my gaze, whispering a hope and a prayer.

'His heart's still beating.'

Jonah and I sat side by side in the hospital, the evening morphing into limbo. This was the waiting area of the damned. I felt numb, but jangled by every fresh outburst of human anguish and pain. We watched in silence as medical teams bundled the bleeding, mangled, drunk and dying under our noses and away to be patched up or dispatched.

Mum was causing most of the commotion. She had been on her feet for four hours straight, accosting every passing nurse, doctor and orderly, demanding news of a boy they had never heard of. They tried to put her out of the way in a room with comfy chairs and an out of order coffee machine, but she broke free and took to prowling the corridors, searching cubicles and broom cupboards with equal fervour.

Jonah explained to me how they had come to the rescue. He hadn't realised I'd gone until he returned from work. In the morning he assumed I'd left early to clean, carrying on as normal to take my mind off things. He tried my phone every chance he got, then discovered I'd left it behind when he got home. Guessing I was at Dan's, he set off in the van to find me.

On the way, Mum called my phone and Jonah answered. She had received a cryptic text from Dan and was hysterical with worry because she didn't know where he lived, couldn't get hold of me, and didn't know what to do. Jonah doubled back and picked her up. The text read: 'Sorry again never again bye xx'

Dan had sent it two hours before. To avoid the rush hour traffic, Jonah drove like a stunt driver down the back streets into Elswick. Mum had been out the van and running up the path to the flat before Jonah had switched off the engine.

I shifted in the plastic seat, Jonah beside me, cool and steadfast. He pulled something from his pocket and handed it to me. My phone.

I had 25 missed calls.

My mind was curiously still, despite the calamity erupting around me. I knew if my mother was somebody else's mother and Danny was somebody else's brother, I would be accusing Mum of overcompensating for previous neglect. And what about me? What had I failed to do when it mattered most? I searched for a response, but found none. Whatever had led to this moment was irrelevant. It was simply happening.

Jonah took my hand and gently ran his fingers over mine. He didn't have to wait with us. He could go home and sleep, but here he was. He had taken charge, telling the paramedics what had happened, and sitting me down as Danny was wheeled away. He bought us all coffee and bullied both me and Mum into eating something, even if it was just a Snickers.

I leant against his shoulder, my eyelids heavy against my eyes, and slipped gratefully into sleep, his arm around me and his heart pounding steadily in my ear.

I walked down the corridor, lino and lights stretching ahead forever to a point in the far, far distance. The stench of decay was barely masked by pungent disinfectant. This corridor was identical to the last, the same painted wooden framed windows, the same heavy double doors at intervals, leading off into forbidden places. I didn't know where I was but I knew I wasn't lost. I took a left, and a right, another couple of lefts, following the endless maze, looking for the way out.

I stopped beside a large corrugated radiator. In the wall above was a tiny window, just like the others. I clambered onto the radiator to peer through the window. It was dark outside and I couldn't see where I was. All I could see was my own puzzled reflection in the dark glass. I opened the window as wide as it would go, and squeezed my body through the gap. The window turned out to be at ground level, and I heaved myself out, hands scraping on the rough gravel.

I found myself standing in a courtyard. The window behind me had become a door. A fine mist fell across my face as I looked about. The courtyard was overlooked by ancient buildings of sandstone, their facades eroded by time. There were four sleek black cars parked in a line, dew drops glistening on the metal bodywork, a thousand reflected moons.

A man emerged from the darkness, tall and rugged with an imposing regal bearing, his face almost obscured by a thick black beard. I stepped forward to greet him, head bowed in respect, for this man was Dionysus, come to claim his own.

Dionysus held up a bunch of golden grapes with a golden key attached. The iridescent metal glimmered in the moonlight as he handed them to me. I cradled them in both hands, stumbling back against a car, overawed. I knew I must accept them, but felt unworthy. To reject the gift would be ruinous.

'But I… I mean, I don't understand.'

Dionysus held me in his gaze and spoke directly into my mind.

'This is for protecting the stone.'

Then he was gone. I was alone in the courtyard, the gold of the key and grapes warming in my hands. I stood perplexed by his statement, turning it round and round, trying to discern its meaning. The stone I knew was the Philosopher's Stone, the alchemical gold, my true nature, Buddha mind. Indivisible, incorruptible like the gold. But the ambiguity had me mystified. I called out to the absent God for clarity.

'Do I get the key because I have protected the stone, or do I need it in order to protect the stone?'

My voice echoed back from the ancient stonework, multiplying and becoming garbled. I had a thought.

'Or is it both?'

Or neither.

Another koan.

A laugh rose, a joy bubble travelling up and bursting in my mind. Laughter cascaded around the courtyard, filling the air with ecstasy.

I awoke with a start to find I had dribbled on Jonah's jacket. I wiped my mouth, and his shoulder, and sat up feeling disoriented. My mother's voice nearby brought me back to the present with a crash. Jonah rubbed my back. He was looking at something over my shoulder, worry lines creasing his forehead. I turned to follow his gaze.

Mum was listening intently to a youthful doctor who was speaking to her with such gravity my insides congealed and I held my breath.

'Daniel has done a lot of damage. At this stage we can't be sure how extensive that damage will be. We need to do more tests.'

The doctor rubbed his eyes and consulted his clipboard. He was clearly exhausted, absently pressing the end of his pen, firing the nib in and out in a frenzied SOS fuelled by adrenaline and caffeine. His eyes found the relevant information and he continued.

'Daniel has been moved to intensive care. The coma could last hours, days, weeks... As I say, we'll do more tests and monitor the situation.'

'Can we see him?' said Mum.

'Follow me.'

The doctor turned and strode down the corridor, Mum racing along behind. Jonah and I leapt up and followed through a labyrinth of lifts and corridors lined with matching doors. I was lost in seconds. A sign for intensive care loomed ahead and the doctor vanished, called away to attend another emergency.

Danny was in a side-room off the main ward, his bed beside the window. Three more beds lay empty. Mum flew at the bed and sat heavily on the side, her hands fluttering over Danny's face and hands, touching him, willing him back to consciousness. I watched from the doorway with Jonah, unable to move.

Danny was surrounded by machines, a drip feeding into the vein in his hand. He looked peaceful, undisturbed by the emotional turmoil roiling around him, measured out by the bleeping equipment arrayed around his bed.

Mum took Danny's hand, tenderly working his fingers, as if counting them. She encased his hand in hers and her head fell forward. I watched my mother's shoulders heaving and her body swaying as her tears pattered down over the sheets. Released from my paralysis as if by a charm, I went to her side, leaving Jonah hovering in the doorway.

I sat on the other side of the bed, hooking my arm over Mum's shoulders and listened as she showered apology and sorrow over her son's inert form. I still felt strangely unaffected, almost as if it were happening to someone else. I wasn't sure what I was supposed to feel. I held onto my shaking mother and thought I must be in shock. Reality would hit me soon enough.

I gazed at Danny's serene countenance and smiled. He finally got what he wanted. An escape, a haven from the world. I knew his serenity wasn't the real thing, that in truth he was trapped faster than he had been before, but in some sense it was okay. Not in the sense of being a good thing, but that it couldn't be any other way. Although I didn't believe Danny trying to kill himself had been inevitable, it did make a kind of sense.

I rummaged in my coat pocket and found a packet of tissues, handing one to Mum and using another to dry Danny's hands of tears.

The following days passed in a blur of endless sitting. Time took on a strange elasticity, each moment taking forever while hours flew by. I took turns with Mum to sit in vigil beside Danny's bed. I didn't know if he could hear me. They had said to talk to him, keep him company as if he were really there, but the one-sided conversation was wearing thin and I was running out of things to tell him. I had resorted to giving him a running commentary on what I could see out the window, making up stories about the people scurrying below.

Today I decided to try something else. I hadn't mentioned it to anyone yet, somehow it didn't seem appropriate, but if anybody needed to hear it, Danny did. I wasn't even sure I could put into words what I had seen, but I had to try.

I slipped off my shoes and curled up on the bed, my head resting on Danny's chest. I wrapped his arm around me, snuggling against him, slowing my breath to synchronise with his. We were afloat on a vast ocean, the beeping monitor a flashing lifebuoy, anchoring us, keeping us safe and showing the way to land, to home.

I gazed up at Danny's sleeping face. I had no idea how to begin, how to reach him. He was lost in his own world, a ceaseless dream; locked into his own mind, prisoner and warden, with no inkling he was even trapped.

'Hey, Dan. I want to step into your dream. Can I do that? Can I come in and tell you a secret?'

Beep. Beep. Beep.

'You are the most glorious mystery and you don't even know it. We spend so much of our time turning away from reality, filling our heads with nonsense, that we miss it. It's right here. Closer than your breath. Closer than your heartbeat.

'I know I scared you, Dan. I'm sorry. I couldn't see past myself. The truth had been stalking me for years, so I decided to stop running and face it.

'I saw that everything I thought I was, was just that: a thought. How could a thought hold onto anything? How could a concept love? I don't know how it happened, but it all stopped, the thinking, the concepts, the mind just stopped. There was no more me. The body was there, this body, sitting there on the pillows, but all I knew was the room, the window with the wonky curtain and the stain on the carpet. I was gone.

'Silly really. It's so obvious. I needn't have made such a fuss. It's almost like my whole life has been one long ego tantrum. What's that saying? A tale told by an idiot, full of sound and fury, signifying nothing. Is that Shakespeare? ...Never mind.

'The veil was torn away, all boundaries dissolved, leaving... fire. Everything is burning, so fierce, so intense. But there's no fanfare, it's no big deal. It just is. Huge and awesome and yet understated, like a whisper that deafens or a light you can't see that blinds. It was as if I'd turned inside out and the whole universe was inside me, only there was no inside or outside, no sense of mine. The fire is alive, everywhere and forever. Simultaneous creation and destruction, birth and death united, happening over and over, all at once, like infinite big bangs in every atom, every cell.

'Chaos and bliss.

'And that's you, Dan. That is what you are. If only you could see it. We get in the way of ourselves, in the way of life. Normally you think of it as you in here versus the world out there, but in reality there's no separation. There's no me or you, just life. There's no time or space either. They're illusions created by our concepts. Don't ask me how that works, I have no idea; I'm going to have to mull that one over. I just know the world is one.

'You know what reality looks like?'

I chuckled as a surge of joy burst into my heart and mind simultaneously.

'It's exactly like this, only lighter. Everything looks more real but less substantial. Normally you'd think something real would seem solid, but it's like all the rules are reversed. It felt like I should be able to see through things. I couldn't. It just felt like they were transparent, buzzing, vibrant and burning. The coffee mug beside me was there, about a foot away, and yet, simultaneously right here, inside me, like I was it looking at myself.'

Beep. Beep.

'Now, I know what you're thinking. Zoe's lost it. She's talking gibberish. Her mind's gone. But you know what? That satori was the single moment of sanity in my whole life. I'm struggling with the words, they get in the way. You have to see this shit for yourself if you're going to understand it, so bear with me a sec.'

I uncurled, sat up and poured myself a glass of water. I glugged back a couple of gulps then wetted Danny's mouth using my finger. I set the glass back on the cabinet and ran my fingers through his hair.

'You know, I can't really say what I just said. It's kind of true and not true at the same time. I can't really say I had satori because there was no me to have it. And I can't even say it happened because there was no time in which it could have occurred. But it did happen, and now I know who I am, or rather, who I'm not.

'We become who we think we are, but that's not who we are. We are life playing with itself, exploring itself through endless variation, improvisation and evolution. You're not really doing any of it – life is.'

I took another sip of water, cradling the glass in my hand. I held it up to the sunlight streaming through the window and smiled as patches of light danced over the walls around me.

'We create these stories about ourselves,' I continued. 'Stuff happens and you weave it into a narrative, a grand drama with you at the centre of the action. And as you tell your story, you create yourself. Fact and fiction entwined, entangled into a life, a person.

'The problem is you think your story defines you. You tell yourself tales and then believe your own bullshit. You build yourself a cage then lock yourself in. Why? Because you think, I'm so small and the world is so big, I'll be safer locked in my cage, I'll be safer if I'm in control.

'But Danny, the point is: you don't have to be scared anymore. You think you're trapped. There you are, you think, shackled in a cave watching shadows on the wall, shadows you take to be reality, because everybody else does too. But reality is outside the cave. You need to come outside, feel the sun on your face and listen to the birds sing. You shake your head at me and rattle your chains. No, you cry, I'm happy here, I'm safe here, you're crazy, there's no such thing as sun and birds, sit down and stop making such a fuss.

'But here's the tragic, glorious truth, Dan. You're already outside. There is no cave, no shadows and no shackles. You're outside in the sunshine telling yourself there is no sun and that you can't hear the birds, even though there's a blackbird sitting on your shoulder singing its heart out right into your ear.

'We forget we're not what we think. We build traps for ourselves in our minds. We feel caged, exiled, but it's all in the mind. You're only trapped because you think you are. In reality, you're already free.'

I felt a hand rest on my shoulder and turned to find Mum standing beside the bed, wonder in her eyes.

'Where did you learn that?'

'Hey, Mum.'

I finished my glass of water and stood, pulling on my jacket and shoes. Mum lowered herself into the chair beside the bed. She looked exhausted, every part of her sagged with the weight of waiting, and her eyes had the bright lustre of someone who hasn't slept in days. I leaned over and gave her a hug.

'It'll change soon. I can feel it,' I said, standing back.

Mum sighed. 'Change which way?'

'That's up to Dan.' I retreated to the door. 'See you in the morning.'

She nodded vaguely, her eyes fixed on her sleeping son. I turned and walked down the now familiar corridor. I felt curiously light, as if I could float out of the hospital and drift home on the wind. Maybe I wasn't eating enough. My mind focused on Jonah. He'd be waiting for me, with food prepared. He was the one keeping me going.

'Zoe!'

Mum's shout startled me and I spun round. She was standing in the doorway to Danny's room waving her arms, a frantic look on her face.

'Quick!'

I hurried back to the room and followed her to Danny's bed.

'He moved. Danny moved. My baby moved.' She cradled her son's face in her hands, searching for signs of life. 'He moved a finger, not a twitch, *he* did it, he's coming back. Danny, Danny can you hear me?'

It was finished.

I stood helplessly by the bed as the machines went haywire, the beeps rising into one, drawn-out electronic line, the line marking life from death. The screech filled my mind, pushing aside all hope.

Danny had stepped into the sunlight.

Two nurses bustled in and wrestled Mum from the bed. Suddenly the room was full of people, and Mum and I found ourselves ejected into the corridor. A crash cart rattled past and the door was shut in our faces.

I stumbled to a chair in the hallway and sank into it, scarcely feeling the hard plastic against my legs. Mum hammered on the door and yelled.

'Will somebody tell me what's going on? That is my son.'

She pushed open the door, demanding to see Danny, only to be gently but firmly refused.

'He's gone, Mum.'

'Nonsense.'

I closed my eyes. I listened as Mum fought like a lioness, clawing her way back into the room, threatening to punch the doctor on the nose if he didn't let her in. The voices began to blur into an incomprehensible mush, my mind was spinning. I opened my eyes and focused on my breathing.

Directly opposite was a tiny window, just like the one I had squeezed through in my big Dionysus dream, only this one had peeling paint. Someone had placed a small vase of carnations and lilies on the sill. Sunlight poured through, falling in blotches on the floor. I felt a cool breeze on my neck from the open window behind me.

Above the hum of traffic, a bird was singing. I recognised the freeform song. It was a blackbird, singing its heart out.

Life going on.

Undone

I was frozen; my body petrified into stone, lifeless and empty. People told me to do things and I did them. If they left me alone, I did nothing. I sat, eyes on the windows, without the energy to even worry if this was unhealthy. The word catatonic seeped through at one point, but I dismissed it as irrelevant. Nothing mattered. My world had shrunk to the corner of the sofa, and there I sat.

Jonah had driven me to the funeral and I sung the hymns. In the back of my mind I could hear my old self having a fit of indignation. Danny wasn't religious, so what was the point of all this hypocrisy, but I couldn't bring myself to get worked up. Jonah sat with me and held me and kept his gob shut. Unlike everybody else. Suddenly the world was full of people expressing their sorrow and making offers of help, even though I knew they'd never liked Danny much when he was alive and were only doing it to make themselves feel better. Jonah was the only warmth left.

The morning after the funeral Jonah got me out of bed, made me get dressed and watched over me as I ate breakfast. I knew it was marmalade on toast because that's what it looked like, but it tasted like cardboard smeared with tangy gunk. I ate it anyway.

'I've made you some sandwiches for lunch and there's some hot pot left over for your dinner,' said Jonah. 'You just need to heat it up, okay?'

I nodded dutifully. I doubted I would eat it, but appreciated the gesture. I looked up at him and tried to smile.

'Thanks, Joe. Don't know what I'd do without you.'

'I don't know how late I'll be. We've got this London show coming up and we must nail the new songs by then. Will you be all right? You can always come over to The Village later, if you want.'

I took his hand and gave it a squeeze. 'I'll be fine.'

He enveloped me in his arms and kissed my neck. I breathed in his rich, musky smell and felt safe, and almost believed what I'd said, for a moment.

'Got to get to work,' he said.

He kissed me once more and was gone. The world hollowed out and I felt myself falling. I curled into a ball in the corner of the sofa, Jonah's lingering scent in my nostrils, and tried to get a grip.

Then it hit me. It was the same aftershave Danny had used. Why hadn't I noticed that before? My head spun. I ached in every bone; I had never felt so tired. There were times I thought I had stopped breathing, my breath was so light and my chest barely moved. *Was my heart even beating?* I checked my pulse – it was still there. I didn't understand how that could be.

I sat in my corner of the world and stared impassively out the window. From my vantage point on the sofa, all I could see were the far edge of the Cluny warehouse, the roof slanting into the sky and stonework overrun with weeds, and the cluster of trees on the far side of the valley. I watched as the air filled with puffs of white, dancing in the breeze. For a moment I was perplexed, thinking it was snowing. *In June?* I lifted my head from the armrest, gazing with wonder as great swarms of whiteness wafted across the valley from somewhere beyond the road bridge. A splodge of white wiggled past the window, giving me a closer look. It was a seed. The trees were spawning.

My head felt too heavy so I laid it back down. I couldn't close my eyes. Every time I did, I saw Danny dying on the bathroom floor. I had only slept through sheer exhaustion. When I did sleep I dreamt desperate dreams within dreams. I would snap out of satori and save him a hundred different ways. I would forgo bliss, fling illumination back into the darkness, to hell with enlightenment if I could just have Danny back. I could free myself any time, I had eternity, every moment, but he didn't.

He needed me and I wasn't there.

I sat through the slow creep of the sun across the carpet, time weaving its illusion through movement. I watched as tiny rainbow orbs danced around the room as light hit the crystal hanging in the window, riveting shards of pain into my heart, making me cry out. Why were my eyes dry? Had I broken myself in my epic quest for truth?

The sun retreated behind the building leaving the living room in murky shadows. I was surprised by pangs of hunger and untangled my knot of limbs from the sofa. I wobbled into the kitchen and heated the hot pot in the microwave. My appetite returned as soon as I began to eat, and I gobbled down several slices of bread along with my vegetables and beans.

As I ate, the setting sun glowed orange against the warehouse bricks outside, throwing shadows of the bridge and traffic across the buildings and trees. I couldn't see the road from the sofa; all I could see were grey shapes moving over stone and leaves. I smiled inwardly as I watched the ghosts of buses and cars pass before my eyes, remembering my attempt to explain to Dan what I had seen. Maybe he had heard. He had been free all along, just as I was now, if I cared to look.

With food in my belly I found myself drifting into sleep. I awoke into darkness, disoriented and confused. I wasn't sure I had dreamed, but must have been asleep for hours. Jonah was at my side, squatting by the sofa, gazing at me with a faint smile on his lips.

'You ate the hot pot,' he said, smoothing the hair from my face.

'What time is it?'

'Bedtime.'

He scooped me into his arms and stood.

'No, I...' I pressed my hand to his cheek. 'I want to walk up. I need to start doing stuff. Been sat on my arse all day.'

Jonah lowered me to the floor and gave me a long embrace.

'That's my Zoe.' He kissed me, then held my face in his hands, looking keep into my eyes. 'Cried yet?'

I shook my head and frowned. I could feel tears, they were there, but they were frozen. I was in limbo.

'Don't worry, babe. They'll come.'

Two days later I was face to face with Ella's Buddha. He hadn't had a good polish for a couple of weeks and was looking neglected. I ran my duster round and round over his head and listened to Ella moving around upstairs. I was keeping out of her way because I didn't feel like talking to anyone and wasn't ready to deal with social convention. All that pretend politeness and posturing felt so unnecessary. I wasn't sure if that was due to the grief or the satori. So much of what I had taken for granted was slipping away. It felt like the inside of my head had been mashed, and what remained was being remoulded into something I couldn't fathom.

'Are you all right?'

I startled and nearly knocked Buddha off his perch. Ella was hovering in the doorway looking worried. I stared at her and couldn't think of a single thing to say.

'It's just that you've been polishing his head for a while, and I just... well, you seem a little subdued, Zoe. I don't mind waiting another week, if you're still not well.'

I pulled my face into a smile, the one I had practised my whole life, the one that meant nothing, the empty mask worn by millions.

'I'm fine,' I said. 'You?'

'Yes, yes, I'm fine too.'

I wanted to hide behind the sofa, dive under the abundant cushions never to be seen again. This was excruciating. Ella was so clearly not fine. She obviously wanted to talk. I took a deep breath and dove in.

'What's up?'

'I just wanted to ask. I haven't seen him, you see, and I just wondered, is he all right?'

I reverted to my blank stare, having no idea what she was talking about. Ella flustered with her hair and blushed a violent shade of crimson. My head filled with a dense buzz as the realisation dawned. She didn't know and I was going to have to tell her. I wanted to run from the room, but Ella was between me and the door and she was speaking again, the words filtering through the buzzing in my brain.

'We left it rather badly, I'm afraid, and he was such a lovely boy, so kind. I never meant to hurt him, and would you mind telling him? Would you tell Danny from me that I'm sorry and...'

'Ella. Danny's dead.'

'What? No. What happened?'

'Suicide.'

Ella stumbled back onto the sofa and perched on the edge, tears falling into her lap, eyes darting about the room.

'Was it... he took my... tell me it wasn't my Prozac,' she said.

I couldn't speak. I watched Ella sob and felt nothing. I was strangely calm. I picked up a box of tissues and sat beside her, feeding her Kleenex until the well was dry.

'Don't you dare feel guilty about the pills,' I said, rubbing her back and pushing aside my own guilty thoughts. Ella swallowed another sob.

'Oh, Zoe. You poor thing. Look at me crying all over you and he was your brother. I'm so sorry.' And she was off again, keening into another tissue like a professional mourner.

I watched the display with fascination and sadness. Here was a woman who hardly knew Danny carrying on and making a fuss, and I was his sister, his twin, and I couldn't feel anything. Weeks had passed and I hadn't shed a single tear. What was wrong with me?

Danny grinning, Danny running, Danny pulling silly faces, Danny holding a crab in his hand, sand smeared over his skin, Danny in a high chair with food plastered over his face, spoon held aloft in defiance.

I sat beside Mum on the sofa at her house, the photograph album spread across our knees. She turned the pages, sighing with pleasure as the memories spilled out. Until now she hadn't been able to look at them. She had rung that morning inviting us over, saying it was time. Time for her to stop crying, at least for today. Jonah had offered to cook dinner and so here we were.

Mum had lost weight, called it her grief diet: 'I won't be recommending it to my friends.' She looked like I felt: like her skin had been ripped off and she'd been flayed alive. I wasn't convinced either of us were ready for the photo album, but she insisted.

'Each time I tried to look at these before,' she said, 'it hurt so much I thought I would die. I even fainted. From the shock. How can anyone endure such torment and live? But with you here, Zoe... You'll keep me strong.'

I wasn't so sure about that.

'Have you got a grater?' Jonah called through from the kitchen. 'Oh, wait, s'okay. I've found it.' We listened to him opening and closing drawers and cupboards, whistling to himself as he worked. He had refused to tell us what he was preparing. It was a surprise treat, one of his mum's specialties.

'Oh, look at this one,' said Mum. 'He was so cheeky that day.' She stuck her finger on a picture of Danny, hands rubbed together in mischief, a grin between dimples. 'You see that dress I'm wearing, a wrap around thing. Danny kept creeping up behind me and untying the bow and I was falling out all over the place.'

I looked at the parade of pictures and felt only confusion. I could hardly remember most of the incidents. If it wasn't for the fact I was in most of the photos, I could almost believe it had all happened to somebody else.

'And look, have you spotted it?' she said. 'The same in nearly every picture.'

I shrugged. 'What am I looking for?'

'His laces. Always coming undone. See?'

She was right. Picture after picture, there they were, dangling, his knees covered in scabs and scrapes from all the times he fell after tripping himself up. I flicked through the pages, image after image, until I couldn't see, my eyes obscured by tears. Wild sobs shook my body, arriving so suddenly and so completely I was engulfed, pulverised into agony. A single thought screamed in my mind: I would never hold my brother again.

Mum dropped the photo album on the floor, kicking it away with her foot, like it had offended her. She wrapped herself around me, cradling me like a baby. I wept into her arms, a current of endurance pulsing between us, binding us together.

Intoxicating aromas wafted from the kitchen and a tantalising sizzle filled the air. Jonah began to sing softly, his voice lilting and swooping, lulling me into peace.

The moist air pressed against my skin, an invisible blanket soaking up the oxygen. It was a typical British summer, heat without sun, and I had been hoodwinked by the thickening clouds into wearing my denim jacket. I slung it over my shoulder and continued my sticky march up Westgate Road, a trickle of sweat gathering at the base of my spine.

Up ahead, loitering on the pavement beside a steep grass bank, were a gaggle of kids. I calculated they must be pre or young teens, bored and restless on their summer holiday. They were watching me approach.

I groaned. The last thing I wanted to deal with was a bunch of mouthy brats with nothing better to do. I took a deep breath and kept my eyes on the pavement as I walked into their midst.

In a moment they had me surrounded and I found flowers being pushed into my hands. Each child had a bouquet of dandelions, primroses, buttercups and daisies they had evidently plundered from the neighbourhood. I was overwhelmed by this random act of generosity and bemused as each mini benefactor checked I had received flowers from them, nobody wanted to be left out.

Finally they were satisfied I had the requisite number of wild flowers and I was allowed to continue on my way. I left them beaming and practically floated the rest of the way to The Village, my posy clutched in one hand, and a faint sense of guilt over my misjudgement playing through my mind.

I offered up a quick apology and let it go while waiting on the doorstep. Linda opened the door, a string of buttercups and daisies nestled in her bushy hair.

'Ah, I see you met the flower fairies too,' she said, with a wink. 'They're probably pixelated on E, or something.'

I followed her up the purple stairs, smiling at the red hearts painted on every other step. 'It's fantastic, whatever the reason.' I couldn't seem to find my old cynicism, it had deserted me. My smile broadened at the thought. 'It's made my day.'

In the kitchen, I found an old jam jar for my posy, putting it in the window with all the other plants. I sat at the huge table and watched Linda prepare dinner. A pile of Sunday papers were stacked on the table, and with a glass of red wine in hand, I steadily worked my way through them. The boys were hard at work upstairs, putting the finishing touches to their latest repertoire, and snippets of songs caroused around the house as they rehearsed.

After refusing my offer of help with dinner, Linda had lapsed into uncomfortable silence, shooting me the odd anxious glance to check I was okay. I was getting used to this response to my Sad News, as others referred to my brother's death, and was surprised to find it didn't bother me.

Danny was dead. I missed him. That was all.

'Do you mind if I ask you something?' said Linda, peering into the oven to check on the roast. To me it looked like she was talking to the bubbling lamb, and I had to suppress a giggle. I put on my most serious face as Linda turned around.

'Ask away,' I said.

She joined me at the table and sipped her wine. 'Whatever happened to that strange gentleman you were seeing?'

The question gave me a jolt. I hadn't thought about Adam in ages. I had been over and over what happened, reasoning it out, then finally pushed it from my mind. It didn't seem that important anymore. Once I had settled on a theory that made sense and felt right, I let it go. Adam had served his purpose.

'I don't mean seeing as in, you know,' she said. 'I mean, he was your teacher, wasn't he?'

'He didn't exist.'

'Oh.' Linda took a longer slug from her wine. 'So...?'

'So, I have a theory. Well, it's Jung. You know him?'

'Anima, animus, all that sort of thing.'

'Archetypes, yes,' I said. 'That's what Adam was. The clue was in the name. He called himself Adam Kadmon, the symbol for the original man. From the Jungian perspective Adam was an image of the spirit, a kind of spirit guide born out of my deep unconscious, the transcendent function.'

Linda placed a hand on my arm, eyes shining. 'This is fantastic. Didn't I say you would meet your spirit guide?'

I smiled and gave her a half nod. She had said guardian angel.

'It's a process of restoring balance in the psyche,' I said. 'I got all screwed up and addled, and Adam shows up to set me straight.'

'So you imagined him?'

'Sort of. It's a primordial idea, much older than any of us. I didn't create it. Jung had a similar experience, only his was an old man with horns and wings, much harder to confuse with real life. Called himself Philemon, and they used to walk up and down Jung's garden having long philosophical discussions, just like me and Adam.

'Actually, Linda, it's probably not strictly accurate to say he didn't exist. Imagination has its own reality. I mean, what is reality, after all?'

'But you know that now,' she said, eyes ready to pop from their sockets in glee. 'Jonah said. He said you did it, you broke through, you saw it.'

I smiled and looked down at my wine. I spun the glass, making the dark liquid dance around and up the sides.

'It's really very simple,' I said. 'Honestly, it's no big deal. It's there all the time, in the gaps between every thought, the seconds before you start to think when you wake up, or when you stop thinking just before dropping off to sleep. When you sneeze. When you orgasm.'

Linda giggled and her cheeks glowed pink.

'We overlay reality with ideas about reality,' I said, 'and then we forget and take those ideas to be reality.'

'So you can't really say your Adam was an archetype,' she said. 'I mean, that's an idea, right? So, he might not be. He might be something else.'

I grinned. 'Touché, Linda. Spot on. The only truthful thing I can say is: I don't know. I don't know what Adam was. The label seems to fit, but you're right, he could be something I can't even imagine.' I shrugged. 'Whatever he was, he was very helpful.'

'So you're not crazy then?' she said, getting up from the table.

I laughed. 'No more than anyone else.'

Linda went to the stove and lifted the lid of a steaming saucepan. 'Better go get the boys, dinner's ready.'

'I'll go.'

I hadn't seen Jonah all day and well... I just wanted to see him. I needed to see his smile and tell him my news. Earlier that day, Felix Baldwin's card had fallen from a book on Buddhism I was reading, fluttering to the floor like a liberated bird. I'd stuck it in as a bookmark months ago, then forgotten about it. Later, in a sublime synchronicity, I ran into him in town. He was people watching on the steps at Grey's Monument, still resplendent in his magnificent whiskers. The final piece of my new life was about to slot into place.

While crucifying my ego and clobbering my fears into submission, I had abandoned all hope of having a normal life, but an alternative future was crystallising before my eyes. Somehow, when we met last year, Felix knew I had something of value to offer. Now I knew it too. I rushed over to say hello and apologised for not calling sooner.

'Been a bit tied up,' I said.

'Not literally, I hope.'

I grinned at him. 'Is the job still available?'

He nodded. 'I knew you'd come through for me, Zoe. I knew it the moment I set eyes on you. We're connected, you know.'

'I know.'

He beamed.

'I have lots of interesting experiences to share with you,' I said. 'You won't believe what I've just been through.'

'Oh, I wouldn't be too sure of that,' he said, and gave me a roguish wink.

I walked up the stairs to the band's practice room. The music had stopped and all was quiet. I was about to push open the door when I heard Jonah speak. I froze, my hand hovering over the bright purple wood.

'I want to bring Zoe with us to London,' he said.

There was a long pause...

'Come on, man, you know the rules,' said Ray.

'No WAGs for away play days,' said Robin. 'You know what happens. It's messy.'

I dropped my hand and pressed my ear to the door.

'Speak for yourself, Daylight,' said Jonah. 'Zoe's different.'

'She'll be trailing around after you, getting in the way, sulking cos you're ignoring her, and then throwing a massive strop cos some stupid tart can't keep her hands out of your pants,' said Robin.

I folded my arms. As if.

'Again, speak for yourself,' said Jonah. 'Look, I'm worried about leaving her on her own so soon after her brother's death. She seems all right, but you never know with these things. I promise she'll behave, and I won't be a dick about it if you won't.'

There was a clicking sound, drumsticks being put down, then Jonah continued.

'We're there to play to the industry, we're working, I get that. I'm not about to fuck it up. Equally, I'm not about to fuck things with Zoe. I'm not leaving her here. Besides, it's her birthday the day of the gig.'

I wanted to run into the room and fling myself into his arms, but stayed put and listened to the silence from the other two.

'No birthday sex in the van,' said Robin, at last.

'Agreed,' said Jonah. 'Let's go eat.'

With a start, I realised they were coming out and would see I'd been listening. I quickly ducked back down the stairs and went into the toilet. When I heard them passing, I flushed the loo and appeared in the hallway, the picture of innocence.

'Hey, babe,' said Jonah, wrapping me in a warm embrace.

I reached up and kissed his cheek, whispering in his ear. 'I love you, y'know.'

He beamed at me and pretended to chase me down the hall into the kitchen. Linda was busy dishing everything up, trying to avoid being hit by Robin, who was standing in the middle of the room crunching every bone in his back and working his arms like windmills.

'Sit down before you take off, will you?' said Linda, plonking the last of the bowls onto the table.

Halfway through dinner a black and white fur ball slid into the kitchen and slithered onto my lap. Maya purred and eyed the lamb on my plate.

'I'll save you some, if you're good,' I said into her ear.

Nobody was saying much, they were all too busy chewing, but I could feel the tension buzzing between the boys. Knowing glances were passing back and forth between Ray and Robin, and both of them were watching Jonah.

'How's it going? Ready for the big gig?' I said to no-one in particular.

Ray smiled and nodded, his mouth full of roast potato.

'We're going to razzle-dazzle them,' said Robin.

'As usual,' I said.

'Actually,' said Jonah, 'the boys were wondering if you'd like to come with us.'

Ray and Robin shot daggers at him and I pretended not to notice.

'Are you sure?' I said, playing along with Jonah's little game.

'We'd really like you to come,' he took my hand. 'Can't leave you on your own on your birthday.'

I put down my fork. 'Well, in that case, I'd love to come. Thank you.'

'Tell her the rules,' said Robin through a shower of peas.

'Don't worry, guys,' I said. 'I'm not going to spoil your fun, wouldn't dream of cramping your style. I'll keep out of the way, okay? You won't even know I'm there.'

I gave Robin a tiny wink. He stopped chewing and had the good grace to blush. Jonah laughed and slid an arm around my shoulders, planting a huge wet kiss on my cheek and leaving a smear of gravy in his wake.

'Oops, sorry,' he said, rubbing it away with his thumb.

'See, this is exactly the sort of thing we were worried about,' said Ray, kind of blowing the whole pretence of it being their idea in the first place.

'Gravy based mishaps,' said Robin. 'Where will it end?'

'You may be interested to know, we're not allowed to have sex in the van,' said Jonah, all mock serious.

'I should hope not.' I grinned.

I hadn't felt this happy in a long time and didn't even notice Maya finishing off my lamb and licking the plate clean.

A Dangerous Book

I clambered over amps and drum cases, and jumped down from the back of the van which was parked in a dingy alleyway behind the NonLocal club, ready to unload. The noise and stink of London enveloped me as I took my bearings, A to Z in hand. The boys were already piling their gear up at the back door. The trip down had been a little strained. With a forbidden female in the van they were unable to let rip and get in touch with their inner primate.

'Hey, babe, what you got planned?' Jonah wandered over and hooked his arms around my waist.

'Just going to have an explore,' I said.

'Okay. We soundcheck in an hour, then we'll meet you at Pizza Hut, say six?'

I nodded and checked my mobile. I had three hours. I stepped out of Jonah's embrace, anxious to let him be. 'See you at six.'

'You forgotten something?' he said.

'Oh.' I stood on tiptoe and gave him a quick kiss. 'Better?'

He chuckled softly and stuck a hand in his jacket pocket, pulling out a small box wrapped in purple tissue paper.

'Happy birthday, babe.'

I grinned and tore off the paper. Ray and Robin started singing a grotesque, out of tune version of happy birthday as I opened the box. An intricately carved dragon pendant lay inside, with fiery crests and wings, and an elegant pointed tail. I held it up to the light. It appeared to be made from black glass.

'It's beautiful, Joe. Thank you.'

'Here.' He took the pendant and placed it around my neck. 'It's obsidian. The woman in the shop said it's for spiritual warriors.'

I felt tears prickling my eyes and flung myself at Jonah, giving him a lingering, deep kiss. The sound of protracted, theatrical coughing drifted across from the van.

'I say, would you mind awfully not devouring our guitarist?' said Robin. 'At least, not until after the show.'

'Ignore him,' said Jonah.

'Who?' I said.

Jonah laughed and gave me another quick kiss. 'Six. Pizza Hut.'

I ambled down the alleyway towards the street assailed by shouts, waves and wolf-whistles from the boys. I ignored them and turned the corner to be sucked into the melee that was London. Determined not to get panicked by the rush, the obnoxious aggression, and the siege-like myopia that afflicted so many of the people I kept crashing into, I kept my pace slow and mindful, going with the flow of life, not the flow of me-first-and-to-hell-with-everyone-else.

I descended into the bowels of the city, along stifling tunnels lined with dirt and graffiti, and squeezed onto a train to take me to the shops. Compared to the Metro in Newcastle, the Tube was a mechanical hell. Even the Tannoy managed to be rude. I hung onto a metal pole as the train rumbled along the tracks, picking up speed, racing through the tunnels. There was no air, I felt suffocated and imprisoned, the noise of the train like a million ghosts screaming in my mind. I had to get out.

At the next station I got off the Tube and forced my way up to the street, to the air thick with traffic fumes and aggravation. I consulted the map and decided to just wander and see where I ended up. It felt good to have no particular direction, to be free to follow my heart. Although, if I were honest, that path would lead straight back to Jonah. I had survived the worst year of my life, largely thanks to him. It could only get better.

A sharp ache punctured my happiness, an ache formed from absence. Every time I felt my mood rise, the Danny shaped fracture in my soul acted as ballast. I supposed it always would.

I wandered the streets, window shopping and people watching. Hundreds of signs shouted out, selling, informing, imploring or just plain annoying. My eyes scanned the consumptive chaos, letting it wash over me, looking for inspiration, something good.

Then I saw it. A battered old sign tied at a wonky angle to a lamppost. It read simply: DANNY'S, with a huge red arrow pointing down another road. I followed the arrow, turning into a deserted side street.

The noise from the main road faded as the buildings in the narrow lane loomed over me. There was something unnerving about this place, almost like it belonged somewhere else. The entire street was shuttered and abandoned. I was the only person and there was no sign of a shop called Danny's.

I followed the curve of the lane as it meandered away from the main road, feeling like I was pushing back some kind of frontier, venturing somewhere normal (sensible) people never went. A shiver ran through me and I laughed at myself. I was telling stories again.

Around the bend I discovered an open shop. I assumed it was open as there was no shutter, but I couldn't read the name, it had worn away over the years. The window was dark. I couldn't tell if it was encrusted with dirt or whether it had been painted; it was simply ancient. A shop lost in time. It was like something out of Harry Potter. Maybe that was it: this was a shop for wizards. I grinned to myself and tried the door. It opened.

A little bell jingled over my head as I stepped inside. The tiny shop was brimming with books. Lines of heaving shelves disappeared into the gloom at the back. A man appeared from behind a stack of books, and I had to bite the inside of my mouth to stop myself laughing. He was short and portly with a long flowing beard, like a hairy weeble. He definitely wouldn't look out of place at Hogwarts.

He gave me a long appraising look with his piercing black eyes. I knew that look. It was the same look Adam had, uncompromising and unfathomable.

'Are you real?' I said.

The man's eyes twinkled and he smiled. 'You're new.'

'Don't live here. Just visiting.' I ran my eyes over the shelves. 'What kind of books do you specialise in?'

'Dangerous ones.'

'Sounds ominous,' I said with a smile.

'Not to you.' He smiled and opened his arms wide. 'I was about to put the kettle on. Would you like a cup of tea while you browse?'

I grinned and nodded. 'Don't get that kind of service in Waterstones.'

'Don't get these kind of books in Waterstones,' he said. 'Milk? Sugar?'

'Just milk thanks. I'm Zoe, by the way.'

He stepped forward and offered his hand. I took it – a good, firm grip. He was real all right.

'Nice to meet you Zoe by the way. I'm Daniel. One tea coming up.'

I chuckled and watched him disappear behind the books. So this was Danny's. I turned my attention to the overflowing shelves. Mum had given me some money for my birthday with explicit instructions to treat myself to something nice – 'none of your usual second hand nonsense, love.' So the real reason for my ramble through the shops of London was to find something I truly wanted. I had been unimpressed by everything I'd seen so far, it was all so unnecessary. But there might be something here. I decided what I needed was a dangerous book and plunged between the shelves.

Moments later Daniel reappeared with a generous mug of tea, plonking it on a shelf next to me.

'Don't worry about moving things around. Get stuck in,' he said, before ambling back to the counter at the front of the shop, his own tea in hand.

I sipped at my tea and gazed at the mountain of books. There was no way of being systematic about this. Daniel's system, if he had one, was anarchic. Perhaps it had started out ordered, evolving into its current state of disarray as customers moved the books about as they searched. It would be hopeless if you were looking for something in particular, you would be here all day. Thankfully, I didn't know what I wanted, allowing myself to be guided by instinct and curiosity. An interesting cover or intriguing title would grab my attention and I would look it over, waiting for my intuition to give me a nod. It felt like I was looking for something specific, I just didn't know what it was. I would know it when I saw it.

And there it was, jammed in and almost hidden behind another book. As soon as I saw it my heart did a little flip. It was called *The Dragon of Delusion*. My fingers ran over the dragon pendant Jonah had given me just two hours ago. A coincidence like that was not to be sniffed at. This had to be the book for me. I yanked it out, pulling another book with it, which fell to the floor.

Ignoring the book on the floor, I ran my hand over the cover of *The Dragon of Delusion*. It was quite plain. I had hoped for a cool dragon picture at least. I flipped it open at random and read a couple of paragraphs. It was dull. Disappointed, I returned it to the shelf. My intuition must be taking the piss, making connections where there were none. Remembering the escaped book on the floor, I stooped to retrieve it.

With a jolt, I sprang back like it was a snake about to bite. I clamped my hand over my mouth and stifled a yelp. My heart was pounding so fast I thought it would burst through my chest and splatter over the shelves. I was looking at something impossible. It simply couldn't be.

The book was lying face down. On the back cover was a photograph of a man smiling up at me with a familiar twinkle in his eyes.

It was Adam.

I leaned forward and gingerly picked up the book, half expecting it to disintegrate through my fingers or vanish in a puff of smoke. I turned it over. It was called *Addled* and was written by a man called Aidan Sinclair. The blurb told me it was the story of this man's spiritual journey, from broker to Zen monastery and beyond. I flipped through the book and found more pictures. One in particular caught my attention: the author standing outside a Buddhist temple in Japan grinning at the camera and wearing the same posh suit, with cravat, as Adam.

Adam was Aidan. He was real.

My head was literally crumbling. I didn't know what to think. Why had he called himself Adam Kadmon? Why hadn't he told me the truth? Why hadn't Jonah been able to see him? I needed to read this book, right now.

I picked up my empty mug and went to the counter. Daniel was concentrating on an obscure book about alchemy. Perhaps he really was a wizard.

'Thanks for the tea,' I said, placing the mug on the counter.

Daniel looked up from his reading. 'Ah, yes.' He nodded at the book in my hands.

'You've read it?' I said.

'Interesting fella. They say he can travel.'

I was about to protest that anyone can travel, but then realised he must mean something else. My confusion must have shown because he smiled at me as he took the book.

'Astrally,' he said.

'Oh. Right,' I said, none the wiser.

'Shamanic flying.'

I nodded and pretended I knew what he was talking about, handing over my cash. Daniel came with me to the door and waved me off.

'Come again, Zoe.'

'Oh, I definitely will. Thank you.'

'Happy travelling.'

I dodged through the bodies and bags clogging the floor in Pizza Hut. The boys were already seated on the far side of the restaurant, deep in conversation. They didn't notice me until I was standing over them, beaming like a deranged beauty queen.

'I found him,' I said.

Three blank faces stared up at me.

'Look.' I handed the book to Jonah. 'There's a picture on the back. I was searching for the wrong name.'

I sat beside Jonah who was turning the book over and over in his hands, worry running all over his face.

'Babe, it might just look like him.'

'What about the suit? Here.' I took the book and flicked through to the photos, shoving it back into Jonah's unresisting hands. 'The details are exactly alike. How could I have imagined it so accurately? Either he's real and he was there, or I'm the most amazing psychic ever.'

'What am I thinking?' said Robin.

Jonah shot him such a hostile look the drummer ducked behind his menu and hid. Jonah turned to me and put his arm around my shoulders, scooching me into a warm hug.

'Let's just eat,' he said into my hair. 'We'll talk about this later.'

The four of us ploughed through an enormous pizza with piles of toppings and salads. While we ate, the boys perfected their set list, Ray clearing a space to scribble down three sheets in bold marker pen.

Jonah kept half an eye on me throughout. I had *Addled* propped up against the condiment collection in front of me, intent on devouring more words than food. I could tell Jonah was worried. He probably thought all this madness was behind us.

When we got back to NonLocal, he took me backstage to the dressing room while the others got drinks from the bar. The room consisted of a long counter below a filthy mirror running the full length of the room, and a handful of battered chairs. Doodles and messages had been scrawled on the walls and mirror by previous headliners, making sure the world remembered they were there. Stacked in the corner were the band's flight cases and bags.

I stood in front of the mirror, oblivious to the grime, reading *Addled*, while Jonah closed the door. He stood behind me, watching. I glanced up and caught his eye in the mirror.

'Please will you stop reading that thing,' he said.

'I need to find out how he did it,' I said, turning round to face him.

Jonah didn't look happy. Surely he couldn't be jealous all over again. Could he? I dumped my handbag on the counter. I didn't want to fight.

'What's wrong?' I said, in what I hoped was a calm and reasonable voice.

He put his arms around me, running his hands over my hair, messing it up and smiling to himself.

'I don't know, babe. I want you to be happy, that's all.'

'Then I need to read this book.'

'I get that, Zo. It's just... I thought it was finished with, the Adam thing, and I don't want anything to happen to you that-'

'That makes me go crazy again.'

He nodded sadly. 'You know the worst thing? I keep pushing the thought away, but it keeps coming back. All through dinner, you sitting there reading, so sure you've found him, and it's like it's bullying me, making me think it, over and over, running through my head like some kind of delirious streaker.'

'Will you get to the point,' I said softly. 'You're turning into me.'

'What if she's right?' he said. 'What if you're right, Zoe? What then? Suddenly we're living in a world where you can have long conversations with a man I can't see, and what the fuck is that all about?'

'I know. That's why I have to understand how it happened. I can't let this go now. Don't you want to know the truth?'

He nodded, but with a heavy heart.

'You're scared I won't be able to handle it.'

'Not that... I don't know, Zoe. I don't know anything anymore.'

'Welcome to my life,' I said.

NonLocal was crammed with bodies. I sat at the bar watching the heaving mass pulsate before me. Up on stage, Jonah closed his eyes against the glare of the lights, his guitar humming in his hands. I marvelled at the way he sucked up the energy of the crowd and then poured it back out through his voice and his guitar. Upturned, expectant faces, eyes wide, drinking it in, his music lifting and embracing, rolling and crashing inside every head.

I beamed as the song ended (one of my favourites), the last note faded into a roar of voices and hands crashing together. I turned back to the book in my hands, unable to resist the lure of truth. Out of the corner of my eye I saw Jonah look up and over the crowd. Perhaps he could see me sitting here, head buried in my book instead of his music, but it was no use. I couldn't wait. I told myself I could read it on the drive home, I had all the time in the world, I didn't have to do it right now, but it kept drawing me back. I was helpless; captured in another man's stories.

It may have been my imagination, but as the gig blistered on it seemed to rise in intensity, the music developing added edge and urgency. Jonah sang like a man possessed by both an angel and a demon, wrestling to the death, and the crowd adored him for it.

The post-show fallout passed in a blur of pumped hands, bear hugs and hysterical declarations of undying love. Robin had been right about that much, it seemed. Jonah came away with a fistful of business cards and promises. It looked like they were going to have to 'do' London in the very near future to capitalise on the excitement generated tonight. Packing up and loading the van took longer than usual. Their new friends insisted on helping and only succeeded in slowing everything down, with generous offers of floors to kip on and sumptuous feasts for free.

I kept out of the way and sat on the steps of a fire exit in the alleyway, doing my best to ignore the exuberance around me, deep in concentration on *Addled*. I glanced up a couple of times to find Jonah watching me surreptitiously. I couldn't tell if he was annoyed or amazed. I beamed at him, sending as much love his way as I could muster. He took a step back and his mouth dropped open, as if the love beam had actually hit him in the chest. Having recovered, he started to laugh, and wandered across to my perch, chuckling all the way.

'I have never known anyone so infuriatingly single-minded as you my whole life,' he said.

'Is that good or bad?'

'If you keep smiling at me like that: good, extremely bloody good.' He walked backwards to the van, blowing kisses to me with both hands, making me laugh along with him.

'Smile like what?' I shouted.

'Like two million watts,' he shouted back. 'That, Zoe, is dangerous. Stopped my heart. A Full Beamer.'

With the equipment packed into the van, the hangers-on finally wandered off into the night, chattering about their fresh discovery – the band of the decade – and the four of us were left alone. Ray climbed into the driver's seat. Jonah had driven down, so he got to sit it out on the way back. Robin climbed up front, leaving the back seats for me and Jonah.

I ambled across to the van, nose still in *Addled*. Jonah appeared in front of me.

'Ready to go home, babe?'

I closed the book and kissed him, hooking my arms around his neck.

'You were fantastic tonight,' I said. 'I know I was reading, but I heard every note. You guys rocked.'

He grinned down at me. 'Good is it?'

'You should read it.' I stepped back and hugged the book to my chest. 'But I'm not done with it yet.'

The drive north lapsed into contented silence once the meta-analysis of the gig and the grandiose plans for the future had been fully investigated. I kept reading while the discussion zipped about my head, and Jonah didn't seem to mind. I caught him staring at the photo on the back cover a couple of times, like he was trying to rustle up some kind of animosity towards the man who nearly drove me insane, but he didn't seem able to maintain it. In the end, he sat back and watched the night fly past the window as we trundled up the motorway. Ray drove steadily and Robin dozed off, curled up on the double front seat.

Sleep crept up on me too, my head filled with words and possibilities and questions. My eyes closed and my head lulled forward, the book toppling onto my chest. Then all was darkness and silence.

Jonah's fingers gently running across my cheek pulled me out of sleep. He kissed my forehead. 'Wake up, sleeping beauty, we're home.'

I roused myself and looked out the window. We were driving over the Tyne Bridge, the lights on the quay hanging in the darkness along the curve of the river. The streets were deserted, and in no time Ray was pulling up outside our flat. Jonah slapped him on the shoulder.

'Thanks, mate. I'll pick up the van sometime tomorrow.'

'No problem,' said Ray. 'Want a hand with your amp?'

'Nah. S'all right.'

Robin stirred in the passenger seat. 'Are we there?'

'Nearly,' said Ray.

Jonah leaned over and grabbed Robin's hand. 'Later, mate.'

'Later,' said Robin.

I was dazed from sleeping so deeply for so long and in such an uncomfortable position. I clambered stiffly out the van and stood outside the flats, swaying slightly and staring into the chilly darkness. Jonah retrieved his guitar and amp, and waved the van off, watching it disappear up the street, taillights blinking in the night.

We stood together in silence for a moment. Then a slow, rising panic ran through me, gripping my heart, as I realised I'd lost my most precious possession. Patting my pockets and rummaging in my bag didn't help.

'No, no, no, no...'

'Chill, babe.'

I looked at Jonah, frantic. He smiled and pulled *Addled* from his pocket with a flourish. Relief flooded through me and I gratefully snatched the book from his fingers. Jonah sat on his amp and looked up at me, his face unreadable in the darkness.

'I wanted to hate him,' he said. 'Adam, or Aidan, or whatever the hell he's called. I wanted to take his stupid book and sling it out the window, to be lost forever on the M1. But he kept smiling at me. The way you smile, your full beamers.'

'You read it?'

'Bits,' he said. 'It's all there. All the stuff you told me. The car engine bursting into flames, the journey around the world, and then the monastery in the forest in Japan. All the details match.'

I nodded.

'But I looked through the whole book, Zoe. There's nothing in there about special powers or weird shit.'

'You sure?' I rifled through the pages. 'I'm only halfway through. You couldn't have read the whole thing, Joe.'

'I skimmed. But it's okay, babe. We can ask the man himself.'

I looked up so fast I nearly gave myself whiplash. 'What?'

'How do you fancy a trip to New Mexico?'

Dream With Open Eyes

I rubbed my eyes and tried to wake up. My head felt fuzzy from dozing and now we were flying over the mountains and I didn't want to miss it. The plane banked, descending through a haze of cloud. I pressed my face to the window, watching in awe as the Rockies rose up below us, glistening in the autumn sunshine. Without moving from the window, I reached around behind me for Jonah, patting his arm and gently shaking him.

'Joe, Jonah, wake up. Joe, you've got to see this.'

He stretched and leaned into my seat, his stubble rough against my neck. He gazed down at the jagged peaks wrapped in a green blanket of pine and aspen, and let out a long, satisfied sigh.

'Yep,' he said, sitting back in his seat and closing his eyes, a huge grin spread across his face.

'Yep?' I looked at him in astonishment. 'Is that all you have to say?'

'What else is there?'

'It's just so...'

'Yep.'

I giggled and turned back to the window. 'We're here all right.' I wiped a smear of breath from the glass, sucking in as much of the view as I could. It felt like my eyes weren't big enough to see it all, and in a wild moment wanted to smash the window, stick my head out and laugh into the wind.

'Thank you,' I said.

'Mmmm?' Jonah was dozing off again.

'For this.'

I turned back to him and rested my head on his shoulder. He had made the most incredible sacrifice. After saving for years to visit his ancestral home, he had blown it all on bringing me here. All his hopes and dreams abandoned just so I could find Aidan. Whenever I thought about it, it made me cry with joy and amazement. I ran my fingers over Jonah's jaw line and down his throat, and a tiny smile tugged at his lips.

'I was looking forward to seeing Trinidad,' I said.

He turned and kissed my forehead. 'Another time, babe.'

'Jonah Nelson, you are the most beautiful, gorgeous, wonderful human being.'

He chuckled. 'You are very welcome.'

'You know my mum would've paid for this, if I'd asked.'

'I wanted to do this for you, Zo. After... everything, y'know.'

'It's just... I don't want it to be a waste. What if we can't find him? What if he doesn't want to see me? I can't just show up, I mean, he was pretty cross last time I saw him.'

'Will you chill, babe?'

Jonah took my hand and kissed each finger in turn making me giggle, until I snatched my hand away and lunged at him, kissing him with such passion and ferocity we were assailed with a flurry of tutting from the elderly couple across the aisle. Jonah pulled back, grinning.

'We will find him and he'll be overjoyed to see you,' he said, scrunching his fingers through my mad hair. 'You did read his book, didn't you? It's not like he's a monster nutcase. Nah worry yourself.'

I did as I was told, sitting back in my seat to enjoy the rest of the flight. It was Jonah's turn to worry as we came in to land, gripping the hand rests and gritting his teeth. I tried to soothe his nerves, but was enjoying myself too much; taking off and landing were the best bits as far as I was concerned. I loved the lurch in the pit of my stomach as the plane left the ground, and the sensation of a great hunk of metal careening along, impossibly fast. I swallowed, opening and closing my mouth like a delirious goldfish, to make my ears pop, as the plane hit the runway and rumbled to a standstill.

Jonah breathed out in relief. 'You're a maniac.'

I giggled and stood to get our bags from the overhead locker.

We emerged blinking into the Albuquerque sunlight, dazzled by the sheer amount of space surrounding us. Up ahead, rising in waves into the air, were hundreds of giant hot air balloons, suspended in multicoloured grandeur against the crystal blue sky. Jonah had timed our visit to coincide with the balloon fiesta because he thought I would enjoy it. I was enchanted, gazing up into the sky with childlike delight, practically hugging myself with glee.

'Joe, this is great. Look, there's one shaped like a dog wearing a hat.'

'I expect he's practising for the Special Shapes Rodeo later in the week.'

'Can we come back for that? After we've found Aidan.'

'Course.'

He took my hand and led me, like a child, to the shuttle stop, wheeling our luggage with his other hand. I nearly tripped over my own feet with my eyes fixed on the sky. We balloon spotted all the way out of town, until the bus dropped us in Santa Fe.

After a quick lunch of green chilli enchiladas with blue-corn tortillas, and Jonah had coaxed the recipe from the chef, we left the hire car at the hotel and ambled downtown, merging with the dusty, narrowing streets lined with adobe boutiques and galleries. I found myself drawn left and right to displays of turquoise jewellery, Native American tapestries, a carved saint lurking in an alcove, and wacky sculptures fashioned from scrap metal. Mum would love it here; art and life burst upon you from all directions. There was so much to take in, I started to believe I had developed attention deficit disorder and had to remind myself why we were here.

While Jonah bought himself a dashing Santa Fean hat, I consulted the directions to the Zen centre I'd pulled off the internet before we left England. In no time we were walking up the flagstone path winding between stubby pinon trees. Water trickled into a large flat granite bowl and a contented stone Buddha shaded himself beneath the wide branches of a juniper tree. More rust coloured adobe buildings, sculpted from the earth, greeted us, and once inside the main reception we were transported to Japan.

Polished wooden beams and floors glowed with a soft orange light and an atmosphere of extreme calm emanated from every corner. I caught myself smiling for no reason and turned to Jonah. He was smiling too, his new hat clutched at his belly. We beamed at each other, until a polite cough from behind got our attention.

A young man, casually dressed with his long hair trussed up in a pony tail, was waiting patiently for us to explain our presence. I felt a cool draft of air drift past and out of the corner of my eye noticed a small nun carrying a watering can. She moved silently and deliberately, measuring out water into the assortment of plants lining the reception room, her black and brown robes hanging about her like a tent.

I suddenly felt foolish. I didn't know where to begin with my crazy tale and could feel a rash of embarrassment running up my throat and across my face. I rummaged in my bag and found Aidan's book.

'Um... I don't know if you can help. I'm looking for someone. He used to come here.' I handed the book to the young man, who looked at it with curiosity. 'He's been teaching me. Well, sort of... I haven't really met him. I mean, well, I kind of have, except... I don't know. Jonah couldn't see him and I could, so I don't know if he was really there or not. I wasn't even sure he existed at one point.'

I laughed my best hysterical laugh and ran a nervous hand through my hair. The unearthly peaceful man flicked through the book and turned to the back cover. Aidan twinkled up at him and he smiled back.

'When I met him... um... what I thought was him, he called himself Adam Kadmon. But then I found his book.'

A childlike chuckle bubbled from behind the spikes of a yucca and the nun stepped forward, leaving her watering can on the floor. She appeared to float across the floor, joining the young man holding the book, and peered at the photograph. Her face danced with the most joyful smile I had ever seen. It seemed to light the whole room.

'Sounds like Aidan is up to his old tricks again,' she said, chuckling like a wind chime in a light breeze.

'Do you know where he lives?' I said, fighting the urge to laugh along with the nun. Her happiness was contagious.

'Oh yes,' she said. 'Do you have a pen?'

I handed over a biro and my Lonely Planet guide, and she scribbled directions in the margins.

'He lives outside Taos, just up the road,' she said, without looking up.

'Does he have a phone?' I said. 'I don't feel right turning up out of nowhere.'

The nun handed back the guide and biro, and wrapped her hands around mine, gripping them warmly and smiling deep into my eyes.

'If he wants to see you, he'll be there,' she said. 'If he doesn't, he won't.'

I nodded and smiled my thanks. I glanced at the map to check the distance to Taos, anxious to get there today. It wasn't far, but there were two routes.

'Which would you recommend, the high road or the low road?' I said.

'Both are good,' said the young man.

'The low road is faster,' said the nun.

We retraced our steps to the hotel and picked up the car, stocking up on flagons of water on our way out of town. The altitude was starting to take effect and I could feel a tightness gripping my head, as if the weight of all that sky were pressing down on me. I gulped great mouthfuls of water and swallowed a couple of ibuprofen.

'I don't think I'm designed to be up this high,' I said, passing the water bottle to Jonah. He swigged and drove, the mesa spread out either side as we barrelled down the empty road. Blue-green sage and grasses with flashes of yellow flowers and clumps of pinon and juniper huddled together against the arid climate, all rolled by. The mountains rose up against the horizon like a forbidding wall stretching into the sky.

The air felt cleaner up here, it clarified everything, opening out spaces in your mind you never knew you had. I could imagine how you might feel small in a place like this. The sky and the mountains were so vast they defied imagination, making everything else seem irrelevant. They were timeless, mythic. I felt myself spilling out into the spaces around me, every petty thought vanished against the immutable landscape, leaving me empty and full of peace. I had wondered why Aidan settled here; now I understood.

A shadow fell across the road and slid into the brush and away. I looked up. Soaring above us was an enormous hot air balloon. As I watched, flames appeared in the hollow under the canopy and the balloon rose, drifting away from us. I hung out the window and waved, the wind blasting my hair flat against my skull.

The balloon was ice-blue, the same colour as the sky. If you squinted or glanced at it quickly, you might believe it wasn't there, rising and rising, following the line of the Rio Grande.

'Balloon!' I shouted, and waved some more, as Jonah took the turn onto the gorge suspension bridge. The blue-green plateau plunged beneath us as we drove over the gash in the earth, ragged walls falling away into a shimmering river on the valley floor.

'Oh, Joe.' I transferred my wonderstruck vision from the sky to the void under the bridge, the ancient rocks making me feel positively prehistoric. I beamed at Jonah, who kept his eyes firmly fixed on the road.

'Don't ask me to get out and look,' he said. 'I ain't ready for that yet.'

I chuckled and checked the directions scrawled in my guide book. 'Not far now.'

A couple of miles down the road strange shapes appeared to rise from the earth, aerials and makeshift turbines sticking out at odd angles. Flashes of sunlight reflected off the windows of homes buried in the ground, like sunken spaceships waiting for the mother ship to return. Jonah turned off the main road and the car rumbled down a dirt track, sending up clouds of red dust in our wake.

I peered through the windscreen, the heat haze shimmering over the sage bushes and yuccas. Further up the track I could see a man standing in the middle of the road. He didn't seem to be doing anything in particular, just idling, hands in his pockets, like he was waiting for something or someone. As the car approached, he turned to face us but didn't move out of the way. There was something familiar about him, but the clothes were all wrong. He was wearing a pair of scruffy jeans and a loose linen shirt billowing in the breeze. He should've been wearing a suit.

A spasm of electricity ran through my body and I leapt from the moving car, leaving the door flapping behind me. I ran towards the man, laughing with joy, and threw my arms around his neck – his solid and very real neck.

Aidan chuckled softly and unwrapped my arms, gently putting me at arms length so he could look into my eyes. I worried briefly that I'd made a faux pas by hugging him, but pushed it aside. He didn't seem annoyed. He was smiling at me. I smiled back, letting all thoughts drop into a chasm larger than the Rio Grande gorge.

Aidan nodded, as if satisfied with something, and pulled me into another warm clinch, making me giggle with delight.

Jonah pulled up beside us, and Aidan let go of me to direct him to park outside an adobe earthship set back from the road. The only straight lines in the house were the long line of windows facing the sun. Every other surface was curved and the walls were packed with old tyres and tin cans.

I stood with my mouth hanging open. I had never seen anything so ridiculously fantastic in my life. Aidan watched me, amusement playing over his face.

'I'll put the kettle on,' he said.

Jonah and I wandered dumbstruck into the living room. The glazed adobe floor studded with straw was swathed in bright geometric patterned rugs and the walls curled over us, not a sharp edge in sight. It was like something out of a Gaudi dream: voluptuous curves, hand moulded organic shapes and coloured glass embedded in the walls glinting like precious stones. Two generous sofas faced each other over a carved wooden table and broadleaf plants spilled from the corners. The overall effect was of being embraced by the space, like being in a five-star womb. I had never felt more at home.

Aidan appeared carrying a tray cluttered with tea things, and smiled to himself when he saw we were still gawping at our surroundings.

'Sit down, sit down,' he said, placing the tray on the table. 'I'll give you the grand tour later.'

'Your house is spectacular,' said Jonah, lowering himself into one of the huge sofas.

Aidan smiled at him and poured the tea. I sat opposite Jonah, my mind whirling with questions. Here was the man I had been talking with for months and he seemed just the same, and yet there was something else, something I couldn't quite grasp. He was absolutely at home here in this impossible house, but watching him doing mundane domestic tasks felt weird. Somehow I hadn't expected this. I didn't know what I had expected. It would have been even stranger to find him being waited on, served by disciples, aloof on a high cushion, condescending to his lowly deluded followers. But he was just ordinary. There was even a guitar in the corner, propped up beside a yucca. I wondered if Jonah had spotted it yet.

Aidan handed me a bowl-shaped cup brimming with green tea, which I cradled in both hands.

'How was the trip?' he said.

'Pretty good, except for Jonah doesn't like flying much.'

'Ah,' said Aidan, as he joined Jonah on the sofa opposite. 'But you're still alive, eh Joe?' He patted his knee affectionately.

Jonah nodded and grinned, his embarrassment draining away under the force of Aidan's compassion.

'I was scared stiff of flying once too,' said Aidan.

'We know,' I said. 'We read your book.'

'You mean there are still copies knocking about? How fantastic.'

I pulled *Addled* from my bag and handed it over. He took it, beaming like a proud parent, running his fingers over the cover, then handed it back.

'So that's how you found me.'

He gave me one of his penetrating looks and I felt the pressure of all my questions rising up. Where to start? I glanced away and focused on the tea tray, trying to concentrate and get my thoughts in order. Beside the pot was another cup. I frowned. Jonah and Aidan both had theirs, as did I.

'There are four cups,' I said.

Aidan glanced at the table. 'So there are.'

I watched my teacher closely. He didn't seem worried he had brought in too many cups. There was none of the usual head scratching, or self-deprecating jokes about senile dementia and senior moments. He simply wasn't bothered. It was just a fact. There were four cups, no big deal. I had been wrong about him. He wasn't ordinary at all.

I felt idiotic, as I was about to ask what would probably turn out to be a stupid and obvious question: how can you be in two places at once?

'It's a bit like telepathy,' said Aidan, fixing his eyes on mine.

Jonah looked back and forth between us, confusion in his eyes, wondering what he had missed. Aidan had just dipped into my mind, or had appeared to. From the inside it was pretty strange, but from the outside it must be mystifying. Aidan placed his tea cup on the table and stood.

'I'll show you,' he said.

He sat cross-legged on the rug beside the table and closed his eyes, immediately entering a meditative trance, a faint smile lifting his features. Jonah and I exchanged glances and waited. I drained my tea and placed the cup on the tray, the china clinking against the pot.

In the corner of my eye something moved. I turned. Standing in the doorway was Aidan wearing his familiar dapper suit, hands in pockets and grinning. I smiled up at him and chuckled.

Jonah's head jerked round, his mouth falling open in shock. He lurched from his seat and dropped his cup. It fell to the floor, breaking against the table leg and leaving a dark stain as the tea seeped into the rug.

'Holy shit,' he said.

His eyes bounced back and forth between the two Aidans, one sitting peacefully on the floor, the other standing in the doorway, both looking equally real. 'Holy fucking shit.'

I grinned at the standing Aidan. 'Why the suit?'

'It's my travelling suit. D'you like it?' He gave us a twirl, then vanished.

Jonah stared at the empty space vacated by the be-suited Aidan. The sitting Aidan opened his eyes and unfolded himself, standing slowly using the table for support. He went to Jonah and took his hands, jolting him back to attention.

'How? How?' said Jonah.

Aidan winked at me over his shoulder. 'It's magic.'

He guided Jonah back into his seat and poured him another cup of tea, placing the broken cup on the tray. I gawped at the shattered fragments of china, mind stuttering and gears crunching, as the implications of what I was seeing erupted into chaos in my brain. I knew exactly how Jonah was feeling.

'You knew he'd break the cup,' I said, in a daze.

'Not exactly,' said Aidan. He sat beside Jonah and watched me trying to work it out. 'Thinking about it won't help, Zoe. You know that.'

'Yes, but... Did you know I was coming? You were waiting in the road. Or is that just something you do? For fun?'

'I figured you'd show up eventually,' he said.

'So you've been hanging around for a while, then?'

'No. I had a dream last night.'

'Okay,' I said, mind going in slow motion. 'So with the cup, you put it on the tray because...?'

'I just picked up four cups, Zoe. I didn't think. I didn't know what would happen. We needed an extra cup and there it was.'

Jonah was rubbing his head and shaking it slowly back and forth, as if trying to dislodge a stubborn fly from his nose. I was pretty sure things were about to get a lot worse for him, but I couldn't stop now. We were knee deep in paradox and about to sink up to our necks.

'I mean, it's not like it would've been a huge problem to run into the kitchen to pick up another cup,' I said. 'Isn't it a little bit like showing off?'

Aidan laughed. 'It's the universe showing off, yes.'

'The universe is definitely taking the piss right now,' said Jonah, slurping his tea.

'You said it was like telepathy,' I said. 'Did I imagine it all then?'

'Yes and no,' said Aidan. 'The image you see is a projection, a tulpa or thought form, created by our imagination. You imagined it, I projected it, but as you know, Zoe, we are not two.'

'A tulpa?' said Jonah.

'It's like a hologram,' said Aidan. 'Usually described as the etheric double, created by the mind through concentration and visualisation. It's an illusion.'

'So you weren't really there,' I said.

'No.'

'But you were there in my imagination.'

'Not your imagination, Zoe. Ours. Life's.'

Jonah put his tea cup back on the table. 'I don't mean to be rude, but you're sounding like a crazy person.'

'Think of it this way,' said Aidan. 'When you're talking with someone on the phone, do you imagine them on the other end?'

Jonah and I nodded. 'Sort of,' I said.

'Okay,' Aidan continued, 'So what's the difference between us talking on the phone and us talking imaginatively, sitting on concrete seats sheltered under the branches of a tree?'

'But that's a real place,' I said. 'I didn't imagine that. And you were on the other side of the world.'

'Are we really separate?' he said.

'At the level of Pure Awareness, no, but... hang on. Are you saying we could all do this? That I could be anywhere just by imagining it?'

'Zoe, most people's minds are scattered to the winds. You know how hard it is to discipline your mind.'

I nodded and grimaced. I still struggled with it, despite the satori breakthrough.

'We don't know how to use our brain yet,' he continued. 'It evolved so fast and we're lagging behind. For most of our history animal survival was paramount, just living through the day was an achievement, still is for too many people. Others are fortunate enough to have moved beyond the basics, creating more complex lives as a result, but that means we must think to survive and we keep screwing up. We seem to have mislaid the user manual for our minds and so are hopelessly addled.

'You asked if you could be anywhere you fancied, just through imagination. Tell me Zoe, is there anyplace where you are not?'

I gazed at Aidan. What he was saying sounded insane, irrational and impossible, and yet I knew it made a crazy kind of sense. He was talking about a whole different order of reality, one beyond thought, beyond imagination. When he referred to 'me', he didn't mean the ego, or personal self. He meant the True Self, which wasn't really a self at all. It was nowhere and everywhere. It was impossible to conceptualise; the words were getting in the way.

'It seems like an awful lot of trouble to go to, when you could just pick up the phone or get on a plane,' I said.

Aidan smiled and nodded. 'We have mastered our material reality. Of our inner, spiritual reality we remain dangerously ignorant.'

'Can I ask a question?' said Jonah.

Aidan turned to him and twinkled. 'You want to know why you couldn't see me.'

Jonah nodded, dumbfounded.

'We hadn't met yet,' said Aidan. 'Imaginatively speaking.'

'But neither had we,' I said, recalling our first encounter in Morrisons.

'Oh, but we did, Zoe. In a dream.'

In a flash I remembered the shadowy street and Jonah driving the little car. It had probably been too dark for Aidan to see him, hunched behind the steering wheel, camouflaged by his mahogany skin. Aidan had stood in the middle of the road, just like today, only in a cravat.

'It was your dream,' said Aidan. 'You came to me and I responded.'

'How did I find you?'

'You needed me.' He leaned back in his seat and opened his arms wide. 'You're more powerful than you realise, Zoe.'

The sun was setting behind me and the mountain glowed red like a blood orange. I was sitting on the low wall running around the roof of Aidan's earthship, a bank of solar panels shining in the fading light, drinking in the last of the rays. From below came the sound of Jonah strumming the guitar, his voice carrying across the vast plain, evaporating into the parched air.

In a short while the singing stopped and I heard footsteps approaching the roof. Aidan emerged from the trapdoor and joined me, as the guitar strumming continued.

'He's had the shock of a lifetime,' said Aidan, sitting beside me, 'and there he is, singing and playing like there's no tomorrow.'

I nodded. 'In many ways, he's better at this Zen stuff than me.'

We sat together in silence, listening as another song played out and the crimson mountain darkened, the red congealing into dusk.

'You know,' said Aidan, 'they say if the mountain likes you, you can stay.'

I looked at him out of the corner of my eye. It felt different now, almost like we were friends rather than teacher and student, closer to equals. I pushed that thought aside, aware Aidan was able to read me so clearly, because it seemed, well... immodest.

I laughed at myself, making Aidan look at me sharply, his face slowly transforming into a magnificent smile.

'I'm glad you came,' he said.

'Why didn't you tell me what was going on?'

'You had to doubt me. Disillusionment is the beginning of wisdom.'

'You let me think I was insane,' I said, trying to keep the reproach out of my voice.

'First of all, Zoe, I didn't let anything. You thought you were insane. Second, insane, sane. They're just words.'

'Easy for you to say.'

'The only true sanity is freedom,' he said.

I took a deep breath, my eyes on the darkening mountain. I could feel the one question I needed answering, the only question that really mattered, galloping to the front of my mind. I had spent the last few months refusing to think it, letting it go every time it raised its ugly, twisted little head. But it had to be faced. I had to know.

'Aidan, I need to ask you something.'

I could hear the wobble in my voice and took another calming breath. Aidan turned to face me, compassion and understanding already in his eyes.

'My brother killed himself. He did it the same day I... the satori... y'know. I was in one room, meditating, and he was in the bathroom, and... why couldn't I stop him? Why didn't I see it or feel it? My mind spread out everywhere and I didn't know what was happening. I should've been able to save him.'

Tears ran down my cheeks, the great void of grief hollowing out my insides, making me feel like I would collapse inwards on myself, implode like a light going out. Aidan put his arm around me and I leaned into him, resting my aching head on his shoulder, my tears making a dark stain on his shirt.

'That kind of thing requires special training, Zoe. It's a skill,' he said softly.

I sat up and wiped my face dry on my sleeve, sniffing back the remaining tears. I knew I was being irrational, that there was nothing I could have done to save Danny, but that didn't stop me thinking it.

In fact, there were a lot of things I couldn't stop thinking. I had expected enlightenment to change me. I thought I'd be floating in blissful oneness, beaming at the world from a position of unassailable serenity. But nothing had changed.

'Why am I still having all these crazy thoughts?' I said. 'I mean, I thought it would get easier once I knew the truth, but I'm still tormenting myself. I'm still getting caught in the stories. I know Danny's not really gone, he's part of me. Not in some silly sentimental way, but...

well, I know you know what I mean. It's just: I'm not enlightened. I'm still me.'

'Who else would you be?'

I frowned at him and dug my fists into my thighs in frustration and sighed. Aidan was watching me and smiling. As usual.

'You need to keep practising,' he said.

I laughed. 'Now how did I know you were going to say that.'

'It does get easier, Zoe. You've done the hard part. Now you know the truth, it'll be harder to stay away from it. Most people don't get it first time. It's a big shift in consciousness, revolutionary. Individuals who jump straight into full enlightenment are very rare. For the rest of us mere mortals, it takes effort and time. You'll have more satoris and more challenges to face. Just do your best.'

We sat companionably on the wall watching the last of the light fade from the sky. I could feel the heat radiating from Aidan's body at my side, and something deep inside me relaxed, as if it had been holding its breath. It circled and curled into a ball and began to purr. I was home. Peace enveloped my mind and I wondered how I had ever doubted anything. A tiny smile tugged at my lips and a sigh of deep happiness rose through my being.

'Zoe?'

'Mmmm?'

'Can I ask, how do you feel about God now?'

An immense laugh erupted from deep in my belly. The more I thought about my old atheism, which was really one enormous defence mechanism hidden behind knee-jerk cynicism, the more I laughed.

'I really was an idiot,' I said between giggles.

'Do you believe in God?'

I stopped laughing and squinted at Aidan through the gloom. He was smiling benignly, his face shining in the rising moonlight. A spark glinted in his eye. He was up to something.

'I don't think the question makes sense,' I said. 'It's like asking if I believe in you or myself, or those solar panels, or the pinon trees, or the mountain. The whole debate between atheism and theism is a sideshow. It's not even a real conflict. Both sides are illusions. The only rational position you can take on that issue is agnosticism. And that's not sitting on the fence, that's acknowledging we don't really know anything.'

'What about faith?' he said.

'Faith is just how you deal with your blind spot.'

'Which is?'

'Our consciousness is on a self-referential loop, so we can't get outside ourselves to see ourselves clearly. Just like we can't get outside the universe to look at that either. So there's a lot of things we'll never see because that loop creates a blind spot. No matter how hard we look, we'll never get it. That's why it's called the Great Mystery of Life. And that is what people call God. Faith is how you live with the uncertainty of not knowing, whether you put that faith in religion, or science, or money, or whatever.'

I looked at Aidan, suddenly worried I was making a complete tit of myself. 'Does any of that actually make sense?'

He laughed and patted my hand. 'I'm not convinced life is supposed to make sense.'

'The mystery is meant to be lived, not understood,' I said, nodding like an old sage.

'Careful Zoe. You can't live inside a concept. This is why you must practise. You must ground your insight, live it, allow it to deepen, take your time. Life is your guide, not your thoughts about life.'

My life had changed so much in the last year I barely recognised my old self. I had woken from my dream and been granted the grace of freedom. The punch line to the Cosmic Joke had been delivered at great cost. I had never been exiled, never abandoned or betrayed, never slung unceremoniously from the garden. I didn't need redemption. There was no-one to redeem. I was never born and would never die.

I could never be separated from my one true love, not even in death. Danny may not be physically with me, but I see him everywhere I am: in the black mountain, the air on my skin, the glowing moon, in every leaf of grass and every beam of light.

I stared up into the darkening sky and let my mind spread into the vastness, reaching out across the mesa and mountains, finding no boundaries, my home being anywhere I chose.

The desert air was stiffening and a shiver ran through my body. The music had stopped and after a spell Jonah's head appeared through the trapdoor. His eyes and smile gleamed as he joined us on the wall. I leaned into him and he wrapped an arm around my shoulders, protection against the encroaching chill.

'I suppose we should be getting back to the hotel,' I said, my breath dancing around my face.

'You're welcome to stay,' said Aidan, gazing into the sky.

No-one spoke for a while. We were beyond words. We sat together on the roof, huddled against the night, the mountain invisible in the darkness, and watched as the sky filled with stars.

∞

About the Author

Jessica Davidson started life as a musician and sound engineer, and produced demos for rock bands before ending up in a cupboard from where she recorded a talking newspaper. She began to write in an effort to make sense of it all.

Addled: Adventures of a Reluctant Mystic is her first novel, which was inspired by her experience of spiritual awakening.

She lives in her head, but can usually be found in the UK.

www.jessicadavidson.co.uk

For loads of extras and behind the scenes action, visit Zoe Popper's blog:

zoepopper.wordpress.com

Printed in Poland
by Amazon Fulfillment
Poland Sp. z o.o., Wrocław